Biker Daddy

Kara Kelley

Published by Stormy Night Publications and Design, LLC.
www.StormyNightPublications.com

Cover design by Korey Mae Johnson
www.koreymaejohnson.com

Images by Shutterstock/FXQuadro, Dreamstime/Marsimo, and Dreamstime/Dary423

1st Print Edition. July 2018

ISBN-13: 978-1724306661

ISBN-10: 1724306669

FOR AUDIENCES 18+ ONLY

This book is intended for adults only. Spanking and other sexual activities represented in this book are fantasies only, intended for adults.

CHAPTER ONE

Drew

Drew looked up from his school sketchbook, the stench of the alley making his stomach roll, and glanced at his father, AKA Trigger or Prez, across the street. His father held some dude's shirtfront, probably scaring the shit out of him. He could have been a dealer, a junkie, or a pimp, but whatever he was, he owed the Grinders something.

Just another day in paradise, Drew decided and rolled his eyes before returning to his drawing. He leaned the book against the handlebars of his dad's Harley and made a swooping motion with his pencil under the yellow glow of the street lamp. The line was bold and swift but so was the river he was drawing.

He was good, and not just for a twelve-year-old kid either. His art teacher said Drew had a talent that he'd never seen in a lifetime of teaching. The words had made Drew's chest flutter with pride a moment before the promise of hope evaporated, taking his pride with it. He'd never be an artist. He'd never be anything other than a biker and for now that meant he 'kept six' or lookout for the Grinders. That was his life. He was the youngest member of the Skull Grinders MC, destined to take his father's place as president one day and no one got out of the Skull Grinders unless they were in a body bag.

Drew glanced up again, hoping the guys were done because he had homework and his top rocker and one percenter patch wouldn't get him out of detention, but his heart jumped into his throat at the sight.

His dad had a gun pressed to the dude's temple. Drew swallowed, almost choking as his mouth dried. The guy had his hands up, begging, blubbering pleases and promises to do better. The look on his face was so fear-filled, Drew's own gut quivered. Drew's instinct was to stop his father. He hated the way the big man was nothing more than a bully, but when a flicker of movement caught Drew's eye, he yelled out instinctually.

More movement in the alley alerted Drew that a young boy was following several steps behind the man who had caught his attention, and before Drew fully realized what was happening, the man rounded the corner and was shot to the ground. A guttural shout of pain ripped from the man's throat as he clutched his chest and fell, the bag of takeout he'd been holding spilling out beside him. The sound of the gunshot registered milliseconds later, loud enough to make Drew's ears ring. Drew turned his head slightly, and his eyes widened in horror as he saw his father holding the gun, a look of pure satisfaction on his dad's face.

Tears pricked behind Drew's eyes and he glared at the still figure on the ground. The little boy stood frozen, hidden from everyone's sight but Drew's, staring at his father. A dark spot grew at the crotch of the boy's pants.

"Nosy shithead." Drew's father spat the words at the man lying on the ground as if they were something vile on his tongue, and they echoed off the brick and pavement.

His dad had shot an innocent man and it was Drew's fault.

"You got a real sharp eye, kid." His dad spun and walked casually back to the man his MC brothers were roughing up. Bile rose in Drew's throat and his sketch pad dropped from his trembling fingers, fluttering beneath the Harley's back tire. He ran for the bleeding man, sliding on his knees at the last second, scraping denim and flesh across the pavement. The others were too busy to notice as he pressed his hands over the bleeding chest wound.

"I'm so sorry. I didn't mean to. Please don't die." Drew's voice was a high-pitched whisper that he barely recognized. He looked at the boy. His pants were wet down both legs now. He was no more than

five. "Run!" Drew's eyes darted behind him where his father was still busy. "Run, kid, run!"

The man tried to speak, looking frantically at his boy and Drew leaned closer, hearing nothing but a gurgle escape his blue lips.

"I'll make sure he's safe," Drew said, figuring the man was worried about his son.

Drew stood, his glassy eyes finding his father again. His father's gun, pointed at the guy he'd been threatening, rang out and that man fell too. A lifeless lump and a vacant stare as the dead man's head lolled to the side. Drew's gut rolled and his skull felt like a balloon filled with helium. Tears fell from his eyes as he looked back down the alley.

The kid hadn't moved. Drew jogged to the kid, grabbing his arm and shoving him behind a dumpster. He put his finger to his lips to tell him to stay quiet. The boy, wide-eyed with terror, nodded. Drew stared for a moment at the bloody handprint on the kid's arm where he'd grabbed him.

If Drew hadn't yelled out, the man might have lived and this boy might not have been traumatized—he might have still had a father. Drew whispered an apology to the kid and went back to the father, holding his hands over the wound again, before anyone noticed where he was.

The man's lips formed the words 'thank you' and then he was gone. His eyes were vacant as Drew hovered over him, holding pressure on the bloody hole. Panic welled inside him. The guy was dead and his child, so young and innocent, had seen everything.

"Is he dead, kid?" Drew nodded at his father's question, looking at his hands covered in sticky blood. "Come on."

"Hey, I got his patch name, Trigger. Reaper… the kid's just like a fucking reaper sending them off to the other side."

Drew didn't move; his eyes were frozen on his hands. His bloody palms.

"Kid, we gotta move it." Sirens called out in the distance. "He did good, didn't he?" his dad said and Mauler, the vice president, made an agreeing grunt. Dingo, his sergeant at arms, howled and barked, but Drew was too numb to move. A family had been destroyed. Somewhere someone was waiting for her husband and kid to come home with

dinner.

"Jesus, Trigger. We gotta go. I'm not going down for murder," Dingo said, making Drew look up. His father walked his bike to Drew.

"He's earned a drink tonight, eh, boss? Somethin' strong so he'll grow some hair on his balls," Mauler said with a chuckle but before Drew could protest, his father grabbed the scruff of his jacket and yanked him to his feet.

"Get on, Reaper," he demanded, his eyes showing impatience. "And wipe the goddamned tears from your face. You're acting like a fucking pussy."

As they sped off, Drew pressed his face into the back of his father's leather cut and ignored the loud roar, vibration, and the ruckus of laughter and hoots as they outrode the law.

He didn't want a drink. The only things he wanted were for the two dead men to be alive again. And for him and that kid to have normal lives.

• • • • • • •

Drew shot up from the couch, sweat coating his entire body. Hating the recurring nightmare he had at least once a week, Drew threw his legs over the side in frustration and rubbed his bearded face. Goddammit. He needed a drink. Leaning his elbows on his knees and resting his face in his hands, he fought to ease the jitters the nightmare had left. He'd done his time. Drew had served four years in a youth offender facility and had done two more of parole. But no matter how much penance he'd done, no matter how illogical it was to feel responsible when he was only a kid, he'd never be free of the guilt.

Drew rose, looking at the clock. He hadn't meant to fall asleep but he hadn't slept more than an hour the night before. Drew stretched his long body before yanking on a pair of black jeans and pulling a black Metallica t-shirt over his head. He shoved his hands through his shoulder-length hair and grabbed the plain leather cut off the back of his kitchen chair.

Shoving his feet into his black, mud-crusted biker boots, he headed for his Harley with only one thing on his mind—rot-gut whiskey. He could afford better, but he didn't deserve it.

As he started the bike, the rumble of the easy rider filled him with one of the few pleasures he allowed himself, and it made him close his eyes a second before he drove off. There was nothing like having a hog between your thighs, except maybe a woman's mouth, but today that didn't interest him. Bad whiskey, straight up, with nothing to cool the burn from his gullet.

The only biker bar in the small town of Fell was mostly empty at just past two on a Wednesday afternoon, which suited him fine. He had no more interest in company than he did a picnic in a field of daisies.

"Fitz," Trevor, a part owner of Last Resort Bar and Grill, said with a nod as Drew clomped into the dimly lit establishment. "What'll it be?" The people of Fell only knew him as Fitz since he'd changed his name to Andrew Fitzer after leaving the Skull Grinders MC.

"Ten High, straight up." Drew threw himself onto a stool and ignored the grimace on Trevor's face.

"How you stand that shit I'll never know." Trevor shook his shaved head and poured two fingers in a glass. Drew waved his hand for more before slumping against his forearms on the bar and hitching his booted foot on the railing of the stool.

"You sell it," Drew answered with an irritated sigh.

"Only because you ask for it, and I'm guaranteed to empty the bottle weekly and the Iron Code appreciates your business." He slid the drink to Drew. The Iron Code, the local MC Trevor was a patched member of, was the other part owner of the bar. "You should choose a top shelf in honor of Ray today."

Drew lifted the glass and saluted before taking a liberal gulp. He clenched his teeth, hissing as the burn turned his gut to lava. Thinking of Ray, the man who had unofficially adopted him after he'd run away from the Skull Grinders, heightened the fire in his belly. He still couldn't believe Ray was gone.

"Ray didn't drink, so if this drink was in honor of him pushing up daisies, I'd be slinging back milk." He shook his head. "*Fucking* chocolate milk."

The thirty-something biker with the road name Gunner, for his time in the military, chuckled deeply and put the Ten High back on the shelf. Drew admired his cut with the Iron Code patch on it. They weren't a one-percenter club like the Skull Grinders and although they were often rowdy and toed the law at times, especially when it came to keeping justice in their town, they did more good than harm. They were the kind of MC that Drew could understand the appeal of. They were a brotherhood that had each other's backs—*a family*.

"Any action I should know about?" Drew asked as Trevor swiped the bar with a cloth. He asked every time he came into Last Resort. At Drew's request, Trevor kept an eye out for any MC members coming into town. Trevor didn't know which club Drew was watching out for or why and he didn't ask. Drew sure as hell wasn't offering either.

"I wasn't going to tell you this until after Ray's funeral, but Loki was on a poker run and a couple of Skull Grinders were at one of the stops showing your picture around."

Drew's fist tightened beneath the bar. He'd been looking over his shoulder for a decade and had never been mollified by news that they hadn't gotten any closer and this was why: Drew knew one day they'd catch up with him.

"Don't worry, he didn't say a thing and none of the other Iron Code members would either. You know Loki wants you as a prospect. Ever since you fixed up his bike, he's been bugging me about it. You turned that piece of roadside shit into a highly coveted machine."

Drew nodded, relieved that he hadn't been found, but still edgy at how bold the Grinders were getting in their search.

"Hey, Fitzie." A bleached blonde with blood-red fingernails and a matching fringed leather skirt leaned close. The smell of her cheap-ass poison perfume made his eyes burn like his gut. Her low-cut shirt showed off too much of her sunburned, freckled cleavage.

"What do you want, Layla?" There was nothing friendly about his gruff voice, but Layla only giggled and ran a red talon across one of his fully tattooed arms. He'd done some of them himself and she was always fawning over them. She wasn't really looking at them then though. She was looking at Trevor with a taunting gleam in her eye. Drew glanced between the two with narrowed eyes.

"Just thinking you might want a little company. My roommate's out."

"He's your *son*, not your goddamn roommate and no, I don't want any fucking company."

"Sheesh, you don't have to be so rude, Fitz. It's not like you haven't warmed my bed a hundred times." She leaned against the bar, ran her hand up his arm to the bicep, and rolled her eyes playfully.

Drew's eyes found the bottle of Ten High and focused on it, but he didn't fail to notice the flicker of discomfort on Trevor's face as his eyes slid by. The sight of Layla made Drew sick, but the look in Trevor's eyes made his gut sink. His hand tightened on his glass, his fingertips whitening.

"Three, Layla, three fucking weak moments. *Three.*" He held up his long paint- and grease-stained fingers to aid his point. "Go home and clean the beer bottles and hash stink from your trailer before your son gets home." His jaw ticked at the thought of her six-year-old, Brent.

Trevor started slamming shit around behind the bar, but Drew ignored it, lost in thought.

Drew had woken up after his final weak moment to find the boy sitting at the shitty Formica table that doubled as his bed, overloaded with ashtrays and beer cans. His sweet face had been crunched in concentration and his tongue sticking out as he colored on the inside of a pack of cigarettes. Some shit cereal with zero nutrition was getting soggy beside him.

It had been like seeing himself at that age. He'd stayed, made the kid a real breakfast, and taught him a bit about drawing, but then he'd left, getting out of Layla's filthy trailer before she got her lazy ass out of bed. He dropped by often to check on Brent, and when his mother was shit-faced he'd take him to have dinner at the diner and then to the cliff house to paint, but that was as far as things had ever gone between Layla and him.

"Asshole," Layla spat, letting her hand fall from his arm, and waved to Trevor for a beer. Trevor growled as he slammed a can of Coke on the bar.

"Get home and clean up for your kid, Layla, or this'll be your last drink here ever." Trevor's hand flexed when she huffed, but she nodded.

"Fine." She grabbed the can, mumbling, "You're both assholes."

Drew took another swig of whiskey. *That I am, Layla, that I am.*

"Don't you pick up the kid from school in an hour?" Trevor crossed his thick arms, staring Layla down. Drew knew Trevor looked out for the kid too.

"He ain't fuckin' yours, Gunner, so mind your own business."

Drew scratched his beard, watching the bartender's teeth grind. Perhaps there had been a possibility Brent was Trevor's, but Layla had fingered some guy from the next town over who'd been unfortunate enough to stop at the diner where she worked one night after having one too many. He was too decent to ask for a DNA test, but not decent enough to do anything more than pay child support. He never saw the kid.

"This place is my business," Trevor said and leaned one of his bulky arms on the bar so he could get closer to Layla. "No alcohol for mothers driving to pick up their kids is a company policy. It's also a club policy." His long finger stabbed the bar top as he made his point. Drew knew Layla had wanted to be part of the Iron Code for years, and when Trevor refused to give her his property patch, she attempted to become one of the club whores. That didn't go over well either and she'd been out in the cold, nothing more than a hang around.

"I'll just go somewhere else." Layla flipped her hair and headed for the door, wiggling her ass.

"Don't fuck with me, Layla. I'll call child services."

Layla gave Trevor the finger. "Try it, that asshole already did." She pointed at Drew and walked out, lighting up a cigarette as she did. Drew shook his head.

"You did?" Trevor's brows rose, and Drew mentally chuckled at the man's surprise.

He'd done his best to fly under the radar over the years, to keep his good deeds—however insignificant—as quiet as his sins. If he had any reputation at all, it was for laying low and not getting involved.

He was sure Trevor would be shocked to know that Drew had donated millions of dollars in commissions to Victims of Violent Crimes, the charity he'd founded when he'd sold his first piece of artwork six years ago when he was only twenty. But not nearly as surprised as he'd be to learn that Drew was the real artistic genius in town, and that he'd only hidden behind his friend and mentor, Ray Moore, to keep his father and the other Skull Grinders from ever finding him again.

The low-lit bar brightened a moment as the door opened and slapped shut. When Trevor's eyes widened from their usual half-lidded state and he smoothed his beard and black t-shirt, Drew knew someone had walked in when Layla left and that someone was female. Drew had the urge to look with Trevor's reaction, but not even Julia-fucking-Roberts would interest him that day. Then some dick playing pool smashed his cue across the table, and Trevor rushed his leather-clad ass to the trouble. He was burly, muscled, and broke men in half without breaking a sweat. He needed no help, even if Drew was edgy and could use the distraction. Besides, all Trevor had to do was remind the unruly patron he was destroying Iron Code property and things would end quietly.

Drew glanced at the stool beside him as it was gently moved aside so someone could lean against the bar. An expensive female scent wafted up his nostrils. Why was it he couldn't go to a fucking bar in the middle of the day to get shit-faced and get some goddamn peace? There was ten feet of bar, but the woman chose the part closest to him.

He glanced to the side, his gaze scanning the woman from the bottom up and not making it to her face as she was looking toward Trevor and the ruckus. She was short, and wore a flowered skirt, cream blouse, and wide-brimmed hat that was only suitable for a fancy-ass garden party or visit with the damn queen of England. She wasn't someone who belonged in a biker bar, let alone one that was affiliated with an MC.

"Can you tell me how to get to Tonalonka Camp?" she asked, her voice honeyed but with a velvety tone that was nothing like the kind of sickly sweet voice Layla used to get a man's face between her thighs. He curled his lip.

Big city stink, prissy-ass clothes, and a sweet voice meant to lure someone into a false sense of security. It had to be that fucking reporter who'd been hounding him.

"How many times do I need tell you, lady? I'm not going to talk to you and if you set one high-heeled shoe on the property, I'll toss you off it onto your city-girl ass." Drew chugged the final swallow of whiskey and stood, the stool scraping back loud enough to be heard over the scuffle at the pool tables. His six-foot-four frame towered over the woman. She took several steps back and gasped, but he ignored her and walked out of the bar.

He scared people all the time. He was tall, inked with most people's nightmares and pierced, and had perfected a scowl he used to keep people at a distance, particularly women. Only women like Layla braved it, and as if on cue, she was touching him again before the bar door slapped shut behind him.

"Sure you don't want some company?"

A snort was his only reply. Why he'd ever put his dick in that… his thought halted. He knew why he'd fucked her. He deserved nothing better than Layla, the whore of Last Resort. Men like him made their beds and needed to shut the hell up and lie in them.

Then again, Trevor seemed to have a thing for her, so maybe Drew was missing something.

"Come on, Fitz, I'm horny."

"Go flirt with Gunner, Layla. You two seemed to have some long overdue business by the look of things."

"Pfft, whatever. Gunner's a prick."

Drew's long legs straddled his hog, and he revved it until his jaw vibrated. He didn't look back as he peeled out of the lot, not even to see if the bitch from the big-city paper had followed him. She'd never keep up anyway.

As the scenery flew by, Drew tortured himself further by finishing the sequence of events in his mind that he didn't get to see when he woke too soon from his nightmare.

"This your drawing, Drew?" His teacher held Drew's sketchbook open to the picture of the river he'd been working on several weeks ago. The one he'd dropped in the alley. It had a tire mark across the top. Drew stared so hard at the paper in his teacher's hands, his eyes blurred.

He swallowed hard and looked back at Mr. Marks, noting his thick brown mustache twitched anxiously. Drew's gaze swung to the tall man in the brown suit beside him. The suit's eyes were hard, eager, and greedy.

"You a cop?"

The man's brow rose and his lips pressed slightly. "Yeah. Detective Dick Brighton." He shoved back his suit jacket and set his hands on his hips, as if daring Drew to remark on his name.

Drew nodded slowly. He wouldn't lie. Not about this. He'd seen the news. The dead man had been an off-duty cop and his young son had been so traumatized he was left mute. Drew also knew the police had his prints. His bloody hand had left them on the kid's arm.

"It's mine, Dick." Drew narrowed his eyes at the detective, playing the part of badass so well even his dad would be proud. "How'd you find me?"

"The sketchbook is from our school board." His teacher's voice was higher than usual and it shook, forcing Drew's eyes back on him. "And I saw you working on this drawing in class a few weeks ago."

"You're going to have to come with me, Andrew Trigger."

"Detective Brighton, he's a good kid. He really is," Mr. Marks said pleadingly. The detective snorted.

"He's just another punk kid vying for a place with the Skull Grinders." He shoved Drew forward as Drew looked back at his teacher, and the place that had made him feel normal, for the last time.

"Actually, Dick, I'm the future president." He wasn't bragging, although it probably sounded that way. Maybe if he was in jail for the rest of his life he'd never have to pull a trigger himself.

Drew glanced at his wrist where the Skull Grinders ink used to be as he idled at a stop light. The scar was ugly, always a reminder of where he'd come from and who he was. He may be a good-looking son-of-a-bitch, or so he'd been told, but in his soul, he was as ugly as that scar. The rest of the tatts that covered his arms like sleeves were his way of owning his inner demons.

He revved the bike and sped ahead to cut off a pretentious-looking guy in a BMW eyeing him scornfully. Drew gave him the one-finger salute while driving off. He just wanted to ride, get Ray off his mind, and take in the fresh air. But no amount of riding could rid him of the thought that sat just beneath the surface. *Addianna would be coming. His Addi, probably still wearing pigtail braids and cutoffs.*

Addi would come for her uncle Ray. And for better or worse she'd stay—at least the rest of the summer.

Ray's letter, fresh in his mind, made Drew open the throttle and fly down the highway. The wind burned his eyes, the speedometer made his heart soar, but his promise to Ray anchored him to Fell County, even when instinct told him to get as far away as possible.

CHAPTER TWO

Addi

Addi drove up the winding campground lane, flicked off the air conditioner in her rental, and rolled down the windows. A small rush of humid air filled the car with the scent of evergreens, damp earth, and wood smoke. She felt the tension she'd had since pulling into the Last Resort Bar and Grill ease.

It was lucky the bartender had given her directions, otherwise she'd still be in that bar stewing over the rude, dark-haired biker with the bearded, square jaw, set so tight she was sure it might crack at any moment.

He'd obviously mistaken her for someone else. Someone who hadn't needed to talk herself into entering the biker bar in the first place—who hadn't been hyperventilating like a 'fraidy-cat over thoughts of being made a drug mule, or getting stabbed or dragged into the bathroom and defiled. She shivered.

Addi wrinkled her forehead in thought. Who had the biker thought she was? An aggressive woman with a thing for bad boy bikers? Maybe that's why the blonde biker chick had sneered at her. Perhaps she thought Addi was encroaching on her territory.

Uh, no way in hell, lady. You can have him and all the other scary bikers! Note to self: no biker bars from now on—not even if you're desperately lost and starving. She smiled to herself as she imagined what her write-up on Last Resort Bar and Grill would be.

Last Resort Bar and Grill has charm only a masochistic, leather-clad hillbilly with a fetish for pain, abuse, and bad whiskey would appreciate. Ambience you need only experience if you stopped for chili cheese dogs at the roadside food truck two towns back and needed to use the facilities or ruin the seats of your brand-new Mercedes. And if for a second you're fooled by a brooding, unbelievably rugged, gorgeous man—run. His anti-charm will peel the good-naturedness right from your DNA. The name says it all—only go in as a Last Resort.

She chuckled, reminding herself she had a real article to write for *Charm & Adventure Magazine* and the bar didn't fit either category. Although it certainly was an adventure for her. Her phone buzzed, interrupting her thoughts. She glanced down.

Dear old Dad.

She ignored it for the moment to take in the scenery. It was his fourth call since she'd left home, and not a single one about how she was doing after the sudden death of her uncle. He'd already asked her where his blue sweater was, what channel his favorite show was on, and if she knew how to fix his printer remotely. Oh, and he'd ended each call asking if she thought she could wrap things up sooner and get home early.

Another buzz made her growl and she glanced down even though she secretly hated herself for it. Thankfully, it was Daniel this time.

"Have you made it?" Her editor and best friend's voice sounded slightly panicked. He was a bit of a worrier. But at least he was worrying about her and not about himself.

"Hey, Danny, I'm just pulling up the drive. I had a little trouble getting directions. I'll call you back and tell you about it when I've got a minute."

"I just needed to know you arrived safe. Take your time, okay? And call me if you need anything. Even if it's just to complain about mosquitoes, snakes, bears, or any sexy country boys."

"Thanks, Danny." She chuckled. "Especially the sexy boys part, I'm sure." Her chest filled with warmth for her friend and she almost, *almost,* got emotional.

"Talk to you later, hon."

Daniel and his husband, Steven, were Addi's closest friends. Steven owned the magazine she wrote for but he also wrote some of the adventure articles. And although Addi had done many an interview for Steven on his adventure pieces, she only wrote the charm stuff. There wasn't an adventurous bone in her body.

Steven had written a piece on Uncle Ray's camp five years ago when it changed from a sleepaway summer camp for boys to a family campground.

She had only stayed at Tonalonka for one summer when she was sixteen. It was supposed to be one of the last summers of carefree adolescence before she had to start worrying about university, but her mother had died that spring and she was plunged into a dark place. Addi thought of the tall dark-haired camp leader who'd let some light back in. Drew Trigger had been her first kiss. Addi's teeth clenched, anger replacing the nostalgia. He'd ended up breaking her heart and wrecking the camp with his biker club though.

Addi had been closed off from the world before camp; she'd gone to school, done her work, and come home. She'd made supper, cleaned the house, and done laundry because her dad was always buried in his office. And a broken heart only added to her need for solitude.

Shaking off the memories, Addi concentrated on her surroundings. The driveway was more than a kilometer in length and through dense forest. It was also gravel and full of holes that jolted Addi around in her seat. Her empty stomach churned and she reached for her bottle of water.

She hoped her uncle had something in his cupboards, otherwise she might not make it down this path again without ruining the interior of the shiny rental. She was only there to drop off her bags before heading to the funeral home.

The forest canopy opened and Addi removed her foot completely from the gas pedal, letting the car idle into the clearing. As she rolled slowly, she got her first view of the camp in ten years. She drew in a breath. It was still beautiful, but nothing could have brought her back except the phone call from her uncle's lawyer telling her he was dead.

"I'm sorry, Addianna. Your uncle's had a stroke." The words had hung on the line as she'd fought for air.

"I—is he okay?" She'd told herself not to panic until she'd heard everything but the fact that Uncle Ray's lawyer was calling had her head spinning and heart plummeting.

"No, hon, I'm sorry. He didn't make it."

"Oh, God." She sucked a rapid breath through her teeth. "Uncle Ray. I was—I just booked my holidays last week to come see him. He'd asked me to come. He wanted to talk to me about something." Addi clenched her jaw to keep the howl of pain inside.

They had always been close—he was more of a father than her blood one. Uncle Ray had been at her house for every holiday, special event, or just simply when she'd needed him, and they Skyped weekly, sometimes more. Now he was gone. She closed her eyes and buried the pain. There would be things to do. Arrangements to make, people to call, an obituary to write…

"Yes, I know. He'd told me. I'm so sorry. Can you come earlier?"

"Of course."

"Addi?"

"Yes?"

"There's a man living at the camp. He's been with your uncle for years. They were very close."

"Oh." The emotional stupor that came from to-do list-making spread from her chest outward, sweeping away the torrent of grief that had been building inside her and allowing her to remain calm and

reasonable. How hadn't she known her uncle was gay? She'd been friends with Daniel and Steven for over five years and Uncle Ray knew that. Why hadn't he told her? She could add 'console Ray's boyfriend' to her to-do list. "Okay."

"I just didn't want you to be startled."

"Of course, thank you." Calm, cool, and apathetic.

"Call me when you're ready to set up a meeting to discuss the estate. There are things we need to deal with after you put him to rest. At your uncle's request, I delivered a letter for you and one for his friend to the camp. You'll find yours in the office desk. Please travel safe, Addi, and if you have any questions in the meantime…"

"Yes, okay, fine. Thank you, Mr. Turner. I'll leave right away."

And she did. Nothing could have stopped her. Not her fear of flying, not her article that was due on the quaint B&B in cottage country, not even her urge to curl in a ball and weep until she was an empty shell. Uncle Ray had always been there for her when she needed him and she'd be there for him now.

Her chest fluttered and her eyes blurred before she blinked them clear. *Oh, Uncle Ray.* The flutter turned to pain and she kneaded a fist between her breasts to ease it.

Addi glanced at the cabins scattered along the edge of the forest across from the clearing and the mess hall, office, and showers. There was one cabin in the front though, that her eyes stuck on longer than the others.

It was painted a sunny yellow with blue gingerbread trim, and it had been built just for her. *Addi's special place*, her uncle had called it. The purple and pink clematis still climbed up the side of the adorable little cabin, only now fuller and more mature.

Uncle Ray had planted the climbing flowers her second day there. He'd wanted her to feel at home. Now, seeing all the work he'd done to make it a home away from home for her brought on more grief. He'd been the only one who ever did things for her.

No siblings.

A dead mother.

A flake of a father.

And now no Uncle Ray.

She was completely alone in the world.

Overwhelming loneliness crowded her lungs and she began hyperventilating.

The roar of a motorcycle assaulted her ears and further increased her anxiety as she searched the car for the empty brown pastry bag she knew was somewhere. She'd hated motorcycles ever since Drew's biker club had stormed the camp and left it a smoldering mess.

Seeing the paper bag, she lunged for it, crinkled the end, and started breathing into it. *In, out, in, out.*

In her rearview mirror, a bike kicked up dust along the driveway. It slowed but didn't stop as it came up behind her. The rider, all in black, leaned to the side and went around her car. She watched the bearded man, wearing one of those half cap helmets with an airbrushed skeleton playing a guitar on the side, slide past her. His mirrored sunglasses covered his eyes, but his grim mouth, framed by a wild beard, said it all. He wasn't a friendly man.

How many unfriendly bikers were there in this town?

Addi's eyes narrowed. How dare he look at her with that flat, hard-lined mouth. She lowered the bag and pulled her car over to park in a spot with a sign that read Anglers Parking Only. Her uncle's spot.

The bearded man killed the engine on his bike right where he was.

She tugged her coral-colored sun hat on her head and slid on her big sunglasses, but before she could unbuckle and open the door, the biker was at her window. His brow creased as he eyed her—not that she could see his eyes behind his mirrored sunglasses, but she felt it. It was probably the cream silk blouse and flowered skirt that threw him off. He'd probably never seen a woman dressed in anything other than short-shorts and tank tops before.

She flicked her long hair off her shoulder and narrowed

her eyes right back at him. His mouth tightened further and his jaw clenched.

"Goddammit, didn't I already tell you? I'm not doing the fucking interview. Get the hell off this property." His voice was low, deep, and raspy enough to send a shiver down her spine. She clicked the seatbelt open quickly and was about to climb out but as he pulled off his helmet, she froze.

He was the same brooding, ruggedly handsome man from the bar. His scraggly beard begged for a trimmer, or at least a comb, but suited him more that way than she cared to admit. It only enhanced his sexiness.

"Did you follow me?" she demanded when she found her voice.

His head pulled back in shock. "What the hell are you talking about, lady? I live here."

She examined him further noticing his black leather vest was open and the t-shirt he'd been wearing earlier was gone. She swallowed hard. His chest was bare beneath the vest. His muscles, although well-defined, weren't overly bulky and were tanned and smooth except for a smattering of chest hair. He wasn't some sweaty hairy beast. His arms were covered in tattoos, and although they were pretty scary-looking they also gave her a zing of excitement in her belly. She hadn't felt that since she was a teen. All things dangerous terrified her now and this guy had danger written up and down both arms. His eyebrow cocked up and Addi stopped gawking and cleared her throat.

"I'm sorry?" Addi's voice went up in pitch at being caught ogling him. *Gee, like you've never seen a hot guy before.*

"Good. Now go away," he said, pointing toward the road. The sound of his voice vibrated inside her. He smiled menacingly, and his perfect teeth made her eyes widen. This man could be a model—well, if he wasn't a biker.

"I'm not," she stammered, feeling confused.

"Not what?"

"Sorry." She grabbed the bag she'd dropped and began breathing in it again. He set his hands on his hips, looked skyward and swore. Insulted, she put the bag back on the seat. She wasn't going to let him intimidate her!

"I—I." Why did she feel so tongue-tied? *Because I hadn't expected to see a biker at my uncle's and I've been traveling and I'm exhausted and grieving and darn it, he's a rude jackass!—And most likely my gay uncle's boyfriend.* She gave herself permission to be a little undone.

"If you weren't, then why'd you say it?" He fingered the hair in the divot beneath his extremely sensual mouth as his lips curled into a snarl.

"Who are you?" she asked, attempting to open her door. He didn't step out of the way to let her though. He leaned down into the window and glanced around the rental as if assessing whether he should let her out or not.

"That's the wrong question. You know who I am and I know who you are, and I've already told you, I'm not interested, so turn your rental around and get the hell out of here. No amount of money will change my mind."

"I think you've mistaken me for someone else and if you wouldn't mind, it's been a heck of a day and I'd be rather pleased if you'd stop shouting at me."

He pulled his bottom lip through his teeth. "Really? *You'd be rather pleased?*" He mimicked a high-pitched feminine voice and crossed his arms. "You *are* a writer, yes?"

She frowned. "Yes, how'd you know?"

He sighed as if the last of his patience was gone and he was ready to do as he'd threatened in the bar and toss her out on her butt.

"Lady, I'm tired of your games. I'm not doing the interview on Ray, or showing you his last works, so you can *fuck off.*"

She frowned at his awful language but spoke as if she hadn't heard it. "I'm not *that* kind of writer, Mr. Biker. I write for *Charm & Adventure Magazine*. And my boss already did a write-up on Tonalonka Camp five years ago." Addi had no interest in writing anything about Uncle Ray except an obituary and eulogy.

Her heart sank at the thought and once again she attempted to rub away the hurt with a fist to her sternum.

"Did you just—" He paused and a smirk pulled the corners of his mouth upward. It changed his whole face at least what she could see of it not hidden by his sunglasses. "Did you just call me *Mr. Biker*?" His chuckle and sort-of smile unfortunately made him even more attractive.

"Well, uh, yes, I guess I did." She felt her cheeks flush. He leaned way back clutching his abs and laughed heartily.

"Name's Fitz," he said in a lazy drawl. "Camp isn't open right now." His eyes fell on her luggage. She looked over her shoulder at her expensive bags, a gift from Daniel and Steven. "This isn't your kind of place anyway, lady."

"I know it isn't open," she said, looking back at him, narrowing her eyes further. She wondered if she'd get wrinkles from holding the expression for too long, so she relaxed her face.

"Ray just died," she stated plainly. A queer feeling crawled in her chest at him examining her things again. Would he steal them? She suddenly became aware that they were very alone and far from civilization. Her breath quickened and then she regained her self-control. No, this was Uncle Ray's boyfriend, wasn't it?

"Are you… uh… the man who lives here at the camp… with Ray?"

"I live in the maintenance trailer here in the camp, yes. Who're you?" His right brow arced above his glasses and he frowned again, this time looking puzzled. "Besides a *Charm & Adventure Magazine* writer." His hand rose to shove back his gorgeous, although messy, dark hair.

"I'm Ray's niece." That got Fitz's attention. He straightened and stepped back, pulling open her door. His lean but well-conditioned torso made her stare again as he did. He even offered a hand as she climbed out, but Addi ignored it. She thought she might feel better standing, but the man still towered over her—it wasn't some trick fear had played on her in the bar. He was big—huge even.

She looked up. He looked down and plucked the hat from her head. There was an unreadable expression on his face, but it was one that made her gut flip and flutter. She swallowed hard. And then she saw it. He recognized her.

"Addianna Moore." She nodded. "Where's your pigtail braids?" he asked, smoothing a palm over his bearded chin as he assessed her and then he snatched her sunglasses too. He chuckled. "Yep, that's you. I'd recognize those brown eyes anywhere."

"Oh." He must have seen pictures of her. Uncle Ray was always showing off the school pictures of her in his wallet. And pigtail braids was her hairstyle choice back then. "And you're my uncle's… er… *friend*?" She tilted her head as he leaned back onto the heels of his big black boots.

"You could say that, but friend doesn't really cut it," he said and put his large paw out for her to shake, and it was a paw—a ginormous one like a grizzly bear's. Addi looked at it too long, thinking he'd just further confirmed what she thought when the lawyer said '*There's a man living at the camp. He's been with your uncle for years. They were very close*,' and he took it away, shoving it in his jeans pocket.

Her eyes lingered on those jeans a moment—well-worn and snug, belted with a thick black strap of leather. His stomach was trim with a line of silky hair that ran beneath the belted jeans, making her eyes long to follow it.

"Do you know what happened?" she asked with a tremor in her voice, suddenly looking back to his face. His mouth softened and he reached out for her. His warm hands wrapped around her upper arms and she swallowed hard, but didn't stop him—*couldn't.*

"I found him." He pulled her in for a hug and she ignored the awkwardness of his naked chest against her silk-covered one and allowed him to offer comfort. She hadn't shed a tear. She was on a mission. Get to Uncle Ray's, plan the funeral, and figure out what came next. But in his arms, warm and safe, she wanted to let go and *feel*, feel her loss while someone who shared it held her together.

Fitz's skin felt warm against hers. With only her blouse separating them, she not only felt his heat, but the beat of his heart.

She pulled away, tucking back into the open door of the car, even though she'd like to have stayed there for another hour. She was tired and she knew her day was only beginning. He probably needed comfort too.

"I'm sorry for your loss." She gathered a big breath.

He looked taken aback by her condolence. "Uh, thanks… thank you. He was like a father to me." He shuffled back, putting some more space between them.

A father? Ray was like a father to his boyfriend, Fitz? Um…

Suddenly, Addi couldn't help it, call it a stress reaction, but a giggle burst out of her. She pressed the back of her hand against her mouth and tried to hold it in, but nothing helped, especially when he looked so confused.

"I'm sorry." She bit back her smirk, attempting to control her laughter. "It's… it's… the stress." She swiped at the leaking water from her eyes.

His brow wrinkled and his hands found his hips. "Maybe you've mistaken *me* for someone else."

She shook her head, trying to control herself.

"Besides being Ray's friend, I'm the caretaker here and I was in the middle of purchasing the place."

All the humor evaporated instantly and her jaw slackened at his words. Purchasing the place? Her uncle was selling his beloved camp? He would never!

Oh, hell no!

"There's no way in hell," she said, stepping away from the safety of the car and slamming the door while closing the gap between them. His set jaw was no deterrence as she advanced on him. She poked a short French-manicured fingertip into his hard, bare chest.

"What are you trying to pull, you swindling scoundrel biker bully? My uncle would never sell this place—not even to his *friend.* It was his whole life and just so you know I'm not some long-lost niece, buster! I talked to my uncle almost every day and Skyped with him weekly! And just because I didn't know you lived here doesn't mean anything." She took a moment to breathe and calm herself. Her face flamed with anger. "He would have told me if he was selling the place."

Fitz's face turned down at the spot on his chest where she poked and he frowned. She had overreacted. She hugged her arms around her middle and looked away. God, she was exhausted and not acting like herself at all. She had just poked a *very* large biker in the *very* bare chest.

"Uncle Ray would have told me," she repeated, quieter, almost contrite. Was this what his letter was about? "He built this place for his deceased wife and son. It meant everything to him."

"First off, he didn't want you to know because he knew you'd want to come to his rescue. He's broke—*he was broke.* And second, little girl, you ever poke me again and I'll show you what a scoundrel I can be." His mitt-like hands came off his hips and he crossed his thick tattooed arms.

"Broke? No way! Do you know how much his paintings go for? *Hundreds of thousands!* There's no way he was broke. And don't you threaten me," she retorted, her temper flaring again.

"Yeah, well, he liked giving his money away. And it wasn't a threat. It was a promise." His fingers pressed deeper into the skin of his bicep.

"Not to his detriment, you caveman!"

A smirk twitched behind his facial hair and she clenched her fists, a growl escaping.

"It's no joke!"

"I'm no caveman, baby girl. I believe in *women's* rights and equality." His voice was rich, raspy, and tinged with sexy innuendo and then just as suddenly as it came, it left and the amusement fell from his face. "However, I have no qualms about putting a deserving *little girl* over my knee if she can't keep her damn hands to herself and her temper in check. And that's what you're acting like, aren't you, babe?"

"We'll just save the rest of this money conversation for the lawyer," she snapped in hopes of ending the fight she was too tired to continue. Besides, she felt heat creep down her body to inflame her core as she realized what he'd just said. "Did you just threaten to spank me?"

"Nope." He uncrossed his arms and positioned them back on his hips. "Again, it was a promise. And just so you don't get your panties in a twist, the sale became void as soon as Ray died. He hadn't gotten around to signing the papers." They faced off for a long pause before he shook his head and opened the back door of her car. She watched in shock as he reached in to grab her bags.

"Come on. Let's get you settled and then I'll take you to the funeral home. I only came home to feed Ray's fish. I don't feel much like being here today. As taciturn as Ray was, this place is too quiet and empty without him."

Carrying her bags, he strode off on his long legs, leaving her to scramble after him. *Taciturn? Who used the word taciturn in regular conversation?* She decided to leave the hot topic of him buying the camp and spanking her for the moment until she'd seen to Uncle Ray's arrangements, had some food and some much-needed sleep. Then she'd be capable of shredding him without losing her cool.

Tomorrow that biker was in for it. She huffed and then hauled ass to catch up to him. *Did he say fish?*

"Uncle Ray has a fish? Like a goldfish?"

He shot a smirk over his broad shoulder at her. "It's no goldfish, baby girl."

When he called her that, her belly squirmed. No one had ever called her that. Not even just *baby*. She'd had a few 'babes.' *Hey, babe, wanna go for a drink? Hey, babe, you mind? You're blocking the game. Hey, babe, can I give you a ride?* But they didn't count.

"I can take that," she said, reaching for her suitcase. He only quirked that damn eyebrow at her again, making her gut flip.

"Even a scoundrel like me wouldn't let a lady carry her

own bags." He left her behind to head down the path to Uncle Ray's cabin. She didn't try to catch up then. Her heels were sinking into the soft moist pine bed and if she moved any faster she'd probably break an ankle.

"What the hell are in these anyway? Bricks?"

Yeah, for the wall I'm going to build to keep you away from this camp.

"I was supposed to be heading to a posh B&B in cottage country. I just grabbed my already packed suitcases and went straight to the airport."

He made a huffing sound—she thought it may have been the start of a chuckle, but she wasn't sure.

"Bikinis don't weigh this much."

Now she huffed. "It was a business trip." She rolled her eyes. "I was doing an article for the magazine and I don't wear bikinis."

He glared down at her, now at his side. His face moved slowly as he clearly examined her body, leaving a sizzling path of heat.

"Why not?" he asked his expression seriously perplexed. *Was he blind? Were those mirrored sunglasses he wore distorting his sight?*

"Because girls with my figure shouldn't," she stated plainly and looked away.

"Why the hell not?" He sounded offended.

"Because I'm thick."

"Thick? What the hell does that mean?"

"Solid."

"Solid?"

She sighed. "I'm fat!"

He stopped at that and set her bags down, grabbing her upper arm again, this time to spin her, stopping when she'd gone full circle and faced him again.

"Christ!" He pressed his mouth sternly. "Says who? Who the hell would call you fat? Those curves should have warning labels, they're so dangerously enticing. Only an asshole looking for a plastic doll would call you *thick, solid,* or *fat.* You're goddamned perfect!" Oddly, even though his words were complimentary, he sounded angry—as if her looks pissed him off.

She crossed her arms and gave him a challenging look to hide her insecurity. His mouth only firmed further and she found her gaze dropping to her coral high heels uncomfortably.

"Fuck the bikini, you should skinny dip anyway." He released her, sounding even more irritated and picked up the suitcases again. He made it five big strides before Addi started following. How the hell had they just had that conversation?

And why had his words left her both flustered and overheated in places that shouldn't be in her current situation? Or at all, since he was a biker and they were dangerous and she didn't do dangerous. And why the hell was he so aggravated with *her*?

Uncle Ray's cabin was in great shape—not like the other cabins. His was freshly painted and even had a new covered porch on the front. She liked the rocking chair sitting on it, but it made her laugh. Uncle Ray was not a rocking chair type even if he was seventy-two. She looked at Fitz and smirked.

"What's so funny?" Fitz asked as he set her bags down to open the door.

"Just the rocker," she said. He grinned crookedly a moment before he entered the cabin.

"What?" She hurried up the porch after him.

"Nothing," he replied from inside, scratching at his beard. "Just a gift I gave him that had him chasing me clear across the camp with a pellet gun aimed at my ass." She bit her lip to hold back her laughter at the image of her small uncle chasing the very big man in front of her and picked up her bags to bring them inside.

"Oh, no. You're staying in *your* cabin. We're just at Ray's to feed his fish." He pushed his glasses up onto his head when he got inside, and even with the low light she saw he gave her a look that said, 'don't argue' and yet it made her want to, twice as hard.

"What do you mean *my* cabin?" How the hell did he know about her cabin?

She looked around the inside. She had been fooled by the outside. Inside, it was run down and creaky and even smelled a little like mildew. Fitz was testing the floor with his large booted foot in a spot where it looked to be sinking.

"The yellow one with the clematis. It's yours," he said, not looking up from his task.

"Oh, I forgot all about that thing," she lied. It was where she had really bonded with Uncle Ray early that summer. Fitz shot her a look that told her he knew she was full of shit, but she only continued looking around Uncle Ray's cabin.

"What are you doing to the floor?"

"Checking it. The roof was leaking and Ray wouldn't let me in to check for water damage after I fixed it."

"Oh."

There were two bedrooms: Uncle Ray's and a guest room with a bathroom between them. Besides that, there was a kitchen area with a scarred two-person table open to the living area with an old checkered brown sofa and threadbare chair and an ancient, but not antique, coffee table. The only luxurious thing about Uncle Ray's cabin was the massive rock fireplace—oh, and… *Holy crap*, an enormous almost wall-sized fish tank.

Both were meant for a fancy million-dollar cottage in the Muskokas, not some camp cabin and certainly not one that looked as run down as Uncle Ray's on the inside. By the look of the floor, that tank and the huge fish in it were living on borrowed time.

Fitz scooped some smaller fish from a bucket on a table and dumped them into the tank. The big fish stilled a moment, flicked its tail in a sharp movement, darted, and gulped all but one.

"What is that?" She pointed a finger at the thing that

would surely give a barracuda pause. Fitz looked up at her question and in the light of the window she saw his eyes were blue. He smiled and her heart skipped a beat. It wasn't one of his flirty or sarcastic smiles, it was genuine and it went right up and crinkled the skin around those stunning blue eyes.

She frowned, staring. *Those eyes.* She'd only seen eyes like that once before. She mentally took away his beard and shortened his hair. Chewing her lip to hold in her gasp, she blinked. Andrew Trigger—hero, first kiss, first love, and first heartbreak. Addi's mind was pulled back in time to when he'd broken her heart.

Addi stood, rooted to the spot in front of the cabin that was deepest into the woods. Four older boys occupied it, but it was the one standing in the doorway—filling the doorway, actually—that she was there to see.

"What do you want, Addi?" His voice, normally warm, was achingly cold. She immediately felt a shiver.

"I haven't seen you today." She paused, watching his mouth firm. He looked around disinterested, so she continued. "I wanted to see you." Her words sounded lame even to her own ears.

"I'm busy."

"Oh." Her eyes watered but she blinked them clear, annoyed at her own vulnerability. "What are you doing? I thought you might wanna teach me how to swim today like you promised." She shoved her hands in the pockets of her shorts.

"I'm packing."

"Packing?" Her breath stuck.

"Yes, Addi. I'm finally leaving this dump."

"It's not a dump." Anger flared. It was one thing to treat her badly, but her uncle worked hard to make the camp a fun place. Her face heated and she crossed her arms both from the upset and to hold herself together. Why was Drew being so mean?

"My family's here to get me. I was forced to be here, so I made the best of it."

"What are you saying?" she demanded, frustrated by the quiver in

her voice.

"God! Do you need me to spell it out?"

"Actually I do, 'cause you're not making sense." A tear slipped down her face and she angrily brushed it off. For a flash she thought she saw his eyes soften. It was only a second but it felt like years as she read his face. He was sorry. Sorry he was saying the things he was. He didn't mean them. Then again, she loved him and was probably imagining it to lessen the crushing pain he was causing.

"Addi, this job was my first step to being integrated back into society after four years in a young offender detention facility. Your uncle reported directly to my caseworker. When he asked me to watch out for you, I did. I had to. But if you think I felt anything beyond an urge to be out of the system, you're wrong. It was just a helluva a lot easier to keep an eye on you if you were following me around like a lovesick puppy."

"But… Are you teasing me? Is this a joke? I love you." Her voice shook, so she took a breath and added to her statement in an accusing voice. "You said you loved me too!"

He looked over his shoulder at the deep chuckling from inside the cabin and Addi felt her face drain. She peeked around Drew, the boy she had trusted with her life only minutes ago. A scruffy blond man, dressed in leather with silver studs and a tattoo of the devil on his neck, was tossing stuff into a duffel bag. "I love you," he mocked in a squeaky, fake feminine voice.

Her boyfriend laughed cruelly then and she felt as if her heart, previously cracked with his cold words, explosively shattered.

"Let's hit the road, Reaper. Your dad has plans for you."

"Right, Mauler," Drew said, looking over his shoulder and then curled his lip at Addi. Tears were free-flowing down her cheeks by then and no amount of anger could stop them. "Get lost, crybaby. I've got shit to do."

"You're an asshole and I wish I never met you."

She took three slow steps back, before spinning. Her uncle stood among more men in leather, the camp vandalized, smoldering in places, beyond recognition. Their eyes met briefly, his defeated and worried, but she was already running away. Running deeper into the forest, away from her uncle, who'd asked a jerk to look out for her and away from the boy she'd thought loved her.

"Remember how Ray was always talking about the granddaddy of all fish in the lake? Ray had the best tall tales about this giant fish and well, he finally caught him."

Addi was only half listening as she stared. Fitz was taller, thicker, and with the beard and shaggy hair she hadn't noticed, but his eyes—they were a dead giveaway. She swallowed hard, her heart pounding like a jackhammer in her ears.

Addi walked over to the tank and peered at the fish, frowning, still deep in thought. His name was Andrew Trigger and he said his family called him Reaper. She'd never heard the name Fitz before though. But it had been ten years. A lot could change in ten years—even a name, because this man was no doubt the boy she'd once loved.

"It's a pike. A carnivorous fish with sharp teeth. Ray'd always warned the boys that this guy could bite off a toe," Fitz said and gave a snort of laughter.

"I remember," Addi answered with double meaning, quietly and Fitz continued.

"A few of those boys told scary stories about that fish around the campfire. This kid, Markus, screamed bloody murder one afternoon, swearing it was after him. It had all the campers in an uproar. When he got out of the water, it was an old piece of rope wrapped around his leg. He never lived that down." She felt his eyes on her, which made her turn.

Why hadn't he said anything?

She bit her cheek. Maybe he didn't think she remembered him. She hadn't right away, but that was only because he'd changed so much and she couldn't really see his face with the beard and glasses.

"Uncle Ray was amazing with kids," she whispered and caught Fitz's nod. His eyes were closed and he gathered a breath before he opened them again.

"Anyway, he caught this beast a month ago. It had been

injured so he kept it in the tank until it was ready to be released. See the scar along here?" He pointed and she leaned closer and nodded.

"I remember him mentioning something about it. He was going to put it back in the lake this week." She rubbed her hands over her face. "Said it deserved a second chance."

"Yeah. A second chance," he repeated, a little dazed. Emotion welled in her so she swallowed hard, rubbed her sternum and changed the topic.

"Where'd he get the tank? It's ginormous and beautiful."

"Ginormous, huh?" Fitz grinned, ruining his big, tough biker look once again. He looked boyish wearing the teasing look and it made her chest flutter.

"Yes, it's a mix of gigantic and enormous," she defended, setting aside the knowledge of who he was for the moment. Straightening her shoulders, she stuck her chin higher. His brows rose and he bit his lip, almost hiding the smirk on his rugged face.

"Certainly," he said through a chuckle. "Artistic license and all." He licked his bottom lip after he released it and Addi's belly squirmed.

"Artistic license nothing. It's military slang from the 1940s." It was easiest to hide her vulnerability behind useless facts.

"I see." He was still looking at her as if she was the most amusing thing he'd ever set eyes on when he continued. "I got the tank from The Old Inn on Main Street. They finally closed and gave it to me for free as long as I moved it myself."

"And you did?" She cleared her throat. "Moved it yourself?" She looked at his muscular arms and swallowed.

"Nah, I had help." He winked. "Not even Arnold could carry that alone."

"Your biker club help you?" she probed.

He smirked again and she felt like a silly little girl at his mischievous look.

"I'm a lone wolf, baby girl. Did my time in a motorcycle

club and didn't much like it. Being a one-percenter isn't all it's cracked up to be."

She looked closer at the fish, bending at the waist to eye it. "Was it the one that vandalized the camp?" She peeked at him and watched as he shoveled a hand through his shiny dark hair.

She realized after she said it, it was a stupid question. She'd basically just given herself away. Now *he* knew she remembered him.

He didn't say anything, just looked at her intensely as if he was reading her mind. Her gut dipped and she changed the subject, looking back at the fish—this time at the lone one swimming, unbeknownst to the danger it was in.

"How was he, Drew? This last little while." Her voice was barely a whisper, but it was filled with emotion.

"Aw, baby girl." He was about to come to her again when she straightened, clearing the emotion from her throat.

"Can you give me a minute to change? I want to go see him now." She went and grabbed one of her bags.

Drew nodded, hid his soft expression under hard features, and left.

"I'll be back to get you in ten minutes. I can't go dressed like this." He picked up the other bag. "Wear a jacket. It gets cool on the bike." Before she could protest, his boots clomped loudly off the porch. "I'm taking this bag to your cabin."

She swore under her breath. The hell if she was getting on his bike. She started sweating at the thought alone. She could find her way to the funeral home—in her nice, fully loaded, five-star safety awarded car.

She washed up in the little bathroom, wondering how on earth Drew had ended up back with her uncle after what he'd done to the camp. Her uncle was forgiving but that was crazy! Drew had destroyed it with his biker friends.

After getting dressed in a pair of capri jeans with embroidered flowers down the legs and a pink, lace-trimmed peasant top, she looked through Uncle Ray's cabinets. She wanted a few crackers to put in her belly, but there was nothing like that in her uncle's cupboards. There were cans of baked beans and soup, and some hotdogs in the fridge but not much else.

She was just sneering at the outdated package of hotdogs with green fuzz growing in the corner when Drew knocked.

"Come in," she hollered. Swallowing hard, she tossed the hotdogs back in the fridge.

"You ready?" She turned, still holding the fridge door open to see him standing at the door with a helmet in one big hand and his leather jacket in the other. He looked good. His hair was wet and combed, although still a little wild with natural waves, and his beard was tidier too. The bleach-white t-shirt was a contrast to his dark hair, tanned skin, and piercing blue eyes. She looked at the tattoos he wore like sleeves up his arms again. He cleared his throat so she stopped gawking and he pointed at the fridge.

"You hungry? Ray doesn't have much. He'd been feeling like shit so he didn't want to go shopping this week. He wouldn't let me do it for him either." Drew came to the fridge beside her and opened the door wider, looked at the hotdogs and frowned. He smelled clean and yet still woodsy with a hint of campfire and... paint thinner?

"I've been bringing him dinner from my place, complaining my woman overcooked again and was wasting my money so he'd take it."

"Your woman?" she stammered. *His woman.* Addi tried to picture the woman who would be this man's lover and felt a tinge of jealousy as if ten years hadn't passed between them. She was once *his girl.* "Someone else lives here?"

"No, no one lived in the camp but Ray and me. I don't have a woman. I'd just say that so he'd eat what I brought him." Drew's eyes were pinned intensely on hers, making her heart quicken its pace. "There's been no one serious since you, Addi."

Her heart thudded harder against her ribs and her breath

stuck. *What the hell did that mean?* He let the refrigerator door close, but they never broke their stare. She licked her lips. The silence was killing her. Why didn't he say something else?

"You know before you took your glasses off I didn't recognize you." She waved her hand, rambling. "And I misunderstood when the lawyer told me a man lived here with my uncle." She looked down to break their fervid stare.

"He said you were very close. I dunno, but the way he said it I got the impression you were my uncle's boyfriend." She looked at the helmet in his hands and shook her head, feeling her cheeks heat. "No, not hungry at all." She pointed at the helmet. "And I'm not getting on that death machine with you."

"Wait." He started laughing and she looked back up at him. "You thought I was *with* your uncle? And then when I said he was like a father to me—" He paused to laugh harder. She loved the way his eyes crinkled when he laughed.

"Baby girl, trust me, I'm *always* the daddy in a relationship." His brow arced at her and she felt a tickle in her gut. She licked her lips again and warmth began to spread through her. *He's always the daddy?* He must have noticed her reaction because his mouth curled on one side and his eyes drilled hotly into hers.

"And honey, my bike is not a death machine. You can trust *Daddy* to keep you safe." He winked and her breathing sped up. She was sick and *twisted*, she decided. Her dampening palms and panties proved it. He had just turned her on by calling himself *Daddy—twice.* And Jesus, she was about to bury her beloved uncle. What the hell was wrong with her?

"Besides, you have no clue where you're going. We'll get there faster on my bike."

"Nuh-uh." Addi shook her head, waving her hand, palm out, at him. "My rental has a GPS and plenty of life-saving airbags. I'll find it just fine."

His chest rose in a sigh. "You're still damn stubborn. Just

like your uncle." He crossed his arms. "Follow me on the bike."

"Why? Why are you back here?" she asked, surprised the words in her mind had come out. He looked down a moment before finding her eyes again.

"You have questions and I'll answer them, but for now we need to get to the funeral home."

She set her jaw as he left the cabin, effectively cutting off her opportunity to demand answers. Why the hell did he think he could control everything? What made him the boss?

Because he's a daddy. She put her hand on her forehead. *Oh, God.* And as much as her mind hated the idea, her body loved it.

"Screw you, pal," she grumbled under her breath and followed. He could demand all he wanted, but he couldn't make her follow him. He hurt her, broke her heart and her uncle's, and maybe it was a long time ago and he'd forgotten, but she hadn't.

She knew she was being unreasonable, but she was hangry, and hated when men thought they knew best. Especially men she'd once loved; *man*—just one.

And dammit, being a bitch was unavoidable; she was scared to see her strong uncle lying in a coffin—scared she couldn't hold back her fear, grief, and exhaustion much longer.

Especially with Drew around, bringing up her past, comforting her and making her feel things she didn't want to feel. She didn't want to crumple.

CHAPTER THREE

Drew

Addi had become a beautiful woman. He knew she would, but seeing her exceeded anything he could have imagined. If only he hadn't assumed she was that sleaze reporter Rebecca Snow… if he'd actually looked at her before he'd been such a jackass, he'd have known in an instant. Those almond-shaped eyes had always undone him—so dark and deep, practically bottomless. And God, her spunk was like Sriracha sauce, heating him to his very core.

He had the urge to go to his studio and paint her right away. Which was often the only way to remove obsessive images from his mind. He knew he'd be distracted until he'd painted her. He'd painted the girl countless times, but he wanted to paint *the woman.*

There was an insatiable itch—no, a burn—in Drew to drop her bag and run, full speed, to his studio on the cliff and barricade himself inside, lose himself in creation, to paint her naked, in the middle of an orgasm, her head tossed back and her hair wild, her hands gripping a red silk sheet. His heart pounded and his cock hardened. He'd loved her with the innocence of youth, and he'd lost none of that love, but now he *wanted* her like a man wants a woman.

But Addi needed to be taken care of. And he'd promised Ray. He remembered it as if it were only yesterday.

"I need you to promise me something, Drew." Ray's gaunt face stared grimly at Drew as he reeled his line back a little, tugging his fishing pole slightly. Drew did the same in hopes of drumming up interest in their bait.

"What's that, Ray? Not to screw that new waitress in your bed while you're getting your tests done in the hospital?"

Ray chuckled. "Nah, go ahead. It's the closest I'll get to any action now." It was Drew's turn to chuckle then as Ray looked skyward and smiled. "She has some rack on her. One look at her in that tight uniform brings Ray Junior back to life in seconds."

Drew laughed harder, rocking the small fishing boat, until Ray looked at him seriously.

"It's Addi."

"Addi?" Drew swallowed hard, his throat suddenly dry and the image of the waitress naked disappeared as quickly as it had come.

"When I'm gone, I need you to take care of her for me." Ray's mouth firmed and he held up a hand to stop Drew from speaking.

"I know how you feel and I know it won't be easy for you." He rubbed his neck beneath his collar-length gray hair. "She's got no one, Andrew. No one who takes care of her—even as a young girl.

"I'm the only one who could ever take care of her, besides you. You took care of her that summer, Drew. I know you did. Once I'm gone, she'll be lost. She'll pretend she's fine. Hell, she'll probably act like she could run the world on top of everything else. She's stubborn like me, but I know you'll see through her smokescreen."

"But—"

Ray cut him off sharply. It wasn't a tone he used often so Drew shut up. "I know you love her. I even know you don't think you deserve her, but she's my baby and I deserve to know she'll be cared for."

"Ray, I'm not good for her and you know what happened last time you asked me to watch out for her."

"You were only doing what you thought was right to protect her.

She needs protecting. That girl needs to be set straight sometimes. I know you know that, too." He looked at Drew and Drew's heart kicked up a notch. "You're a born leader, kid. And I don't mean like your father wanted. You're a good man, even if you don't see it. You've gotten more from me than you ever did from that no-good bastard named on your birth certificate."

Suddenly Ray's line started reeling fast. He gripped the fishing pole with two hands and arched back, pulling and winding the line in repeatedly. The little boat swayed and Drew held the sides.

"I know I owe you, Ray—"

"Bullshit!" He was out of breath. "You've been taking care of me and my place for years. This ain't about owing, this is about love." He huffed but when Drew attempted to take his rod, he growled. "You're like a son to me. She's like a daughter. I love you both and I need you to take care of her. Promise me, dammit!"

And so Drew did. And he wouldn't break that promise—not for anything.

Addi needed him.

She always had, and even if Ray hadn't asked him to care for her, he would have. He couldn't resist. As self-destructive as it was, she tugged at him as if there was some unseen gravitational pull between them. She played the part of taking care of herself, but just like Ray had said, he saw beneath that façade.

He'd be there for her—keep her safe—but she was off limits for him. No matter how much he loved her, she was not *his* and never would be. Not when it could put her life in danger.

Addi deserved better than someone hiding from a family with connections to drug cartels, brothels, and bloody murders—a family that would hurt or kill anyone Drew cared for as punishment for him leaving. He and his past were too dark for her.

Drew looked between the Harley and the Norton. He wouldn't take the Harley. He'd just finished fixing up a '69 Norton and had wanted on it since he'd found it hidden like an unpolished gem at an estate sale. He planned to auction it off for his Victims of Violent Crimes charity, but wanted to enjoy it for a few weeks first.

Well, Ray was supposed to auction it off. Drew put everything was in Ray's name so Drew could stay anonymous. He couldn't risk alerting the Skull Grinders of his whereabouts.

How would that work now? Ray had nothing and refused to take anything from him, but on paper, he owned it all. He was the name on the paintings. He was the name on the accounts, the charity foundations, everything except Drew's Harley (that was under his legally changed name, Andrew Fitzer)—Ray even held the deed to Drew's studio on the cliff. No one would ask questions or dig into his past and former name without provocation, but if Andrew Fitzer was known as the rich and famous artist who'd founded several charities, they might.

Drew hadn't expected Ray to die so soon and he didn't know how their arrangement would work now that he had. Drew hadn't thought that far ahead. Ray was still young. What's seventy-two when people lived well into their nineties now? Truth was, the few times Ray brought it up, Drew refused to talk about it. Ray was all he had.

Addi didn't know how things worked between him and Ray—no one did. It didn't matter though; even if he lost it all, he was okay with it. If it went to Addi, it was fine by him. She'd do right by the charities.

He sat in the parking lot of the funeral home, straddling the Norton, which rode like a dream, watching the road for her. She had given him the slip quickly and since she had a GPS, he hadn't bothered to double back and get her. She obviously needed the space and he was enjoying the Norton too much. He was quickly regretting that he hadn't turned back for her though. He looked at his watch and frowned. Getting off the bike, he headed to the giant wooden polished double doors.

A tall dude with a beak-like nose met him in the foyer.

"Good afternoon, I'm Colin."

Drew nodded and looked around the dimly lit funeral home. There was incense hanging heavily in the air and it made his lungs itch.

"Is there someplace I can wait for my friend? We're meeting here to make arrangements for Ray Moore."

"Of course, sir." He swept a hand to the left and bowed slightly. "Right this way."

Drew was a big man, not afraid of much, but ever since he was a kid, having been witness to two violent deaths, places like this creeped him out. And the dark decorations and heavy curtains blocking out the light didn't help.

The waiting area was probably once a bedroom in the old Victorian house. It had some chairs, a sofa, and some side tables with plenty of tissue boxes and fake flowers. He looked around feeling claustrophobic until he noticed a corner set up with coffee supplies and a kettle. The area was only slightly less depressing than the rest of the home, but the promise of coffee eased some of his edginess.

A steaming Styrofoam cup in his hand, he walked to the sofa and sat, tossing his jacket on the armrest. Looking at his watch again, he ground his teeth. He'd bet the coffee in his hand Addi was lost. It reminded him of when they were at camp and he was just starting to fall for her.

"What are you doing?" Drew looked at the girl, Addi, with her knees tucked up to her chest sitting on the ground. Startled, she yelped, her eyes wide and wild.

"I'm on a walk." She lifted her chin while she spoke. She was different from the girl he'd saved from drowning the week before.

"You're on a walk?" He furrowed his brow and set his hands on his hips. She was cute and the kiss they'd had still played through his mind every night even though he regretted it.

"Yes." Her bee-stung lips turned out in a petulant pout.

"And why are you sitting if you're on a walk?"

"Because if you ever get lost in the woods, you're supposed to stay put." She scooped up some aromatic sticky pine needles and tossed them

unconsciously to the side.

"So which is it, are you on a walk or are you lost?"

She looked at him then—straight at him with her exotically tilted dark eyes, making his head spin. Her lashes were unreasonably long and the freckles scattered across her honey-colored nose and cheeks made his gut clench. She was both annoying and alluring and he couldn't decide whether he wanted to drag her back to her uncle or to kiss her again.

First, he shouldn't give a damn and second, she was a good girl, the kind he avoided. Hell, she even had pigtails. Sixteen-year-olds with pigtails were definitely good girls.

"I haven't decided yet." Her haughty tone irked him but not in an entirely bad way. His brows rose and he scratched his head.

She was the only girl at Tonalonka. She had a sadness to her that made his own chest ache—maybe because he was sad too. Ray had asked him to look out for her and at first it pissed him off so he hadn't promised him anything.

He didn't want to be responsible for the camp owner's niece. He also didn't think a guy as smart as Ray should trust him with his precious niece. Drew was bad news after all—a parolee. But he'd already rescued her once. She'd intrigued him since then. She was a loner like he was, but more captivating was the way she acted as if she was above all the activities and fun. Especially when her eyes and longing looks told another story. She was scared. Maybe even terrified. So he'd followed her quietly when she went to the woods.

"You haven't decided?" Drew asked.

"That's right. Are you going to keep repeating everything I say?"

"Uh, no, saucy pants. Are you planning on deciding soon?"

"Maybe. Why do you care?" She set her chin on her knees, still looking at him with those big brown eyes.

"Because I need to decide whether to rescue you or not."

"I don't need to be rescued. I'm no damsel in distress." She let her legs fall straight and crossed her arms. She might've looked less vulnerable if her lip wasn't stuck between her teeth.

"Too bad, I kind of like rescuing damsels."

"Well, find another one, Prince Charming, I'll never be your damsel."

"Fine, but if you're lost and staying put, what is it you expect to happen if not to be rescued?"

"I haven't decided that yet either." She looked away. He wanted to slide one of her pigtails through his fingers.

"You're very indecisive."

She turned to him and smiled then, and it took his damn breath away. It was like being socked in the gut, but it didn't hurt—in fact, it was thrilling.

"Yes, I am." She reached up to him and he took her hand to help her to stand. He wanted to keep holding it, but she took it back.

"Would you walk me back?" she asked casually while dusting off the seat of her summer dress.

"No, but I'll rescue you." He smirked at her and she rolled her eyes, but her smile got unbelievably wider.

"You already rescued me once. I have a once-only limit on being rescued," she said.

His eyes narrowed but he couldn't hide his smirk. "Is this because you think I'll be mad at you for doing something dangerous again?"

"No!" Her chin rose higher. "I've done nothing dangerous! Besides, you're not my camp leader. I'm not your responsibility."

He grunted his reply.

"I haven't!"

"Camp leaders are responsible for all campers, not just their assigned kids."

"Well, I'm not a camper. I'm just here visiting my uncle," she said haughtily.

"Is that the cop-out you're taking?"

Her eyes narrowed angrily at his words and she slammed her hands on her hips. He could barely hold back his smirk.

"I never cop out of anything." Her words were strong and severe and her cheeks were flushed with anger.

He held up his hands. "Okay, okay. Truce?"

She visibly relaxed and let out a breath audibly as she nodded.

"Good. I'd hate to have the cutest girl at camp mad at me." He grinned crookedly at her and she rolled her eyes.

"I'm the only girl at camp."

"Come on, it'll be time for dinner soon. I'll walk you back." He

took her hand again and when it trembled in his, he held it tighter and before they'd even made it halfway back, Addi was walking pressed against him.

Drew's memory faded as he heard Colin speaking from the foyer. Standing, he set the cup of coffee down and walked out of the room.

The woman standing with Colin was a ginger, with a sharp expression, big black-rimmed glasses, and a skirt too short for the business wear she'd obviously been going for.

"Would you mind if I had a word with you?" she said, her smile wide.

"Who are you?" His cold words made Colin look queerly at him. But Drew's instincts were good, *very good.*

When you spent four years in a young offender facility, you had to develop an aptitude for sensing danger, bullshit, and bat-shit crazies. You also needed a powerful body and a fight-to-the-death attitude. That's what kept you safe. Especially when your father was the president of the Skull Grinders.

The woman looked at Colin and then back at Drew and bit her lip. Her lips were thin and painted with some pale pink glossy shit. She tugged on her navy skirt and took a tentative step toward him.

"Would you mind, Colin?" she said, not looking back. The slim man nodded politely and walked away.

"I'm Rebecca." She stuck out her small hand, nails painted the same pink as her lips, but Drew ignored it. "Can we talk about Ray?" The woman gestured back to the room with the coffee and Drew wondered if she was a grief therapist or something. He didn't hide his impatience though. He sighed forcefully, walked to his spot on the couch, and fell into it. He didn't need to talk about Ray to anyone—least of all a fucking stranger.

Once the woman sat, he spoke. "I think we should wait for his niece. I'm just here for moral support." He let out another breath and looked back to the door.

"Oh?" Her perfectly shaped eyebrows pulled tighter. "You did live with Ray, didn't you?"

What the fuck did that matter? "Yes, as the caretaker of the camp, but his niece is his family."

"So, you were just an employee?"

"Well, no, not quite. We were friends." He puckered his brow. "Who are you?"

"I thought we established that. I'm Rebecca."

He flicked an eyebrow skyward and smoothed his beard. "Actually, we haven't. Telling me your name doesn't tell me who you are, does it?"

"I suppose." Her eyes shuttered before she straightened and her look seemed to sharpen.

"You're that reporter, Rebecca Snow, aren't you? See, you better not be her because I've been telling her to give us some privacy since Ray died. And I'm no longer planning on being nice about it."

Her eyes widened and then hardened.

Not so easily intimidated, huh? "Get the hell out of here." He spat the words with vehemence, his fists clenching in his lap.

The redhead shrank back a little, her confidence faltering. She even had the nerve to look down the hall where Colin had disappeared like she was afraid of him.

"I promise the piece will be tasteful," she said.

"Do I look stupid to you?" He crossed his arms and lowered his chin, giving her a disparaging smile.

"Uh, no." He saw she was chewing the inside of her cheek.

"Then don't play me for a fool. As soon as you called I looked up your work—you love dirt and we both know it. You're one of those word-twisting, out-of-context, rabid-dog writers."

"This could be my break, Mr. Fitzer. *My* way out of writing that trash. I think Ray had an amazing story and I want the world to hear it."

Drew jumped to his feet and by the surprise she showed,

faster than she expected he could move. "You're just a tabloid writer, pretending you're better than the weekly rags, and you always will be." His voice was harsh and loud and her jaw clenched before she opened her mouth to speak. Drew pointed to the door. "Get the hell out of here. The fact that you've been calling me since the news broke about Ray's death without allowing anyone time to grieve and you've now come to the funeral home to get what you want is proof enough you have no morals, Miss Snow. Go, before I toss you out."

Colin came rushing back, looking only slightly more alert. "I've called the police."

Rebecca's mouth curved down in a scowl, which was the first honest expression she'd shown in his opinion, and turned on her heel to swiftly walk to the door. She looked over her shoulder shrewdly and spoke. "Perhaps you have something to hide, Mr. Fitzer. How does a man with Mr. Moore's artistic genius fail high school art class? And how is it a man whose last painting sold for six-hundred-and-fifty-thousand dollars is three years behind on his property taxes? Mr. Moore's life and work with all those charities would have made a lovely story but suddenly I'm more curious than ever about the secret side of his life." She exited the doors with a flick of her hair.

Drew closed his eyes and fought his urge to punch the wall.

"Oh, my, that was quite a bit of trouble," Colin said, and Drew opened his eyes to see the man wringing his knobby fingers at his front.

"You shouldn't have let her in here," Drew growled, anger still burning deep. "What if she got to Addi? That poor girl is grieving and the last thing she needs is some reporter, using her words out of context and writing a trash piece on the world famous artist, Ray Moore, her beloved uncle."

"You're right. I apologize. It's just…" he stuttered, "w-we don't normally interrogate guests who come into the home."

"You patronizing me, Colin? Because I know it's not often you have famous people in your funeral home and perhaps you should have foreseen some issues arising. You need to review your policies, yeah?"

"Yes, of course." He bowed again and Drew bared his teeth before storming back to the room to grab his jacket. It was time he found Addi and taught her a lesson about punctuality.

CHAPTER FOUR

Addi

The roads were all gravel and didn't help her rolling tummy. They also didn't have any freaking signs! Side road this and side road that! *Arg!* She gritted her teeth as she turned on yet another dirt backwoods road. She slowed and smacked both palms on her steering wheel.

Where the hell was the highway? She eyed the GPS screen on the dash with malice. She hadn't lied, this car did have a GPS; she just didn't pay for it, so the SD map card had been removed. Damn car rental places up-charging for everything! And now she was lost and cursing her stubbornness for not following Drew… Fitz or whatever he called himself nowadays, the bossy biker jerk.

She blew out, making her side bangs flip up for a second before flopping back in her face. Even calling him that felt wrong. He hadn't been a jerk—not really. Okay, he'd definitely been one in the beginning, but that was a case of mistaken identity. She spotted a road further ahead and squinted. Even from a distance she could see several cars drive past. It had to be a main road. *Finally!*

Her heart pounded and her palms started to sweat, but

she gunned it, not wanting to explain to Drew that she'd gotten lost when she finally arrived at the funeral home. Dust and gravel flew out from behind the car in her haste and her elation over finding her way to civilization, *without the help of a badass biker*, fell flat with the flashing police lights behind her.

"Damn, damn, damn!" Addi pulled back over. *Could this day get any worse?* At this rate, not only would she not get to the funeral home before it closed, but she'd likely starve to death before she made it back to the camp. She looked at her lap as she turned off the ignition and punched the hazards on. A tap on her window made her look up abruptly. She blinked, temporarily dazed before lowering her window.

"Uh, hi."

"What's your hurry?"

"Was I speeding?" she chirped. The officer's flat, what-do-you-think smile made her shoulders slump. "I'm heading to the funeral home. I've been lost for the last forty minutes and was hoping to get there before it closes."

"Keep up the crazy driving and you won't have to worry about closing time." His words made her shiver and her eyes well up.

The officer's face fell instantly at the sight of her distress. Her uncle's death was too fresh to hear stuff like that and she was beyond done with the horrid day.

She had never gotten a ticket in her life, and certainly wouldn't cry to get out of one, but here she was with tears pooling, embarrassingly in front of the officer with puppy-dog brown eyes and a scar on his lip that made him look slightly rugged. Nothing like Drew though. His kind of rugged was not slight—in fact, if it didn't jump right out and smack you then you were blind or *dead. And there, I've come full circle.*

Addi wiped under her eyes and sniffed. "Sorry. It's been a long day."

"No, I'm sorry. That was incredibly insensitive."

She sniffed again and blinked away the excess water in her lids.

"It's okay. I'm just overwhelmed." She handed over her license and registration. "Can we just get this over with?"

"Uh, yeah."

She let her head fall against the steering wheel and listened to him walk away wondering what Drew thought about her absence. Was he concerned or pissed off? She sat back and groaned.

When the officer returned, he was wearing a solemn expression.

"I'm so sorry about Ray, Addi. He was special to a lot of people. Me included. He'll be missed." He took off his hat and Addi did a double take as he handed her documents back.

"Thanks," Addi said and looked closer at him. He rubbed a hand through his dark blond hair and shook his head.

"I suppose you might not remember me." He fiddled with the brim of his hat. "I was one of the Tonalonka boys."

She nodded. There were a lot of men that were once Tonalonka boys. That's what Uncle Ray's camp did; it turned troubled or lost boys into competent men. With all the skills they learned—canoeing, swimming, setting up camp, wilderness survival and working with others—they gained confidence and trust in their capabilities and other's.

"I was there the summer you were. I was a leader then, but I'd been going to the camp for years." He chuckled. "All of us leaders had a crush on you."

Addi's eyes widened. She was an antisocial, chubby sixteen-year-old who wore sundresses and pigtail braids. She had her nose in a book most of the time. As far as she remembered most of the boys teased her. She shifted in her seat, looking at his blond hair and brown eyes anew. She did remember him. She swallowed hard.

"I'm sorry. I don't remember," she lied.

"Carter? Carter Learner?" he prompted and she shook

her head. He looked disappointed, but tried to hide it with a smile. "Come on. Follow me. I'll get you to the funeral home. The Douglas Brothers?"

Addi nodded, relieved that she wouldn't get lost again, but as soon as she turned the ignition, the car made a click-click-click sound and didn't turn over. She groaned again, feeling frustration build to an almost breaking point.

Carter pulled his squad car up beside hers, lowering his passenger window.

"Won't start?" He smiled sweetly, showing his dimple. "Get in. I'll have someone come tow it to the shop in town."

"Thanks, Officer. I appreciate that." But her gut turned at the thought.

"Please call me Carter."

She blinked, recalling their time at camp. Carter had been there the day she'd fallen from the cliff. The day Drew had saved her life. And although he hadn't been responsible for her fall, he had made a bet with her that made her skin crawl. After that day he'd tried to make amends but she had never let him. That kid was all grown up now though and a cop. She wasn't going to turn away the help he was nice enough to offer over some teenage hormone-induced bet.

She pulled out her phone as he opened the door to his squad car for her. She sent Steven and Daniel a quick text and listened to another voice message from her father. *"Are you coming home soon? The meals you froze are gone and my favorite pants are in the laundry. Some guy from the cell phone company keeps calling too."* There was no goodbye or end to the message at all. No, 'how are you?' nothing. Did he even remember she was there to bury his older brother?

The drive wasn't long, but Carter managed to ask a lot of questions—ones she was too tired and too overwhelmed to answer with more than a word or two, so she was relieved when they pulled into a parking lot.

There was no motorcycle in the lot and a big man in leather, whom she had mixed feelings about, wasn't standing at the door with his arms crossed either. On the one hand, she didn't want to face his interrogation on her lengthy travel time, but she also didn't want to face what was behind the big double doors alone. When Carter's radio chirped a call from dispatch, she left him to attend to it.

He got out just after her. She appreciated his help but she didn't want him there any more than she wanted to be picking out a coffin for her uncle. God, it was all too much. She turned to tell Carter she'd be fine, but he was walking toward a bright blue Fiesta in the back of the lot.

When Addi entered the funeral home, all the air seemed to deflate from her lungs. Her nose tingled and her eyes stung. Weakness crawled up her limbs to her core. It was suddenly *real* and as Ray's only capable relative there was no one else to step in.

Uncle Ray's gone. Her legs buckled and luckily there was a chair to fall back into. How did you pick a casket for a man who'd hated to be indoors—hated being cooped up, needed to watch the sunrise every morning? How did you bury the only person in your family who remembered your birthday, loved popcorn with mac and cheese powder on it, and wore his socks inside out because the seam annoyed him just like you?

"You've done this before," she told herself aloud. "You can do it again." She'd had to do it when she was a teenager for her mom. Hell, she'd had to do worse. She had to make the decision to end life support. The memory hit her hard. Her father's voice was as clear in her mind as it had been that day years ago.

"She's your *mother. It's your decision." Addi's father looked odd, unshaven with his gray-streaked hair mussed, and although his stare was always distant, now it was vacant as well. Being out of his office and away from the house was unusual for him, and it made him seem frail, but it wasn't every day your wife was in the hospital hooked up to life support.*

"What if I make the wrong decision, Dad?"

"Then you live with it—we live with it." He sighed. "That's life,

Addianna." Seeing him looking at his watch, she felt the pressure on her chest triple. "Let's not waste the doctor's time now."

She'd known with how active her mother had been, she wouldn't have wanted to live in a bed hooked up to machines, but God, she hadn't wanted to let her go. The doctor had said even if a miracle occurred and she eventually healed enough to live without life support, she'd still have had full paralysis.

"You can't escape your life, a husband and kid, for fun and adventure when you're stuck in a bed or wheelchair unable to even scratch your own nose." She didn't say it aloud, but thought it. Maybe she'd finally get her mother's attention then. Shame flooded her at the thought. Terrible shame. And she sat at her mother's bedside, took her hand, and nodded to her father and the doctor.

The memory she'd dragged up had been intended to make her feel stronger, but instead she trembled more. It had taken seven long minutes for her mother to become starved of oxygen and die. Had Uncle Ray suffered? She should have been there with him. She should have taken him up on his offer to run the camp with him years ago. He hadn't deserved to be alone.

He hadn't been. He'd had Drew.

"Miss?" A tall, slim man in a dark suit with his hands folded neatly in front of him entered the room silently. "Miss Moore? Addianna?" His glasses were too low on his large and slightly crooked nose, and he smelled of something strong and overpowering. Her breathing quickened, and the scent suffocated her. She gulped breaths faster in hopes of getting fresh air until she was hyperventilating again. She nodded and held up a finger while she bent forward, leaning an elbow on her knee for support.

"I'll get you some water." The man bowed slightly, and his comb-over didn't budge. His eyes, gray and beady, looked both sympathetic and slightly panicked as he glanced at the doors. It made her even more anxious. Shouldn't a man in his position be used to this? She couldn't be the first person to have a grief-induced panic attack at the funeral home.

"Baby girl?" Drew strode in through the double doors, his thick, muscled thighs moving with purpose toward her. She was instantly relieved. His blue eyes pierced hers when she looked up, and although they were concerned, they held no panic. Drew was completely in control. Crooked Nose followed, hovering. Drew turned, suddenly looking annoyed. "Come on, honey." His gentle voice made her lip wobble, and he tried to help her up.

"That's it, gorgeous." He wrapped his arm around her back to assist her to stand, but she didn't have the strength. Her chest was so heavy, she was sure there was a concrete block on it—each breath harder and harder to draw in. God, she just needed to catch her breath. Drew grabbed her behind the knees and scooped her into his strong arms.

"Tuck into me, baby girl. I've got you." As soon as they were alone, he sat on the sofa and adjusted her comfortably on his lap. He didn't speak for a few minutes, just held her, massaging her neck and rubbing her back soothingly. Her breathing steadied, following the lead of his slow, sure touch. She sniffed into his shoulder, not sure if she could hold back the tears battering against her lids any longer.

"Let it out, sweetheart. Holding it in is ripping you up." With his permission, she let out a low trailing whimper and buried her face deeper into his neck. Once Addi started, she couldn't stop and her shoulders began to shake with racking sobs. "That's it, baby girl, that's it. Get rid of it."

The door opened and Colin whispered, "There's someone here who came with Miss Moore."

"Excuse me?" Drew moved Addi gently over to the corner of the couch, kissed her head, and stood.

"What are you doing here?" Drew said in a low, angry tone. It sounded like the quiet warning growl of a Rottweiler or wolf.

Addi blinked and glanced up to see Carter in the doorway. She wiped away her tears quickly and cleared her throat.

"I brought Addi here. I was just in the parking lot dealing with this one." He thumbed over his shoulder at a pretty red-haired woman. *Who was she?*

Drew looked at Addi with knitted brows a moment before looking back at the cop.

"I'll bring Addi home when she's finished here. You can go and take *her* with you." His tone wasn't pleasant or helpful and the last three words were said with tight lips and clenched jaw. He clearly didn't like Carter, but he despised the woman.

"I think Addi would rather ride home in a police car than on the back of an ex-con's bike." His voice was hard and just as full of dislike as Drew's, but Addi still heard a tinge of nervousness in it.

Addi looked between the three. Carter might not like Drew, but he was afraid of him. The redhead's eyes were lit with excitement as she eyed the two men and Drew's jaw twitched. His arms were tightly crossed, but he didn't say anything else. If looks could kill…

"What's going on?" Addi asked as Drew cracked his neck with a quick twist and rolled his shoulders.

"Addi, this is Rebecca Snow, a tabloid reporter, who's been up my ass asking for an interview on Ray since the news of his death went public." His eyes narrowed on the redhead. "I've asked repeatedly for her to respect our need for privacy and time to grieve, so when she showed up here I confronted her with a little more verbal force. Colin was kind enough to call the cops."

"Oh," she answered, eyeing the woman who looked petulant next to Carter. "I agree with Fitz, we'd appreciate some privacy and time, Miss Snow." Rebecca's eyes shot to hers.

"It'll be respectful, Addi and it wouldn't be for the

tabloids. I'd be sending it to *The Sun*."

Drew growled, but Addi rose and went to his side, reaching for his hand. His immediately swallowed hers. "I give you points for eagerness and persistence, Miss Snow, but I need to bury my uncle. Give us our space, I can't promise I'll want to talk to you later either, but I can promise that I won't be speaking to any other reporters." Addi's eyes found Carter's and he nodded.

"I'll make sure she doesn't bother you."

"Thanks, Carter." Addi sniffed embarrassingly, and plucked a tissue from a box on the side table, wiping her nose quickly. "And don't worry about me. Fitz and I are going to the same place. I'll be fine getting home." She didn't know why she said it. She did *not* want to ride on the back of a motorcycle, but she also felt loyal to Drew. Her heart glugged faster as she looked up at him. "He's helping me with Uncle Ray's arrangements." She straightened herself, gathering her strength. "He and Ray were really close."

Again, the redhead's eyes widened in some sort of thrill and her head cocked slightly.

"Besides, you look like you have something else to do," Drew added tersely. Carter looked at the woman beside him with disdain.

"Right. Listen, we'll get together soon, okay, Addi? Talk about old times?"

"I wouldn't think you'd want to remind her of old times, Lerner." Drew's voice was steely, causing Addi to shiver.

"Oh, I think there's some old times she might need to remember," Carter said, his face smug. He took a step forward and Drew stood taller. Drew's mouth curved into a brutal sort of snarl.

Drew dropped Addi's hand and took three giant steps toward Carter. Carter worked his Adam's apple but stood his ground. Addi cleared her throat. "I have no issues with my memory, guys."

"You do remember me then?" He looked at Addi, his

mouth widening in a smile. She nodded. He shifted his eyes to Drew and he lost his smile. "And him? You remember what he did?"

She looked at Drew. She did. She remembered quite vividly how he broke her heart and her uncle's. "Yes, I do." She swallowed. "But we're all adults now and in case you've forgotten, Carter, we're standing in a funeral home."

"Right." He hung his head a moment before looking back at her with remorse.

"Honey, again please accept my condolences on your loss." Drew stepped in front of Addi and she blinked up at his back. Why was he acting like a jealous boyfriend?

Addi peeked around Drew. Carter look irritated, but the redhead was the one Addi was interested in. She was as happy as a cat with a canary. Addi could practically visualize the feathers sticking out of her mouth.

"Hey, you ready?" Drew said gently, pulling Addi's assessing eyes from the redhead and putting his back to the others. He placed his hands on her shoulders. They were warm in the cool, dark room. He looked over his back at the others watching until they left, before looking at her. Colin had been hovering quietly but stepped forward then.

"We'll go to the back and discuss all of the options first, Miss Moore. I can show you several caskets we have on display or if you'd prefer cremation…" Drew's look had Colin closing his mouth.

"If you're not ready, we can wait." Addi tilted her head up to look at Drew and his brows rose in question. Her mind was stuck on how their relationship had ended ten years before.

He bent his knees and crouched until they were eye to eye. "Baby girl? You okay? I can take you home and we can do this tomorrow."

Addi's stomach fluttered. She wanted nothing more than to dive into his arms for support again, but dammit, she couldn't do that. She wasn't anyone's fragile little girl in need of handholding. *Screw that!*

She shook her head both to clear it and to answer his question, and then stepped toward the door. She had never been anyone's baby girl and she didn't plan on changing that. She'd had to take care of herself for as long as she could remember, except when she was with Uncle Ray, but now he was gone. There was no one to rely on but herself.

It was dumb to lean on Drew. She'd learned her lesson before. He wasn't the kind of man who stuck around. Letting him take care of her was just a momentary weakness. She'd be fine once she'd taken care of Uncle Ray, had something to eat, and had some sleep.

"No, I can do this." Addi strode to Colin's side and turned back. "*Alone.*" And walked out of the room behind Colin, trying to put his quickly hidden injured look out of her mind.

• • • • • • •

She'd expected him to be gone when she was finished, and she was holding herself together well until the moment she saw him. He looked up from his spot on the sofa, a foam cup in his hand, and for a full thirty seconds examined her face, searching it, as if he needed to reassure himself she was okay. That broke her.

She'd been heartless telling him she could do it alone. Heartless and selfish and rude. He was close to Uncle Ray too.

"I'm sorry." Her voice shook from emotion and embarrassment. "I shouldn't have dismissed you like that. Actually, I shouldn't have been an ass." She looked at the floor. "You were being nice and taking care of me and I was being a jerk." She looked up, her eyes filling with tears once again.

Drew shrugged, standing up. "Hey, he was your uncle and you haven't seen me in ten years." He held out his hand, she took it and he yanked her close, tucking her in for a squeeze before positioning her beneath his arm. His head dipped down and his free hand tipped her chin up.

"For now you get to be snarky." He narrowed his eyes. "And late. Where were you, little one?"

"I do?" His mouth came closer to her.

"Yes. You're grieving." Her eyes found his lips. They were sensual and soft, bordered by dark facial hair, and calling to hers. "Where?"

"I got lost and the rental broke down."

His brows rose. "No GPS, huh? Liar, liar, pants on fire, babe."

"And if I wasn't grieving, Drew?" Those lips, so close to hers she could practically taste them, quirked at the sides and her heart pounded.

"You, baby girl, would be over Daddy's knee for a long, hard spanking."

She swallowed hard and exhaled a heated breath.

He guided her to the exit and she followed in a stupor. He pulled open the door and the sunshine instantly took away some of the heaviness in her gut.

"Come on, you've gotta be starving by now."

"I. Am. Famished. I haven't eaten today." Addi looked up at him when he paused.

"I asked you if you'd eaten earlier. Did you lie to me twice, baby girl?" His voice was a low rumble and his brow cocked, but he didn't look all that annoyed—he was just giving her that playfully sexy *'daddy'* look.

"No, you asked me if I was hungry and I said no." She gave him a cheeky grin.

"And were you?"

"Maybe." She shrugged and looked away before he could lecture. She was thoughtful a moment as they stepped off the walkway onto the pavement. "Why are you taking care of me, Drew?"

When she turned her eyes, his face was unreadable and he pulled away to reach in his pocket for the keys. She missed his warmth instantly. Why was it she felt so comfortable with him? Even after he'd broken her heart.

"Here," he said in a gruff voice and held out the helmet from earlier. Her stomach quivered.

"Hey, Addi!" She looked up from her transfixed stare at the helmet to see Carter jingling her keys in his hand. The rental was parked next to his cruiser. The redhead sat petulantly in the front seat of his car.

"Thought you might want this." He patted her car and she smiled back as he tossed her the keys, thanking the good lord she didn't have to get on Drew's death mobile.

Drew leaned down close to her ear.

"Baby girl, you'll be on the back of my bike soon enough." His words gave her shivers and she swallowed hard. It sounded way more seductive than it should have, especially with her fear of motorbikes. He straightened, quirked an irritated brow at Carter, and straddled his bike. He kicked the bike to a start, and winked at her before pulling his glasses out of his shirt and putting them on. He popped on his skullcap.

"You comin'?" he asked. Addi continued to watch, dry-mouthed as he kicked the stand back and held the huge, rumbling machine with his thick thighs.

"Hey, you wanna follow me back instead?" Carter asked, but Addi barely glanced at him. Her attention couldn't be pulled from the bearded, tattooed man who waited for her—*her!*

"I'll be fine, but thanks for having my car fixed and brought over." Addi opened the door. "How much do I owe?" she asked, pulling her eyes from Drew's leather-clad back.

Carter's mouth pulled into a dimpled smile. "I don't know anything about cars, but the tow truck guy said it was just a loose spark plug. He fixed it right there. But how about you let me take you to dinner Friday and we'll call it even?"

Drew revved his bike impatiently and Addi felt the vibrations right through the pavement into her pelvic bone.

"Uh, I'm standing at a funeral home. My uncle just

died." She gave him a small shrug. "Not really a good time for a date."

"Oh, right. Yeah, that was dumb." He rubbed his forehead and gave her a flat smile. "How about I just come check on you on Friday? You can give me the funeral details then and I can have a look around the camp."

Addi nodded, wanting to get away and go back and lie down. This day felt never-ending and her emotions and instincts were whacky. Why did the huge scary biker revving his engine, once again acting like a jealous boyfriend, make her feel safer than she had in years?

Safer and indecently aroused at a completely inappropriate time.

Biker Daddy.

CHAPTER FIVE

Addi

When she pulled into Uncle Ray's parking spot in front of the camp office, Addi took a moment to rest her head on the wheel. She closed her eyes, but couldn't really relax with the rumbling of Drew's motorcycle, especially when she thought about the way it vibrated through her. It made her belly coil tight. When he cut the motor, she let out a breath she hadn't realized she'd been holding.

Addi didn't know how long she sat motionless, head against the steering wheel, but it was at least a half an hour before she heard the tap on her window. When she looked up, Drew's face was plastered with concern again.

She didn't want his concern. In fact, she was suddenly angry that he was there *again*. Why had her uncle let him live here? Why had he been selling the place? And why was Drew being so protective and flirty?

Frustration burned in her so hot she threw her head back and shoved the door open, hitting Drew who was standing against it. He had been nothing but nice and she felt like a supreme bitch, but she was suddenly the teen girl who couldn't control anything around her again. The feeling overwhelmed her and she wanted to go curl up and sleep away the world.

"Hey, what's going on? You okay?"

"Nothing. I'm fine," she barked, and squeezed out of the car since he wouldn't budge. "I'm going back to the cabin." She left him standing by her car with the door still partially open.

"Addi?" She looked back. "Your uncle asked me to take care of you. He was worried you'd crumple when he died."

"Thanks, but I'm fine," she answered, but he was staring expectantly. She *could* take care of herself.

"Addi?"

"What?" she shouted, throwing her hands up in exasperation. "Just let me go. I'm fine."

"You seem like a boulder heading toward the gravel pit to me."

Her eyes narrowed. "Yeah, well, you don't know me anymore."

"Maybe, but I have good instincts and you don't seem to have changed all that much." His lips quirked up. "I do miss the braids though." He chuckled when she grimaced at him. "And, baby girl, I moved your bag to *your* cabin."

She growled and covered her face with her hands. "Stop calling me that!" When her hands dropped and she started toward her uncle's cabin, he stepped in front of her like a brick wall.

"Move, Drew. I'm going to Uncle Ray's cabin."

"It's not safe." He paused to look at her, his eyes switching back and forth between hers. "It was falling apart around him and I'm not letting it fall on you. He spent a few days in the hospital a couple of months ago and I broke in and put the fireplace in because it's drafty as fuck in there. I did the windows, put on the new veranda, and gave it a coat of paint, but it needs so much more. He wouldn't let me in while he was here." He shook his head and pressed his lips. "The bloody floor is rotten. I had no idea it was that bad or I'd have fought him harder." He swallowed and shoved his hand through his hair, looking more sorry than angry then.

"What the hell right do you have to do anything around here?" Her eyes narrowed on his clenching jaw and she stabbed his chest with her finger. He looked at it, took her hand and held it tightly, but not uncomfortably, in his.

"You're not setting foot in there until it's safe. And that's the second time you've poked me, little girl. You're definitely in need of some time over Daddy's knee." Her gut dipped.

She knew the floor was rotten from watching him inspect it earlier, but she had no idea how much he'd been taking care of her uncle.

"You've been taking care of him all these years." Guilt swelled inside her. She should have been here. If only she'd known. "He seemed so… well… capable all the time. I had no idea how bad things were. My dad can't function without me, but Uncle Ray—"

He cocked his head and his expression softened. He bit the inside of his cheek. "I loved him, Addi. He meant the world to me. And he didn't want you to know how bad it was." There was a vulnerability in his look he couldn't hide and it went straight to her heart.

He released her hand and lowered his face. "I only wish he'd have let me do more for him, but he was damn stubborn." Drew kicked a rock hard and it skittered toward the lake and then his eyes met hers and firmed. "Apparently, it runs in the family."

Addi smirked. "Perhaps it's in the water here."

He reached out and touched her cheek. "I already fixed your cabin. It was the first one I did when I came back here to fix what I'd done." He paused, watching her face.

She shut her eyes, remembering the way the camp had been in shambles after his club had their fun.

"I added some amenities."

Her eyes fluttered open and his thumb smoothed down and across her lips, making her heartbeat quicken. "To make it nicer for the guests?"

"No, no one stays in your cabin." He dropped his hands and they fisted slightly. She searched his expression and he looked away. When she wasn't being a raving lunatic, she could easily see his grief.

"Your uncle never let anyone stay in it," he added and started to walk away. He turned back a minute, looking broody. It didn't seem like it was her uncle's decision by his reaction, but then again, she was overtired and probably reading into things. Why the hell should he care? He broke up with her, told he he'd never cared, that he had only been with her to please Ray. And that's all this was too, a promise to Ray.

"I'll bring you dinner in a bit and breakfast in the morning. We can talk about your poking problem and the rest of your indiscretions then."

"I can get my own…" She let her words trail off as he growled.

"The hell you will." His pace increased and he effectively cut her off by storming away. His gait was most definitely a sexy swagger, but not the intentional kind. He was a natural.

Addi couldn't help but feel a little breathless watching him in his tight jeans and black scarred motorcycle boots with his shoulders squared and his longish dark hair curling over the collar of his shirt.

As she turned to the little cabin across the gravel drive, fear singed her gut. It was hard enough facing her uncle's place but the cabin held more memories. She and Uncle Ray spent weeks getting it perfected. That was a time she'd cherished her whole life. No one had cared about her room at home or what she liked or didn't.

She entered the cabin and despite her reluctance, smiled widely. It had air conditioning and it was also her dream. The bed was not like the bunks in the boys' cabins or the frilly nightmare she'd had as a teen. It was a cherry wood sleigh bed with a solid yellow quilt and more pillows than anyone needed and everything was spotlessly clean. Best of all there wasn't one bit of lace anywhere. There were bookshelves lined with her favorites as a teen and a cozy chair with a throw blanket over the armrest. Across from the bed was a dressing table that had pretty antique perfume bottles, and silver brush and mirror set.

Addi pulled out the little stool and sat, staring at herself in the mirror. She looked tired. Lines of worry around her eyes and forehead made her rub her face as if that could remove them. There was a modern porcelain bowl and jug for washing up on the dresser top and she stood to reach for it. That's when she saw the beautiful antique iron woodstove. She covered her mouth with her hand as she stared. And then her eyes landed on a door at the back of the cabin, one that was never there before, and her brow furrowed. She thought of Drew's words.

"I added some amenities."

Addi stood and went to the new door. Opening it, she gaped. It was a bathroom—with a claw-foot tub. None of the cabins had bathrooms. All the campers had used the communal washrooms and showers by the mess hall—she'd used the bathroom in the office and Uncle Ray's shower when she had been there.

She looked at the room in awe. It not only had a functioning toilet, gorgeous tub, and a pedestal sink but an antique mirror, more antique-looking bottles, and finger, hand, and bath towels. Why was it so painstakingly decorated with the perfect combination of modern and antique if her uncle hadn't rented it out?

She reached out to the sink. A little divot in the porcelain held different shaped soaps. She picked up an oval-shaped bar and sniffed it. It smelled like lavender. She turned, noticing a metal tray set across the edges of the tub.

One of the little baskets had several bath bombs and another had a gel eye mask. She reached to touch them, too.

The cabin would have been a big seller. She eyed the deep tub and bit her lip. She would love a hot soak with one of those bath bombs fizzing in it, but first she walked through the little cabin again looking at everything anew imagining what her write-up would be.

The pretty butter-yellow cabin with climbing clematis begs to be entered and once you do, you feel like royalty. Suddenly you're swept away from a North American campground to a gorgeous cottage in the European countryside. New delights peek out from wherever your eyes settle. From the modern sleigh bed to the antique fixtures, the cabin is an absolute darling. You won't know whether to throw yourself into the cloud of pillows on the silky quilt or to fill the tub and soak your stresses away. Either way, this is one place you'll forget your troubles for a while.

The cabin was completely out of place in the camp—as ridiculous as glamping. The bunk cabins were rough, with natural wood interiors—plain and basic. The blankets were sleeping bags and the mattresses hard, plastic-covered, and smelled of damp and wood smoke. There were spider webs in the corners and dust and sand could always be found even though they were cleaned thoroughly on a regular basis. It was the way of the outdoors. That was camp life. At least that's how they used to be. But maybe they'd been upgraded too.

She was fondling the expensive sheets on the bed when Drew gave a quick knock and walked in. He took up a large part of the cabin with his towering form. His arms, covered in sleeve tattoos, pulled her eyes again. They were the things of horror films—demons, howling souls being tortured in hell, snakes in skulls, and who knew what other terrors. She looked at his face instead.

"Hi," she said quietly.

He had a faded brown tray, one of the old ones from the mess hall. He set it on the small antique bistro table in the corner of the room by the door, never removing his eyes from hers.

"It's just a sandwich and some milk, but you need something."

"Thank you. For the sandwich and for making my cabin

so gorgeous."

He scratched his beard, looking awkward.

"I'm sorry I've been so crazy. I know I've been rude to you," she added.

"You're welcome." He placed his hands on his hips and cocked his head to the side. "Baby girl, I'm giving you some leeway here because I know you're grieving, but one of these times you're going to push me to the edge. I don't put up with that shit."

She sat on the bed, still pawing the sheets. "Okay." She looked at him through her lashes, his handsome face and intelligent eyes making her heart patter. "I'm not sure I'd be as forgiving as you if it were me."

"Oh, you deserve a good old-fashioned spanking, baby girl—" He smirked. "But like I said, you get some leeway—*for now.*"

"What if even *I* think I deserve that spanking?" She surprised herself with the question and swallowed hard at the throbbing heat that started in between her legs.

"Too bad, sweetheart. I'm the daddy. I decide what you need and when."

She smiled, her heartbeat doubling its pace. "Joking aside, Drew, I thought it was hard when I was a kid, but adulting is no picnic either."

He came and sat beside her on the bed, handing her half of the sandwich and wrapping his arm around her. He watched her with a crooked brow until she took a bite.

"Mmum," she muffled through the sandwich.

"First, I wasn't joking, young lady. If you need a good bottom-warming, I won't hesitate. Second, you don't have to adult with me. I'll help you and if everything gets too much for you and you've had enough, I'll take over."

Addi clasped her lip between her teeth. *He can't possibly be serious about spanking me and taking over, can he?* Before she could ask, though, he moved on.

"Have you decided when to have the funeral?"

Addi looked at her lap, fiddling with the quilt. "They're

putting the obituary in the paper for tomorrow. I'm going to skip the option of visitation. Uncle Ray would hate to be on display." She smirked. "Like a trophy fish." Drew laughed and she continued, feeling somber again. "The funeral will be on Saturday." She looked up at Drew. "I feel like there may be a lot of people that went to the camp as boys that may want to make the trek here to pay respects. I'm going to start going through the files and see if I can't contact some of them."

"I can help with that," Drew said.

She nodded, giving him a small, sad smile before looking around the cabin again. "I'm so tired. I know it's early but I just need to rest. Does my uncle's office pass inspection? Does it still have the old couch in it?"

Drew's finger found Addi's chin and he tilted it so she looked at him. "Why, baby girl? Don't you like your cabin?"

"I don't want to sleep in here. I don't know."

"What if I stayed until you fell asleep?" He let go of her chin and pointed to the floral upholstered chair by the books.

Her heart swelled at his sweet offering.

"Why are you single, Drew? Shouldn't someone have snapped you up by now?"

"Sweetheart, that's a story for another time. Up you get." His big, warm palm swallowed hers, and her heart tripped in her chest. He stood and pulled her with him.

Addi looked at her suitcases and gathered a breath. She was too damn tired to unpack, but she needed something to sleep in. He followed her line of sight and looked at the bags over his shoulder. Nodding at her, he reached over his shoulder and yanked off his t-shirt. He held it out to her, but she only stared at his hard chest.

She was grieving and vulnerable and certainly not in her right mind because the sight of him half naked before her made her middle spasm with need. She licked her lips, wanting to taste the nipples that were hard beads over brown flat disks, the hollows of his neck and, *God*, the trail of hair that disappeared beneath his belted jeans.

"Here," he said, placing the shirt in her hands. "No need to dig around in those bags now." His shirt was warm and as she clasped it to her chest, she could smell him. "Do you want some privacy?" he questioned when she hadn't moved for several moments.

Addi shook her head, closing her eyes. She couldn't stand the thought of being alone, even in the tiny bathroom. Modesty be damned. When she opened her eyes to look at him, his brows peaked in the middle of his forehead and his mouth formed a frown of concern.

"Did my uncle really ask you to take care of me?"

He swallowed hard, shoving his hands through his hair before burying them in his pockets. She saw her own want in his eyes. There was something psychological that happened in times of loss—something that drew people together, made them crave human touch, understanding, and physical comfort, especially from those who shared their loss. That's all this was between them, and she was okay with that. He was the only other person in the world who loved her uncle like she did. They shared that, and that was more than enough.

"Yes, Addi. Made me swear I would give you whatever support you needed. He loved you so much. He knew you'd need someone once he was gone." His voice lowered to a whisper. "Someone like me. Who could not only read through your tough girl act, but deal with your stubborn side."

"Then take *care* of me Drew. *Please*." Her words came out on a whimper, but not the kind that stemmed from a grief-stricken heart; it was one of want, intense need, and carnal urges.

His breath quickened and he looked hesitant, almost tortured at first before he took a step closer, placing his hands on her blouse. By the time he pulled it off her arms, her nipples were tight and begging for his touch. He stared, looking pained again as his jaw clenched. He reached behind her and unhooked her bra. She mewled, arching her chest toward him. His tight expression turned to anger and she blinked in confusion. His hand threaded through her hair and she gasped as he tightened his grip and pulled her head back to devour her mouth roughly. The kiss was thorough, lengthy, and it melted her bones.

"Turn around." His voice was gruff with arousal and demanding. She bit her lip and did as she was told. He ran a hand down her back and she heard nothing but his ragged breathing and her own heart pounding. He took the bra straps in his hands and slid them down her shoulders and off. Her eyes fluttered closed, anticipating his touch—feeling wet and greedy for more. How long had it been since she'd been touched? *So, so, long!* She held her breath…waiting.

His touch didn't come. His shirt was over her head and on her before she could stutter the question she begged to ask…

Why not?

Was he not attracted to her?

"Stay." He lowered her bottoms down her hips and made her step out of them. "Okay, you can turn back around." He pulled back the duvet and sheets. "Let's get you tucked in, baby girl. The last thing you need is an ass like me taking advantage of you."

Addi climbed into the bed, her clit aching, and turned toward the wall. Drew covered her, tucking the blankets tight around her.

"Drew, I understand why you won't…" She cleared her throat. "But, will you lie with me?" Her voice was small and vulnerable and she hated it, but she didn't want to be alone—even after his rejection.

She heard his whispered curse and it stabbed through her like an arrow. He tucked the blanket around her tightly and climbed on top of the covers. She should have known he'd be repulsed by her. She sniffed.

"Angel, you have no idea how hard it is for me to keep

my hands to myself right now. I'm trying to be the good guy for once."

CHAPTER SIX

Addi

Addi woke groggily, wondering where she was. Her mind flipped from home, to Daniel and Steven's, to the B&B, dismissing each thought as it came until she remembered Uncle Ray. The realization had grief pouring over her, cold and heavy like wet cement, and then Drew came to mind. Wide-eyed, she groped the bed for him, and let out a sigh of relief when she felt nothing but cool sheets. She was alone.

Alone. She swallowed a blip of sadness and focused on her embarrassment over asking Drew to stay with her. She gulped, harder this time. She'd propositioned him. *Oh, God.* She pulled the covers over her head and groaned. She had never propositioned anyone in her life.

"Quit feeling sorry for yourself, Addianna Moore!" She kicked a leg beneath the covers, adding to her dramatics.

Gathering a breath, she yanked the blankets off and sat up. With the curtains closed tight, she was disoriented. Had she slept all night? She clicked on the bedside lamp, blinking at the old-fashioned clock beside it. It was seven p.m. She'd only been asleep a few hours.

Knowing she'd need a walk to clear her head and decide what she'd say to Drew before she'd be able to sleep again, she set her feet on the cool floor. She was still exhausted from all her blubbering at the funeral home. How did you apologize for bawling all over someone and then begging them to take you to bed?

She rose, looking down at herself in Drew's t-shirt and her shame deepened. How could she? She'd wanted to be close to another person, sure, bury herself in something that would encompass her, but to push herself on him was inexcusable.

It wasn't just the sex she wanted either, but Drew himself. His presence surrounded her like an ocean of warmth—sometimes tumultuous but always in control and when she gave in to him, calm and soothing.

Screwing him would be like drowning in him. Nothing could get her once he'd fully possessed her. She would be completely his, hidden and free from the world.

Addi pulled off his shirt, bringing it to her nose and breathing him in a moment before grabbing her own clothes, which Drew had folded neatly over the back of the chair.

The sun was lowering in the sky and the heady scent of a fire and grilled meat in the distance made her smile. She loved that smell.

She wasn't sure where to look for Drew, or how to apologize, but she followed the scent of the fire until a vehicle coming up the lane made her head that way instead.

An old VW beetle with too much rust and a bad paint job stopped in front of the office. The blonde from the bar climbed out wearing short-shorts, a black crop top, and bright red heels that matched her lipstick. A little blond boy with big glasses and a cowlick jumped out after her. She reached into the car and pulled out a tray of cupcakes. Addi tugged at her dark hair, thrown haphazardly in a ponytail, and chewed the inside of her cheek.

"How are you?" the woman said in a sickly-sweet tone

that made Addi feel diabetic.

"I'm okay. You?" She didn't look at the blonde woman while speaking but examined the cute kid shoving his glasses up his nose with a marker-smudged finger.

"I'm Brent," he said and held his tiny hand out. "We're here to offer con-dol-enc-es." The big word came out choppy, as if he'd been practicing.

"Well, that's very sweet of you, Brent. I'm Addi." Addi crouched down and took his hand. After they shook, Addi looked at him conspiratorially. "I hope you got to eat one of those yummy cupcakes before you brought them over here." He looked at his mother, who was busily looking around, and then nodded with a wide grin. He patted his tummy and gave her a thumbs up, whispering they'd got them from the bakery in town.

The smile on Addi's mouth froze when she heard Drew's harsh voice.

"What the hell are you doing here, Layla?" Anger contorted Drew's face as he strode like a storm toward them. He opened his mouth, no doubt to say something rude as he seemed apt to do whenever he encountered someone other than her, when Addi took Brent's hand and stepped into his sightline.

"Look, Fitz, Brent and his mom came over with cupcakes."

"Con-dol-ence cupcakes!" Brent said excitedly, skipping toward Drew and hugging his leg. The change on his face was remarkable and before he scooped the kid up, he was all but beaming.

"Hey, buddy! They look awesome. Did you bake them?"

"I did," Layla said, strutting toward him, all legs and ass cheeks hanging out. Brent's expression surely mirrored her own shocked one, but he quickly smiled over Drew's shoulder, putting his finger to his lips. Addi winked and held back a giggle as he winked awkwardly back.

"Come on, let's put these in the fridge," Addi said, and Drew set Brent down. Addi put her hand on the child's back, guiding him away from Drew and Layla. Drew gave Addi one of his assessing looks—the kind where his eyes went back and forth between hers as if reading her like a book. She lowered her face, knowing she'd asked this man to bed her only two hours earlier. Although she couldn't see anything in his expression that said he was annoyed or disgusted with her, it didn't matter because she was disgusted with herself.

"Pick me out a good one, buddy."

Brent nodded and Addi led him to the mess hall. She wasn't even sure if there was still a fridge in there, let alone a functioning one, but again that wasn't the point. She needed to give Drew and Layla a minute, but more important, keep Brent away from the surly man who had started to cuss out his mother.

When Addi looked back, Layla's arms were around Drew's neck and Drew's hands clasped her wrists tightly. Was he removing her hands or holding them there like handcuffs? She shivered at the thought of being handcuffed by his large, strong hands, and then scolded herself. *God, can you think of anything besides sex?*

Addi was just putting the cupcakes in the big old fridge, debating on whether it was cool enough to be working properly, when Brent tapped her on the back. She turned to see the little guy pulling an envelope out of his pocket.

"Here. It's for you." The envelope had the words 'from Brent' scrawled in childlike printing on the front under the scratched-out credit card company address. He had written his name and address at the top on the lines where the return address should go. "That's how they send letters to my mom from school."

"You did it exactly right, Brent. Thank you."

"I'm sorry I didn't know your name then."

"Next time you'll know to write A. D. D. I." Brent nodded with a wide smile that fell quickly at the sound of his mother's holler.

"My mom's calling. I should go. She gets mad when I

don't come right away." He pointed at the envelope. "It's a picture I drew."

"So that's why you have marker on your hands. You're an artist." The little boy glowed.

"Fitz taught me how to draw. He says I'm good. He says I can be an artist someday. He takes me to the cliff house to paint sometimes when Mom's been…" He looked at his feet. "Partying."

"I think if Fitz thinks you're talented, then you must be." *Partying? The cliff house?*

Addi opened the letter quickly and pulled out a drawing of a stream and trees on the inside of a waffle box. It was much better than she'd expected for a child no more than six. "It's beautiful! Fitz is right about you. I'm going to get a frame for this."

"You are?" His eyes were big and round, and he shoved his glasses up again. His toothy grin showed adult front teeth currently too big for his child-sized mouth.

"I am."

Addi stood straight and closed the fridge door, hearing Brent's mom screeching once again for him. "Thank you for the picture. I'll treasure it." He leaned forward to hug her and she gave him a good squeeze back.

"I'm sorry your uncle died. He used to sit with me when I'd to go to work with my mom on Saturdays. He was really nice."

Addi pressed her mouth and gave him a sad nod. "I hope to see you again, Artist Brent." His little face lit with her words and he ran off.

When she walked out a few minutes later, the purple Beetle was kicking up dust and Drew was staring cross-armed and stone-faced. She didn't fail to notice the lipstick on his neck and cheek though.

Unexplainable jealousy burned in her as if she had some claim on him. Before Drew noticed, she jogged toward the woods. Addi not only had no right to be jealous, but being so was ridiculous! She hadn't been involved with Drew since she was sixteen and even then he'd told her it wasn't real. She had no rights to him, now or then.

She was here for her uncle's funeral, not to mess around with Drew, and certainly not to become jealous and obsessive over him. No matter how sweet he was being or how close she felt to him. Or how much he flirted or made her feel special. Or how much desire and arousal he stirred in her.

He's not mine.

Brent was on her mind too. He was a sweet kid but his mother wouldn't be earning any parent of the year awards in Addi's opinion. It brought back her own childhood issues.

Addi felt her knees buckle but caught herself. Being at the camp was stirring up all kinds of emotions and memories—things she'd never really dealt with. She wanted to release all the emotions battling inside so she could pack them neatly away inside herself again, but if she was going to break down, she needed to do it alone. She needed to be away from the man who seemed to catch her at every weak moment. She walked deeper into the forest.

The ground was soft, and her only comfortable shoes were some chunky-heeled sandals that kept sinking into the damp earth, but they didn't stop her from barreling through the natural paths that formed in the woods.

She leaned against a tree and pulled out Brent's picture. She stared at the well-drawn scene. How come she had never seen Uncle Ray paint? Not when she was there for the summer or even over the years when he'd stayed with her for holidays and vacations. She thought of the smudges of marker on Brent's hand. She had never seen Uncle Ray's hands marred with paint.

Running her hands along the rough, damp bark of the tree she leaned against, she breathed in the heady scent of nature. She hadn't gone into the forest the summer she'd been at camp, except once. She closed her eyes, breathing deep. The forest led to the cliffs. The cliffs were where she'd fallen and where Drew had saved her.

"Hey, Addi." One of the camp leaders came out through the door, tossing a baseball in the air. She smiled and nodded at him, remembering his name was Markus.

"You coming with us today?" He swished his light brown hair back and caught the ball, tossing it again before she could answer.

Addi shrugged as she watched him leap forward to catch the wayward ball. Other boys milled out of the hall, laughing loudly, punching shoulders and creating boy ruckus. Addi didn't do anything with the camp boys. They were happy to roll around in the dirt, hike, slide to home base, canoe, and the million other things boys did, but she didn't fit in with the camp leaders either.

It was parents' day so the leaders had free time.

As Markus watched her expectantly, blinking his large brown eyes, she decided that she'd try, especially after Uncle Ray's lecture about how disappointed he was that she wasn't participating or interacting with others.

Addi just didn't like nature. She hated bugs, snakes, rodents, and dirt. Mosquitoes spread all kinds of bad stuff like malaria, and ticks spread Lyme disease. Some snakes had hemotoxic venom that could kill, rodents were the cause of the plague, and playing in dirt could give you tetanus. And ever since her mom's accident, she didn't take risks.

"So?" Addi's mind snapped alert at Markus's terse voice.

She needed to make friends if she was going to be here all school break. After all, she'd come to have a normal summer.

"Can't you make a simple decision?" Markus tossed the ball at her but she wasn't expecting it, so it fell to the ground at her feet after hitting her rounded belly.

"Geez, you can't even catch a ball?"

"Leave her alone," a voice said, making her look up, It was one of the leaders who seemed wiser and more mature than the rest. His eyes, a stunning blue, seemed to carry indifference most of the time, but she saw something else deeper in them.

The other leaders didn't seem to like him very much, but they were respectful. Maybe it was because he didn't goof around like them and they feared him a little. With the kids, he was patient and kind, albeit tough when he needed to be, and they loved him, but he wasn't chummy with the other leaders. He looked threatening now and she could easily picture him flicking any one of them to the ground like a crumb off his Black Sabbath t-shirt.

"Aren't you going swimming?" the leader questioned with crossed arms when Markus didn't move.

"Uh, yeah, you coming, Drew?"

"In a bit. Got something to do first."

Markus nodded and waved the other guys to follow, but Addi continued to watch Drew. She'd heard the others whispering. They'd said he had to meet with his parole officer and that's why he went to Uncle Ray's office every Friday morning, but she didn't know for sure. She just watched his long legs stride away, intrigued by both his secrets and the sadness hidden in his eyes.

"Hey, are we cliff jumping?" Kevin, one of the leaders said, and Addi turned back to watch the group of guys as Kevin sidled up next to Markus, grabbing his ball from midair.

"Hell yeah, we are." Markus looked over his shoulder at Addi. "You coming, Addi? If you're too scared you can just watch. I'm sure Carter could use a cheerleader." He laughed and Carter ran up and put him in a headlock.

When he let Markus go, Carter smiled at her. "You in? Tonight, we're going hang at the beach and drink the beer Alex stole."

None of that appealed. Except she saw her uncle's disappointed face in her mind. He wanted her to fit in, to have some fun.

"She can't do it. She's afraid," Kevin said and threw the baseball at Carter. He jumped up to catch it.

"I'm not afraid." Addi's voice came out in an angry growl.

"Yeah, you are. You're afraid of everything." Kevin's eyes were pinned intensely on her. "I bet you can't do it."

"I'm in on that bet," Markus piped in.

Addi chewed her lip. Would Drew be at the beach later? She looked back toward him. His back was just disappearing into the office. She could dog paddle enough to get to shore, couldn't she?

"I'll do it and you'll lose your bet," Addi said, determined.

"But you never go into the water," Carter said tossing the baseball up in the air. "We thought you couldn't swim."

"Stop worrying, Carter, your girlfriend will be fine. She doesn't need to swim far. She just needs to jump. Jeff can wait at the bottom and help her."

Carter's cheeks turned pink. "She's not my girlfriend, dick."

"I can swim," Addi said, feeling her own cheeks heat with embarrassment. Was slapping at the water like a dog considered swimming? She could keep herself above water for a while anyway. "What's the bet?"

"You jump and we'll never bug you again—even if you don't want to do shit with us—"

Carter pushed forward and cut Markus off. His eyes were heated, eager, and he licked his lips before they turned up in a leer. "You back out though, and we all get to see your tits."

Addi felt sick. Snakes furled in her belly and she fought to keep her pancake breakfast down. Markus started nudging his buddies.

"She won't do it." The group's laughter made the snakes churn faster.

"Let's go."

The guys' laughter became giddier the closer they got to the cliffs. Addi's anger kept her feet moving on the trail and her mind was too focused on winning the bet to think of the creatures lurking in the forest.

She followed them to a spot a few feet from the cliff, and Markus grabbed her.

They quieted as Markus walked her to the edge of the cliff. It was a far drop and she could see the water was choppy around the rocks. She swallowed. What if she hit one? Addi licked her lips, feeling her body sway. It was windy at the top of the rocky outcropping.

Would her father pull the plug?

"Uh, what about the rocks?"

"They only look close. They're not," Markus said. "We've all done this jump, Addi. But hey, if you're backing out…" She turned to see Carter lick his lips again and she shivered.

"I'm not!" Addi swallowed hard again. Carter threw a small log over the cliff and Addi watched it smash into bits. Deciding suddenly that one quick flash of her chest wouldn't kill her like the rocks below, she spun back and that's when she heard a scream. It was from her mouth as Markus shoved a snake at her face. She lurched back, and

the loose gravel on the edge shifted.

She slipped. Her arms pin-wheeled and she fought to regain her footing as Drew ran toward her. His face was a storm of anger and fear. He cursed and lunged for her, but it was too late. He couldn't reach her. Addi felt gravity pull her down.

She was falling faster and faster, and the scream that tore from her mouth at the sight of the snake was nothing compared to the one that came out of her on the way down.

• • • • • • •

Addi was going to die. She didn't want to die.

She hit the water and it stole her breath. Not the water pouring into her mouth but the sheer shock of the cold, hard landing.

Addi struggled, not knowing what was up and what was down, but when her head broke the surface she saw them all howling with laughter at the top of the cliff. Except Drew. She couldn't see him. Where was he?

Water splashed in her eyes as she slapped her hands on the surface. The deep water was so cold, her limbs felt sluggish and heavy. It was much harder than she expected to keep them moving and she felt so exhausted.

She stopped pawing at the water and kicking her legs, letting her head slip beneath the surface. Water swallowed her and filled her ears. It was so calm and quiet beneath the surface. It felt peaceful. Much better than the laughter, ridicule, and embarrassment from above. She just needed a minute and then she'd paddle her way to shore and face them.

Arms grabbed her around her waist, and her limbs, as loose as sea kelp, floated in front of her as she was dragged. She started squirming as soon as she felt ground beneath her feet, but a few seconds later, she was dumped on the rocky sand. Her limbs felt heavy and awkward out of the cold lake, so she lay there sprawled on the ground.

Coughing, her eyes flickered open only to see Drew's fearful electric blue eyes blink at her. She gazed at them, the dark blue ring around the outside making them more intense, suddenly feeling just as much peace as she had in the water. She smiled unexpectedly.

"Are you okay?" Drew's hands cupped Addi's face, and she couldn't speak. His warm touch made her gut flip and flutter and his face, intensely close, transfixed her. He had strong features. Unlike the other guys, Drew's jaw was square and stubbled with more than just peach fuzz. He clenched his manly jaw and yanked her floppy form against his chest, moving his hands from her face to her back.

"You almost drowned." His words were no longer soft and filled with concern, like his expression only moments ago. They were angry instead. He pushed her back and held her upper arms tightly in his large hands.

"You can barely swim!" he said, and she wanted to argue but his angry eyes stopped her. "Why the hell would you even go to the edge?" His eyes seemed to shoot blue sparks.

He shook his head. "Markus will pay for this." He scooped Addi up and carried her through the woods. She had no idea where he was taking her and she didn't even care that he was carrying her like a child or that she was too heavy to be carried. She was too weak and cold to do anything but lay her head on his thick shoulder and wrap her arms around him.

She figured he'd take her back to Uncle Ray, but he didn't. He took her to her little cabin. He kicked the door open and his eyes widened at all the lace and pink. Or maybe it was the lack of similarity to the rest of the camp's rusticness. Addi's cabin looked more like a dollhouse than a cabin—pretty and frilly just like her dad liked everything for her, just like he'd told Uncle Ray she loved. She was so happy that Uncle Ray was taking the time to fix it up with her that she didn't have the heart to tell him she hated frilly pink.

"What the hell?"

She swallowed at his words and started pushing against his chest for him to set her down. He only held her tighter against him and spun slowly to take it all in.

"It's like a princess puked in here."

"It's, it's—"

"Not you," he said simply, and set her on the padded upholstered chair. He licked his lips, glancing at her. "You okay?"

Addi could only nod, embarrassed.

"Can you get changed by yourself?"

Her eyes widened and she nodded quicker this time. Her dress clung to her wetly. The butter-yellow material was almost see-through and she suddenly knew why he looked as if he'd swallowed a lemon. He could see everything.

"I'm fine," she answered in a squeaky voice, covering her chest with folded arms. He straightened, suddenly becoming taller.

"Change. I'll wait outside." He looked at her sternly. "Then we'll talk."

"Um, okay," she mumbled. He'd never even talked to her before this day and now suddenly he was in her cabin and wanted to talk more.

Addi could probably count on one hand how many times she'd heard him speak outside of his time with the campers. She took a breath and shivered. She liked the deep, raspy sound of his voice.

Addi stood on legs as firm as a newborn foal and peeled off her dress. She threw a camp t-shirt over her head and grabbed the only pair of shorts she had. She used them for cleaning. They were cut-off jeans and the button dug into her belly. She pulled on the cut-offs and looked at herself in the mirror above the dressing table.

Drew's knock startled her even though she knew it was coming. Addi called for him to enter.

"Hi," he said, looking stunned by her appearance. "Now you look like you."

"My dad likes me to wear dresses."

"But what do you like?"

She didn't know what to say to that so she just shrugged.

"Sit." He nodded at the chair he'd originally sat her in. She did as she was told and watched him come closer.

"Why?" he asked softly, propping his hands on his hips, knocking the chain that looped from his back pocket to the belt loop on the front of his knee-length shorts. "Why did you stop trying?" His eyes narrowed on hers.

She knew he was referring to when she'd stopped swimming and she only shrugged again.

"Answer me!" Anger threaded into his raspy voice and she wrapped her arms around herself, shaking her head.

"Dammit!" He looked away and she watched his square jaw tick.

"Is it because of your mom?"

Addi's eyes flew wide. How did he know about her mom? Her breath quickened and the tears that stung behind her eyes suddenly spilled over.

"Don't talk about my mom," she said, feeling an all-encompassing hurt and a surge of anger. "This has nothing to do with her."

"I'm sorry, but if you're going to fling yourself off a cliff and let yourself drown, you need to talk about it."

Addi shot forward onto the edge of her chair, clenching her teeth. "I didn't fling myself off the cliff. That dick Markus scared me and I slipped."

His brows rose. "And still you didn't swim."

"I slipped," she said, firmer. "And there was a bet and dammit." She looked away. "And I was just taking a break from swimming. It was cold and my arms and legs felt like lead."

His brow furrowed. "A break? From swimming? That's giving up!" He sat on the bed, rolled his shoulders and spoke calmly. "And what bet?"

She looked away, clenching her jaw. "One I couldn't lose."

"What bet, Addi?" Although the words came out slow and steady, there was an underlying demand in them that forced her to confide in him. The words tumbled from her trembling lips. "If I didn't jump, I'd have to show them my chest."

He growled, angrier than she'd ever seen a person in her life. Her eyes widened and he slammed his hand into the wall.

"I'll kill them!" As soon as the words were out of his mouth, his face paled. He looked ill.

"Are you okay?" she asked, reaching out but Drew only turned to leave.

"You didn't have to agree to that bet, Addi. You're stronger than that."

"No, I'm not."

"Bullshit! Stay away from the cliff. If I catch you there again… "

She grabbed his arm and he stopped, his head down, back to her, breathing ragged.

"I won't go there again."

He spun, grabbed her waist, and pulled her against him. She was still reeling from the shock of his touch, his body still wet and cold from saving her, when his mouth crushed hers.

When he released her, she felt like a hot, wet piece of cooked spaghetti. And then, while she was still befuddled, he left the little cabin, and her heart, beating at the pace of a hummingbird, fluttered against her ribcage.

The reverie made her edgier and she shoved herself off the tree and began to jog. Goddammit, she needed to clear her head, but the more time she spent here, the more time her head was pulled into the past. Everything was too much! With the rough terrain, she stumbled frequently, but caught herself until a root snagged her sandal and she landed face-down in the dirt.

She blew out in relief at not hitting her head off the pile of rocks only a few feet in front of her. Ignoring the sting in her torn palms, she started to push herself up and then froze at the sound of the rattle.

Oh, shit.

Fear pulsed through her. She knew the sound of a rattlesnake. Frozen, ironically in the yoga cobra pose, she searched frantically with only her eyes for the snake.

She was terrified of garter snakes and this was no garter—it was a venomous snake.

Her eyes darted around frantically. She didn't see it anywhere, which was worse than knowing where it was. A mantra of *'oh, God'* and *'what do I do?'* was on repeat in her head when she heard a twig snap to her left. She whimpered. Her lip trembled and her teeth began to chatter. What had she been thinking, wandering into the woods on her own? She had no experience in the woods—nature TV programs didn't count either.

"Don't move, Addi. It's right there in front of you." It was Drew's voice that pulled her from her terror. She couldn't see him—couldn't afford to turn her head, but his calm voice instantly soothed her. The snake shook its rattle again and she spotted it. There was a rustle behind her, and then Drew came up beside her with a branch in his hand. It was forked at the end like the serpent's tongue.

He took three steps ahead and she stared at the thick tread of his biker boots, avoiding looking at the snake aggressively poised and ready to strike in between the crevice of a boulder and the rotting tree trunk. A garbled noise burst from her throat and Drew shot her a stern look.

"I'm going to distract it; you get up and get back."

She was going to nod at first and then realized that was a bad idea. Besides, he was no longer looking at her.

He moved the stick to the snake's side, and it zeroed in on the new threat. As soon as she rose, the serpent's head swiveled back. Drew used the stick again, this time trapping its head in the fork. Addi jumped up and bolted back, before spinning and running twenty feet away. And just to be safe, climbing the nearest tree. She screeched as Drew released the snake and sprang out of striking distance. He backed away, and they both watched the snake dart into the rotting log.

Addi stared, still trembling, as Drew's wide strides thumped toward her. When she finally looked down at him, his brows were knit tight.

"You can get down now."

Addi swallowed and moved her hand to grip the branch differently. "I can't." She looked down at the tree's branches. "I can't get down."

"For Pete's sake. Yes, you can." He looked down, sounding exasperated, and rubbed a hand over the back of his neck. When he looked back up, his eyes settled on her feet. "What are you wearing?"

Addi looked down and wiggled her toes. "Sandals." Her words were matter of fact. "Why?"

"High-heeled sandals?" He looked at her in disbelief. "Seriously?"

"Yes, you're not hallucinating. They are quite obviously chunky-heeled sandals."

"Don't get bratty with me, Addi. You're the loon that

came out into the woods by yourself wearing *chunky-heeled* sandals, messed with a poisonous snake, and climbed a damn tree." He crossed his arms, and again she admired his well-formed biceps.

"They're all I have besides actual high heels, and I certainly didn't expect to bump into a snake."

"I know you know they're here in the forest, and what about bears and wolves? You know they can wander around here too. Especially in the evening. Prime predator hunting time."

"Bears? Wolves?" Her voice was unsteady. Bears were rare but Uncle Ray had told her stories of them occasionally wandering into camp. The boys had always learned animal safety on day one.

"Turn around, lean your belly against the tree trunk, hold the branch, and slide as far as you can until you're hanging. I'll get you from there."

She started to shift, felt the branch sway with her weight, and then went back to her spot in the V-shaped crevice.

"Uh-uh, I think I'll stay here," she said, swallowing hard.

"You can't stay there. Don't be ridiculous."

"Yes, I can." She went to cross her arms but stopped when she teetered.

"It'll be dark soon, the mosquitoes will devour you, and bears can climb trees."

"Oh."

"Come on, I'll lift you down once I can reach your legs."

"You won't drop me, right?" Her eyes narrowed on him.

"Baby girl, you're irritating me. And being dropped is not what you need to worry about when I'm annoyed."

"Okay, okay," she said and gingerly grabbed the branch and slid her bottom across the rough bark. She turned herself onto her belly and slid lower. The bark caught her jean button and it popped open. She scrambled up again but only succeeded in lowering the zipper, and as she let herself fall to swing from the branch, her jeans slid down slowly.

"Close your eyes!" she squealed, wishing the ground

would open so she could fall in it.

"It'll be a little hard to get you with my eyes closed, babe. And if I recall you weren't so shy earlier." He chuckled and she groaned. His warm palms cupped her bottom with only white cotton between their skin.

"Relax into me, as if you're sitting on my hands."

"Okay," she squeaked and did her best to sit on his hands.

"Now let go of the branch."

"Let go?"

"Yes, Addi. Let go."

"But I'll fall."

"You won't fall. I'm right here."

"But…"

"Addianna, you're seriously trying my patience."

She closed her eyes, squeezed them tight, and released the branch. She expected to fall, but all she did was slide down his hard, warm chest to her feet.

He turned her to face him as soon as she was solidly on the ground. They were so close she could feel his breath on her. He tipped her chin up.

"Baby girl, have you ever had a switch across your bottom?"

She swallowed hard again, blinking, and shook her head. "No." Her pulse began pounding between her legs and standing in just her panties with her pants in a lump at her ankles was heating her further. What if he took a switch to her?

"Well, it hurts, not nearly as much as diamondback venom, but enough to teach you not to wander off in the woods alone when you have no experience."

She stumbled back, bent, and swiftly tugged her jeans up. "Thanks for the rescue, Drew." She turned and started walking away. "I have experience enough." She gave a finger wave.

"Then why are you walking deeper into the woods rather than back to camp?"

"Maybe I'm not done exploring."

He snorted and grabbed her arm. "Let's go before I pick a switch and show you what a bastard I can be."

"No way! You aren't smacking me with a stick," she growled.

"You're getting spanked, baby girl, don't doubt that, but if I have to pick a switch you're going to seriously regret it. I'd keep my mouth shut if I were you." He gathered a breath and released her arm to take her hand. "You're lucky I have no love for switches, or you'd have stripes across your ass tonight." He looked down at her and paused, turning to cup her face with his rough palm. "Every swat I give you will be for your own good."

She nodded as much as his palm would allow, and all thoughts of fighting him vanished. She wanted care, even if it came from an ex who broke her heart ten years earlier, even if it came in the form of a spanking. He was right, she was a boulder about to break into gravel, but hanging onto Drew was keeping her whole.

"I care about you. I want you safe."

Again, her only answer was a nod. Her head was full of thoughts about how wrong it was to let a man spank her, but her heart and pussy didn't give a damn about right and wrong.

"That's better. I like my baby girl agreeable."

CHAPTER SEVEN

Drew

They walked in silence after, making it all the way inside her cabin before speaking. His mind had been too busy imagining disciplining her and warring with himself over it. She needed it and they both knew it. He could tell she was aroused. Her face was flushed, and she kept wiggling and pressing her thighs together.

"Wait here, Addianna. I'll get you something for dinner before we deal with your spanking."

Her flushed cheeks seemed to pale. "You're leaving?"

"Only for a few minutes."

"I don't want to sit in my cabin, alone, waiting for you to come spank me whenever you feel like it. Is there something you're hiding from me, Drew? Is there some reason I need to stay here?" Her eyes narrowed, but he noticed she kept her poking finger holstered in the belt loop of her capri pants.

"Don't push me, baby girl. You're staying in your cabin because I said so. And because you seem to find trouble when you're out of it. And because if I catch you anywhere else, I'll find that damn switch."

"Is that what biker daddies do? They lock their little girls up and spank them when they're displeased with them?" There was something in her voice he didn't recognize—something feral, sexy, and tinged with malice.

Was she flirting? Angry flirting?

He leaned toward her, smirking. He brushed a piece of loose hair back from her face, his hand lingering by her cheek. The smell of her, citrus shampoo or body wash mingled with pine needles, intoxicated him. She turned her face toward his left palm, allowing him to cup her cheek.

"That's right, baby girl. That's exactly what biker daddies do. They keep their little girls safe, healthy, and happy—even if that means punishing them. And honey, you're getting punished." Drew's free hand rose and landed with a whack on her backside. Her eyes burst open wide in shock before fluttering closed as he was sure the heat from his hand sank in. Another swat branded her other cheek and she gasped, but kept her eyes closed. His left hand, still cupping her face, was meant to comfort, while his right heated her backside. She needed the spanking, but she needed comfort too.

"Lower your pants, baby girl. Daddy's spanking your bare ass tonight." When she only breathed, he released her face and undid her pants himself. He lowered them along with her panties. His hand cupped her left ass cheek, kneading, squeezing and pulling her against his front while his eyes pinned her in place with his intense stare. He released her bottom and a few swats landed on her bare skin. She hissed at the difference.

"You've been asking for this, babe. Since the moment you got here. Now Daddy's going to take his time with you." Another swat landed, burning his palm but surely sending vibrations through her. Against her, his cock was hard. She grasped his shoulders to hold herself upright.

"What about Layla? You were obviously angry with her today. Is she getting punished too? How many little girls do you have, *Daddy*?" Her last word was full of contempt. The arousal in her eyes turned hotter with anger.

He ground his teeth and dragged her by the upper arm to the bed. He dropped onto it and pulled her across his knees roughly. It was obvious she needed more than a few swats.

"Honey, you're the only one I care enough about to spank, and I'm going to prove that right now."

His hand landed harder this time—unforgiving, not sexy like before—and she squealed. His next swat was hard enough to make her lurch across his hard thighs. There was no sensual pause, no gentle caresses between. He spanked her relentlessly, again and again, knowing his hand ignited a fiery burn with every new branding.

"Ah, no, please." She squirmed, twisting her hips instinctually to avoid his landing palm. He hoped the severity of swats helped her realize her mistake in baiting him. She'd learn to hold her tongue in the future.

"No more poking, babe. No more lying, no more sassing, and no more wandering off. Got me? And Jesus, baby girl, no more jealousy over that twit, Layla." His hand landed in a splat across the middle of both her cheeks so hard she wailed and pelted the bed with her fists.

"Okay! Okay! No more!"

"If you cross me, little girl, you're going to find yourself across my knee again and next time I might not go so easy on you." He pulled her up and sat her on his knee, scooping her legs up so her hot bottom shifted between his open legs. He cradled her while she breathed in and out in little gasping breaths. Her pants were strewn across the room, as were her panties.

"Easy?" she huffed and let a whimper trail from her wobbling lips. "You're not very nice, Mr. Biker!"

He cupped his hand against her cheek. He rolled his eyes skyward and chuckled, but when they came back to hers, his thoughts were no longer on her naughtiness, or how adorable she was. His thoughts were carnal. He wanted her. Her thighs clenched and he smirked.

"I can be, sweetheart. I can be *very* nice." He leaned closer, looking from her eyes to her lips and back again. His lips pressed against hers, lightly at first and then harder until his teeth took her bottom lip and dragged off it.

"Daddy's going to get your dinner and then he's going to hold you until you fall asleep, you got me?"

"Yes, Daddy."

"Good girl." His hand left her face and scooped behind until he was cupping her head. He drew her in again and kissed her sweetly, but once more it was only gentle until it wasn't. It morphed quickly, becoming hot, wet, and eager. It was a pirate plundering her for treasure, it was a robber stealing her wits, it was Adam and Eve tasting forbidden fruit. God, he still loved this woman.

He thought about confessing his love right there and then, but drew in a breath instead. Clenching his jaw, he lifted her, stood and set her on the bed. And then he spun and left her sitting there. He couldn't tell her he loved her. Because they could never be together when his past was always chasing him, it was better she not know.

At the last minute, he turned back. Her mouth was agape, her nipples hard peaks, and her slightly open thighs shiny-slick in the lamplight.

"Don't you dare leave this cabin, Addianna. Consider yourself grounded until I return."

•••••••

He jogged through the forest, avoiding the stumps, dips, and roots. He knew this forest like he knew the back of his hand and he needed to burn away the ache that filled him, first for the love he couldn't give her freely, and second for the trust he didn't deserve. He'd left her once and he'd do it again. He'd do anything to keep her safe.

Dammit! He'd thought it would be fine. He'd thought he was strong enough to resist the temptation of her, but he wasn't. He wanted her more than ever. She needed to let go, share her grief and fears, but once she did, there would be a bond between them so strong it would kill them *both* when he ended it. And it would end.

The Skull Grinders would find him eventually. They seemed to be getting closer. His father had told him countless times he would hunt him down if he ever ran. He would never stop searching. And once he found him, he would be punished for his sins against his brothers. People, places, and things—everything he cared about would be destroyed while he watched. That's why he'd broken Addi's heart. It's why he told her she meant nothing to him.

It was the same with Ray, and the camp. Being sent to Tonalonka to work as a camp leader was part of his release. And it was the best thing that had ever happened to him.

As soon as his full release came due though, they'd come. The roar of their bikes had made his legs itch to run, but Drew knew his father would hurt Ray for information. There was only one option. He had to make his father and the Grinders believe he hated everything about the camp. Addi showing up at his cabin only made things worse. The way Mauler looked at him forced his hand. He had to prove in a big way that Addi, Ray, and the camp were not only just a stepping stone to getting back to his place with the Grinders, but that he'd despised being there.

It was better having the camp destroyed than having Addi and Ray assaulted or worse.

Maybe he convinced them when he had the place destroyed. Maybe they believed he hated it there. Then again maybe they were letting him get comfortable. That was another of his father's tricks.

Either way, he had to stay away from Addi. But Ray…

"Damn you, Ray!" he yelled into the treetops with a roar of anger. He stopped then, slamming his fist into the tree in front of him, before he bent, grasped his knees, and caught his breath.

"She deserves better, Ray. She *fucking* deserves someone as good as she is. Someone untainted by evil." Drew pulled

Ray's letter out of his pocket and unfolded it, letting his body slide down the tree. His hand burned and his knuckles bled but he ignored it. Sitting with one knee bent and his throbbing hand propped on it, he read.

Drew,

I guess I damn well bit the dust if you're reading this. I've been nothin' but a pain in the ass lately anyway. And I bet there's good fishing up here. And my wife. Damn, I've missed her. I'll also finally get to meet my son who, as you know, died with my wife.

I've been dawdling on the sale of the camp for some time. I can see you rolling your damn eyes! The reason is my business, so don't expect a damn answer in this letter, Andrew!

You and Addi are like my own children, and since the sale didn't go through, I feel the camp belongs to both of you.

No matter what happens, the house on the cliff is yours (you built it after all) and five acres around it. However, it cannot be sold or given away. It must remain in your possession for your lifetime. You'll also remain caretaker of the camp, but all big decisions must be agreed upon by both you and Addi, as you are equal owners.

I'd love it converted back into a kids' camp, but I can't force that on either of you. It will however be given to charity if either of you try to break up the property or want out.

Suck it up. These are my wishes and since I'm dead, you can't go flappin' your gums at me.

Love you, son. Take care of my little girl, and damn it, let her take care of you, too. You belong together. You always have.

Ray

He hadn't noticed the P.S. before, probably because his eyes had been swimming at that point in the letter. He swallowed the lump in his throat and finished it.

P.S.

Since I was nothing but a front for these anyway, I've left all the art and control over all charitable foundations to you. No more hiding behind me, Andrew. It's time the world knew how truly good you are—

not just artistically gifted, but a good man too! I've never been prouder of anyone, Andrew. You define yourself by one moment in your past that wasn't even your fault. You were just a child. It's time you look at all the other amazing things you've done in your lifetime. Come clean to Addi. She deserves to know the man who's been in love with her all these years.

You have my blessing to marry Addi. In fact, if you don't I'll personally make sure Saint Peter kicks your ass when you get to the pearly gates.

He straightened his leg, still breathing heavily and shoved his hair back. Inside at the bottom of the envelope was a ring. Ray's deceased wife's engagement ring.

"Jesus, Ray. *Jesus.* Why?"

He rose, rolling his shoulders and flexing the hand he'd punched the tree with, still arguing with himself for being weak and kissing her. He shoved the letter back in his pocket and scrubbed his good hand over his face while heading for his trailer. Damn, he'd known she'd let her guard down for him. Just the thought of it made his furnace burn hotter. Jesus, she had a hold on him. Sweet Addianna.

"She's not yours," he said aloud, angry with himself for the slip.

The burgers he'd made earlier were in the fridge, so he took one out and heated it in the microwave. He'd made a Caesar salad to go with it and portioned some out into a plastic bowl. He had no idea what Addi ate on a burger, so he took the little dish he kept in the fridge with ketchup, mustard, and relish packets in it and plopped a few on the tray. He put lettuce and sliced tomato on a plate along with the now warm patty and a bun. He covered it with tinfoil to keep the bugs out.

It was dark, but he didn't need a flashlight. He didn't really want to face her after he'd fucked up and kissed her, but he'd promised he would. And he'd spanked her. She needed comfort and care. It had been wrong of him to leave her, but if he hadn't, they'd both be naked and tangled in her sheets.

She was sitting on her bed looking a bit stunned when he got to her cabin. "You okay, baby girl?"

She shook her head and tears welled in her eyes.

"Aw, honey, come here." He set the tray down and held open his arms for her. She wasted no time wrapping hers around his waist and tucking into him.

"I shouldn't have left you here after I spanked you. I'm sorry, sweetheart. I should have taken you with me." He smoothed his hand down her hair. She felt so tiny to him, especially since she was tucked in so tightly.

"I felt so alone, Drew. I am alone. So, so alone."

He hushed her when the sobbing started, and rubbed her back, giving her squeezes of reassurance to let her know she wasn't alone.

When the sobbing ebbed, Drew undressed the rest of her, once again pulling off his own shirt for her to sleep in. He kept constant contact with her, whether that was running his hands up her ribs to remove her shirt or simply holding her hand.

"Babe, even with tears streaking your face, you look sexy as hell in my t-shirt." He wiped the tears from her face with his thumbs and took her hand again.

She smiled and sniffled. "It feels good. It feels like you're holding me."

"I am holding you." He pulled back the bed covers with his free hand and nodded for her to climb in. She turned, putting her knee up and when he wouldn't release her fingers from between his, she pulled him in with her.

With the lamp out, and silence except for the sounds of nature outside, he could hear her deep breathing. She was asleep within minutes. Her adventure and the spanking had probably exhausted her.

"You're not alone, baby girl. You're always with me right here." He tapped two fingers over his heart. Tucking her hair back, he kissed her temple and then gently climbing from the bed that was too small for the two of them, he headed for the door. With his t-shirt wrapped around her sweet body, he'd probably be a feast for the mosquitoes, but he didn't care as long as she was comfortable.

The evening was cooler than it had been the week before, and as he walked back to the trailer he felt the bite of it against his bare skin. Knowing he'd never sleep now, he went to the cabins he'd been remodeling before Addi had arrived. He couldn't hammer, saw, or grind without waking Addi, but he could paint the walls. He longed to go to his house—not the caretaker's trailer, but the one on the cliff, the one with his paintings. But he needed to be close to her.

He entered the cabin he'd been last working on and looked at the fresh white walls. He'd already primed them and they were his to paint however he chose. He chuckled, imagining the faces of the guests if he painted his Addianna mid-spanking. The way her mouth formed an O of surprise when it both stung her ass *and* heated her core. He'd known at first the slow spanking had aroused her, and like him, she'd wanted more, but she had opened her mouth and proved she'd needed something a little harsher than some sexy slaps on her ass. That girl needed to know he cared for her and not just because she revved his engine like no other.

He cursed. "Stop thinking about her!" he hollered to the white walls.

He got to work, setting up his paints, deciding this cabin should have a mural of the marsh. Dragonflies, frogs, and a heron fishing with fish swimming beneath and hiding behind rocks and reeds. He'd paint blues and green on the other walls and the beds.

He worked, almost in a trance, losing track of time, stopping only when the mural was complete and daybreak peeked through the windows. He smiled, his paint-splattered hands on hips looking over his work. He could imagine the children that would sleep here, with their eyes growing droopy as they counted the fish and other hidden wildlife.

Drew washed the brushes in his trailer and put them

away; after a quick rinse in the shower to get the paint off, he threw on his workout gear and went for a run. He knew running wouldn't take him any farther from his demons, but it would take his mind off them for the moment.

CHAPTER EIGHT

Addi

Dawn peeked into the little cabin and the sound of loons echoed off the lake. She took a moment to stretch in the cozy bed before hugging Drew's shirt and reminding herself of the night before. Her mouth watered and her pussy clenched.

It was just a spanking, a few hot-as-hell kisses, and some cuddles, she scolded herself. *Grow up!*

But being grown up was exactly what she was avoiding with Drew. She'd been grown up since she was a teenager and it was *over-fucking-rated!*

She rose then, tugging the shirt lower on her legs, and stepped out onto the porch wishing the little cabin had a coffeemaker. One of those pod-using things would be really nice. She could sit on this porch and watch the day begin, sipping delightful rich coffee and remembering every vivid detail of the night before.

She touched her lips, running the pads of her fingers over them. Was what she'd done with Drew wrong? Was it simply her way of avoiding grief? Did it *feel* wrong? Maybe a little dirty, a little naughty, but wrong? How could it be when she felt so light and free? When she felt so cared for?

Mist rose off the lake in the distance, and the damp earthy smell enveloped her senses. She closed her eyes, breathing deep, and when she opened them, she saw a man in the misty distance. For a second she thought it was Uncle Ray.

Just Drew. Her heart fluttered and her belly coiled tight.

If it was *just Drew*, why did her body react like a teen girl crushing on the quarterback?

She went back into the cabin to dress, attempting to ignore the arousal that she'd woken up with.

Addi washed, smiling again at the adorable little bathroom, and pulled on a casual sundress. She had nothing suitable for a rustic campground, so it would have to do. For a moment, she wondered if Drew would say anything about it, but she shook off the thought. She shouldn't care. It was just a game between them—a kinky sexual daddy/baby girl game. And he would be out of her life soon. She needed to remind herself of both of those facts *regularly*.

He was no longer at the beach, so she stepped off her porch and headed there. It was too picturesque to ignore the pull of it.

The lake was hauntingly beautiful as she wandered to the sand and rock shore, thinking again of how her uncle had never missed a sunrise. She pulled her cell out of her pocket and lined up a shot. She'd take this picture to remember him. A lump formed in her throat. Somehow, here in his place, she felt it was wrong for the sun to rise without him.

After the sun was fully up, Addi listened to three more messages from her dad and took a selfie with the lake in the background to send to Daniel and Steven. She didn't have any words, so the picture would have to be enough. The thought of telling her best friends what a muddled mess her head was in—over a guy and her past when she was supposed to be grieving and burying her uncle—was horrifying. They'd think she was crazy and heartless.

Addi didn't hear Drew come up behind her, but felt a

prickle up her spine just as he spoke.

"Morning, babe." Their bodies practically touched and electricity seemed to crackle between them. With a shudder that swelled like a wave about to break, she released a breath.

"Morning."

"How'd you sleep?" His voice was gentle and quiet as if he didn't want to disturb the nature around them or perhaps he didn't want to scare her.

Avoiding looking at him, she watched a family of loons glide by the marshy edge. "Okay, you?" She hadn't slept *okay* at all. She'd slumbered long, dreamless, and peaceful. She caught his self-satisfied smile in her peripheral view.

He leaned down to the shell of her ear. "You slept better than okay, little girl. What'd I tell you about lying to Daddy?" His words tickled more than just her ear and she shivered.

She glared and harrumphed, crossing her arms. Drew's hand found her hip and squeezed—a light-hearted warning that made her breath catch.

"What's that, babe?"

"Fine! I had the best sleep of my life." She stuck out her lip in a pout, playing his game. He chuckled as he turned to face her, looking her in the eye as he plucked at her bottom lip with his thumb. His other hand found her ass and rubbed. The material of her sundress was thin and her body heated instantly. Her pussy tingled with need and her heart kicked up its pace. With heavy eyes, she waited for him to kiss her, but he turned to look out at the water again.

"A good, well-deserved spanking will do that. How's your bottom?" He chuckled when her mouth fell open. She slapped it shut, annoyed by his amusement.

"It remembers."

"Good; it better." He turned to wink at her, and she shook her head.

The crinkles around his eyes made her belly flutter. He looked so carefree with his playful expression and casual workout wear.

He raised his arms in a stretch and she found herself following the path of hair on his rippled stomach. "This place has always brought me peace, but I've never been much of a sleeper and last night not at all. I got carried away painting one of the cabins and then went for a run."

She swallowed, looking back at his face as he lowered his arms. He was sweaty and it wasn't a turn-off at all. She nodded in understanding while chewing her lip; naughty thoughts were forming in her head and none of them involved him rolling paint onto walls.

Stop it!

He smirked. "I run. A lot. Keeps the demons away for a while."

She reached out and touched one of the tattoos on his slick arm—something with horns and sharp teeth showing through a cruel smile. "Seems to me, you'll never escape them when they're under your skin."

He nodded. "Nor should I. I earned every one." He rolled his neck and shoulders, glancing sadly at her. "I dropped off your breakfast, but you weren't there. It's a bun with bacon, egg, and cheese. You never did get around to eating the burger I brought last night."

"I'll get some groceries today," she answered.

"I don't mind making you meals." His brows rose. "Besides, I don't trust that you'll eat."

"Thanks," she answered sarcastically, and looked down at herself. "But I'm pretty sure I didn't get this way by *not* eating." His mouth firmed but before he could start lecturing her, she added, "I'm going to the office. See if I can find contact info for some of the campers."

She heard him call her name, but she broke into a jog to escape.

• • • • • • •

The office was big and rustic with a huge real wood desk

full of grooves and chips from years of use. The seventies-style wood-paneled walls were covered with lots of shelves, filing cabinets, framed photos and letters, but most of all, dust. A square, yellowed-with-age fan sat in one corner with pliers clamping the broken control dial, and she smiled. Right then, she knew Uncle Ray didn't let Drew in here. First, because of the fan, and second because it was obvious no one had set foot in here, besides her, in a long time. Her footprints in the dust were proof.

Addi's uncle was somewhat of a hoarder when it came to paperwork. She clicked the desk lamp on and dust scattered into the air around her. She coughed and attempted to swat it away. Hadn't anyone been staying here this summer? Was that why her uncle was broke? She frowned, thinking of his paintings and what Drew had said about him giving the money away.

Piles of papers in boxes sat on the floor but the desk was clear except for a calendar, a dish of toffees, and a coffee cup that said, *'I'd rather be fishing.'*

Plunking herself in her uncle's chair, she gasped at the tenderness of her bottom. Gritting her teeth and ignoring the thrill it gave her to feel his touch even when he was nowhere in sight, she searched. She was sure the information she wanted was here to be found, but where?

She looked around, feeling a little overwhelmed. She could easily picture her uncle lecturing a group of boys that had been brought in by a camp leader for mischief. She swiveled in the chair a moment. He'd lectured her a few times over the years and although it had stung, it always did her good. Everyone needed a dressing down now and then, and her uncle had done it with both love and strictness.

After searching many drawers and boxes, and several dozen dust-induced sneezes, Addi found what she was looking for: A list of former campers and their addresses in a binder. There were years on the tabs, making it easy to find the summer she was there. Curiosity got the better of her and she looked through the names. Some names had more information listed below them than others. Some were behavioral issues, but most said the kid spent too much time in front of the TV, computer, or gaming system and a few stated the child was being bullied.

Addi leaned back, letting the pages and pages of names from a lifetime of years fan dusty air across her face. She coughed. How would she call all the names? She suddenly wondered if there was a book for the camp leaders as well. She rose to look for another binder.

"Aha!" she shouted, yanking a dusty white binder from a box. "I knew I'd find it!" She didn't bother to go back to the desk but sat cross-legged where she was in front of the box and flipped through the binder. Her finger followed a list and she stopped a quarter of the way through.

Andrew Trigger. Preferred name, Drew. Before she could read any further, a throat was cleared.

She looked up. Drew was leaning against the door frame.

"Hi." He straightened. "Came to see if you wanted help."

"Well, now I have two binders full of names to call." She tossed the binder she held on top of the other with a frustrated sigh. "I'll never get through them."

"I think you'll find a lot of those boys came from the same areas. I'm sure we could just put the obit in their local newspapers with an invitation for former campers and staff to attend. If they don't see it, maybe their parents will. Maybe some of them still stay in contact with each other and the word will get out."

Addi looked at him curiously. "Smart." She rose and plopped into the desk chair, laying her chin in her palm. "Bikers, especially handsome ones, shouldn't be so smart," she teased.

He barked a laugh. "That so?"

She nodded awkwardly, chin still in palm. "Yep, I'm sure that's a rule."

"How about daddies? Aren't they supposed to be smart?"

Her face heated and she bit her lower lip. God, she loved when he referred to himself as Daddy.

He shook his head and walked to her. "Let me look through the binders. I'll pick the newspapers that should get the obit, and I'll use my laptop to set it up with them. You look like you could use a break." His eyes narrowed and he reached toward her to tilt her chin up. "Besides, I dropped off some lunch in your cabin and found your breakfast still there." His brows rose and her bottom tingled. "No dinner last night, or breakfast this morning." He cleared his throat. "Not eating your breakfast is naughty, baby girl. Does Daddy need to remind you what happens to naughty girls?"

She swallowed hard. "Uh, yeah." The corner of her mouth hitched up. "I mean, yes. Please." Her brows wiggled.

He shook his head but smirked. "You're not supposed to want a reminder, Addianna."

"Well, maybe I need your hands on me." She sounded confident but felt unsure.

"Here." He pulled her phone out of his pocket. "It fell out of your pocket when you ran. It's been buzzing like an addict." He handed her the phone. "Call your people."

She looked at her notifications and jumped up so suddenly the chair tipped onto two legs before falling back into place. "There's a Facebook group for the camp!"

"There is? Huh." He winked. "Now who's the smart one?"

She shot him a toothy grin. "No one has ever thought an author was dumb. Now a biker…" She let her words trail off with a snicker, knowing her statement was bullshit.

He grabbed her and pulled her close. "Oh, really?" He fisted the hair at the back of her neck and pulled her head back slightly.

Man, she loved when he did that, too.

"And isn't it a bit dumb to provoke your daddy?"

Her knees weakened and the small smile on his face turned feral.

"Maybe."

He kissed her before she could speak further. Releasing her, he cupped her face gently. "Now, show me this site, babe."

"I made the Facebook group a few years ago when Uncle Ray came to visit me." She pulled it up on her phone and handed it to him. He browsed through the pictures, looking tense.

"Drew, what do you think if the funeral was just for close friends and family and I organize a memorial weekend here at the camp for the old campers and their families? Like in a month or so?" She had thought of it only seconds ago, but it felt settled and right, like she'd planned to do it all along.

"I love that idea, and I think Ray would, too." He set the phone down, tucked a piece of hair behind her ear, and leaned forward to kiss her nose.

"Oh, what size suit do you wear?"

He cocked his head. "I have a suit."

"You do?" She scratched her forehead. "I'm sorry that was probably rude. I just assumed…"

"Assumed that I was a greasy biker who would rather die than wear a tie?" He smirked, so she did too, although her cheeks burned fiercely. "Here's an even bigger surprise: Ray has one too. And we both looked damned handsome in them."

She eyed him, her belly flipping at the thought of him in a suit.

"I don't doubt that one bit—the handsome part anyway—but why?"

He shrugged. "Occasionally your uncle would drag me to crash one of those fancy gallery parties, but we went incognito. No one knew the actual artist by face, so we were in the clear to blend in. He loved hearing what people said." Drew rubbed a hand over his beard.

"Why'd he donate it all, Drew? Why not keep some for himself? Retire somewhere nice. Have someone take care of him for a change." Her eyes stung. "He took care of so many others his whole life, Drew, he deserved better."

"You know Ray, baby girl. He wasn't a complicated guy. He loved hard, and gave everything he had to his passions. Wayward, lost, or misguided boys, and I guess families that lost loved ones because of violence. He was a great man, Addi." He took her hands, rubbing the tops of them with his clean but grease-stained thumbs. "Now no more lollygagging, little lady. Go have lunch and then have a long hot bath. I'll come get you later. Daddy's orders."

She bit her lip again and her thighs clenched to ease the throbbing his words caused. "Yeah, okay," she murmured. "I am a little hungry."

"We'll pick one of Ray's suits together, drop it off at the funeral home, and have a drink around the fire tonight." He smiled. "Roast some marshmallows? Make s'mores?"

"Drink? I could probably use one of those."

He chuckled. "I'm just giving you one. You get into enough trouble sober." He winked. "I have a feeling you can't hold your liquor."

"I can too." Once again, she pouted. "What I can't hold is my s'mores." His brows rose in a stern way and she lowered her eyes.

"Fine. One."

"Good girl." He pulled her in for a quick hug and swatted her bottom. "You're lucky you didn't argue more."

"That so?" she said, mocking his words from earlier.

"I'd stay on my good side. Daddy spanks hard so his lessons are learned the first time."

She poked his chest, her eyes fluttering up innocently. "Like when you spanked me for poking you?"

"Hm, a lesson that needs repeating, I see."

"Seems fairer if you just poked me back, don't you think? A long, hard poking would teach me, Daddy." The last of her sentence was said with a low, seductive voice that made his eyes pin hers and flare with arousal.

He shook his head at her and jabbed a thumb at the

door. "Git, before I spank you and poke you right here over this dusty desk."

"Can we clean it first?"

He stepped swiftly toward her, so she took off, giggles pealing from her.

"You're not taking me seriously enough, baby girl!" he hollered at her back as she ran and he followed.

CHAPTER NINE

Addi

Addi ran until she couldn't hear him chasing her anymore. She slowed to a walk and caught her breath. The smile still on her mouth hurt her cheeks since it wasn't something she did often. She pulled out her cell and dialed her friends as they'd been texting her like crazy when Drew had her phone. Daniel answered on the third ring.

"Hey, honey, how're you?"

"I'm okay. Working on a private funeral and setting up a memorial weekend for Uncle Ray's old camp boys and leaders." Addi walked along the edge of the deepest line of cabins in the forest. It was as far as she wanted to get into the woods.

"I think that's a great idea."

"He changed a lot of lives here and I think they'd want to come, but everyone won't be able to drop everything and come to the funeral last minute. What are you doing in Steven's office? I did call his office, didn't I?"

"Your Uncle Ray was a great man. Again, I'm so sorry, Addi." He sighed forcefully a moment and she heard the shuffling of papers. "Yes, you called his office. Are you aware your other best friend is a big slob?"

She laughed, happy he'd changed the subject to one she could gladly join in on. "Of course I am. I share that office sometimes and I'd have to be blind not to notice. What did he lose now?" She sat at a picnic table outside one of the cabins. It was the one where the campers always carved their initials.

"Nothing important, just the bloody copyedited version of this month's cover story, *Skydiving Adventure at Eighty*. Due at the printers in…" He hummed. "An hour." Daniel growled and then she heard silence, except for the squeak of Steven's chair. He was supposed to oil it weeks ago. "How are you *really* holding up, Ads? Are you eating? Sleeping?"

Addi bit her lip and smoothed her hand over some initials in the table.

"I hate being here without him," she answered, but as soon as she said it she thought of Drew and how much easier he was making things for her. What would it be like if he wasn't there? She leaned over the table to look at the other bench seat. Drew's and her initials were on the seat. She smiled. They were the only ones with a heart around them. He may have broken her heart in the end but the rest of the time was pretty spectacular.

"I bet. We'll come, Ads. Steven and I will book a flight tonight."

"You have so much work though. It's fine. *I'm fine.*"

"Nonsense! Our girl needs us, and besides, I'm married to the boss. I can delegate."

Addi laughed. "I've seen how that goes. You ask someone to do something you normally do, and you break out in hives and end up doing it yourself. You're a bigger control freak than I am."

"Honey, no one, and I mean *no one*, is a bigger control freak than you."

I know one person who is.

Addi heard Steven in the background agreeing, and then

Daniel start to yell about the edited story.

"Tell him he's not getting my macaroni salad for the Labor Day party if he keeps this up."

She heard Steven clearly as she was suddenly on speaker. "How quickly you two forget who the boss is here."

"Pfft. You may own this magazine but I run it."

"I'm creative. We are organized in our own way, right, Addi?"

"Leave me out of this!"

"He might not be alive for Labor Day," Daniel added, sounding aggravated. "He's lucky he found the story though."

"Thank goodness!"

"Now we can come without me needing meds."

She took a big breath and got serious again. "I'm not alone here, guys. You don't have to worry."

"Oh?" Steven's 'oh' was not simple curiosity, it was high-pitched, greedy for details, and accusing, as if he knew the person at the camp was a man and a helluva hot one at that. Her skin tingled.

"He's Uncle Ray's friend, Steven, relax." She knew he'd assume the friend was Uncle Ray's age and let it go. *For now.*

"I'm glad. I hated the thought of you stuck there for months alone."

"What? Months? Why would I be here for months?"

"Oh, shit." Daniel and Steven started bickering, but Addi ignored everything except the pounding of her heart and Steven's slip.

"Your uncle's lawyer contacted me yesterday to make some arrangements from Ray's will." He swore. "I thought you'd know by now."

"What the hell is going on, Steven?"

"Can you pretend you didn't hear any of that?"

"No."

He blew out a breath. "Well, I only know my part. I had to make sure you had the time off for taking care of the will business. Your uncle wanted it arranged that you could work mostly from the camp after he died—at least for three months. Of course, I said yes. I know how you felt about him and I'd do anything for you."

"Three months? Most of my pieces require travel! How the hell am I supposed to pay my bills? And why?"

"He arranged that too. Your paycheck is covered for three months, whether or not you get anything done. I'll get someone from the university to intern while you're away. As for why, I have no clue. "

"Oh." She scratched her head. What was her uncle up to? How could he afford to do that when Drew said he was broke? Was he broke? Was Drew lying or did Uncle Ray have something stashed away?

"Hon? We gotta run, but we'll come for the funeral and stay the weekend. Steven never lets me work weekends anyway."

"The deal is, he works a weekend, I delete *Outlander* off the DVR." Steven grunted. "He's a bully, that one. I ought to fire him."

"You threaten that daily, Steven," Addi said on a chuckle. "We all know you'll never follow through."

"Because I'm the real brains of this operation," Daniel countered smugly. "Take care, hon. We'll see you soon."

"Thanks, guys. I can't wait to see you."

And when they ended their call, she looped around the cabins and headed back to the office with a heavy heart, remembering the lawyer telling her about the letter in the desk. She hadn't seen it, but at the time, she hadn't been looking for it.

The office was covered in footprints from both her and Drew now, and looked awful. She knew her focus on the dirt was more to avoid the letter in the desk. She just couldn't face it yet.

She got the bucket and brush out of the closet and started scrubbing the floor on her hands and knees. She couldn't stop even after she'd scoured and dusted everything. She used furniture polish on every wood surface besides the floor and then began organizing files, ignoring her hands cracking from the harsh floor cleaner.

She was sitting on the floor in the dark holding the letter in her lap surrounded by piles of folders when Drew barged through the doors.

"Addi?" He sounded frantic. "Where the hell are you?"

"I'm here," she said, her voice rough and scratchy from lack of use, dust, and the buildup of emotion. He stumbled into the office, almost tripping over her.

"Jesus, baby girl, I've been combing the goddamned forest for hours looking for you."

She looked at him, her eyes used to the dark room. His eyes fell to the letter in her lap as soon as he clicked on the little desk lamp.

"I'm sorry I missed our s'mores date."

"Have you read it?" he asked, his voice gentler now and filled with a different kind of concern. She shook her head. He looked around the room. "You clean when you're upset?"

She nodded.

"Remind me to piss you off next time you're near my trailer," he said in an attempt at humor that fell flat. He sat on the floor across from her. She wondered how such a big man could fold his legs like that.

"Have you read yours?"

It was his turn to nod silently.

"Was it hard?" She stared at the envelope with her name scrawled in her uncle's messy handwriting. "Reading the last words he'll ever have for you?"

"Hard as hell, babe." His hand touched her knee but she didn't look up.

"I can't do it yet. The lawyer is going to be calling soon after Uncle Ray's funeral and I can't even read the letter." The breath she gathered into her lungs was shaky. "How the hell am I supposed to handle all this shit?"

"It's okay, there's still time. And you're strong, Addi."

"Time?" She said the word as if it was in a foreign

language. "I've been flirting and screwing around with you like I'm still some carefree teenager. It's wrong. My uncle just died and all I'm thinking about is how hot you are, how wet you make me, and how badly I want you to spank me, fuck me, and be my daddy dom *for real*. I'm the worst person in the world." Tears started halfway through her speech, but she ignored them. "I'm not strong, but I'm *fucking* great at avoidance."

"Baby girl." His words matched the sympathy on his face. "You were never some carefree teenager and there's no right way of dealing with any of this. I'm not innocent either, but who says we can't grieve together in whatever way works for us?"

She was *his* way of grieving? Her chest ached with the pain of a thousand wrecking balls landing on it. Here she thought it was just her, but she was no more than a distraction for him too. Just like the last time, this wasn't real. And, God, that stung as if he'd slapped her. She stood, hugged the letter to her chest, and walked to the door. It was no different than when they were sixteen. He was using her then, and he was using her now.

"Don't follow me," she said.

He didn't, thankfully, and she made it back to her cabin without issue. She felt nothing but angry at herself as she tossed the letter on her nightstand. This was bullshit. She needed to sit in her cabin alone and think, but wanted to go out and forget. Bury her emotions about her uncle, her messed-up childhood, and the daddy she wanted so badly it hurt, but her body ached from the work she'd done that day. Scrubbing floors on her hands and knees wasn't something she was used to.

She filled the tub with water and a fragrant bath bomb. She stripped, tossing her filthy summer dress in the corner and stepped into the deliciously soothing water. It was so hot it stung but she sank into it regardless of the tensing of her stomach muscles and burning of her skin. She hoped it would burn away the wrong she'd done.

She scrubbed herself quickly, shaved, and paused, staring at the hair on her pussy. She chewed her lip and swiftly ran the razor over it until it was bare. She ran her hand over the smooth skin and slid under the water until her nose was the only thing above the hot, mollifying liquid.

She thought of her time with Drew, tried to remember anything that happened between them that indicated it wasn't real. She couldn't think of a single thing. It was time she confront him. She needed to know. What the hell he'd been doing then and what the hell he was doing now.

Addi bolted straight up out of the bathtub, not caring that water splashed onto the floor. Determined and wanting out of the confined space of her cabin, she dried off and quickly cleaned the mess.

Pulling on a cotton skirt and blouse with buttons up the front, she walked out into the chilly dampness of night. It had been getting cooler after dusk as they were in August, but it was still warm during the day. The ground thumped hollowly as she made her way through the pines. She should have grabbed a flashlight, but the moon was almost full and cast a little glow through the scattered treetops and cabins helping her eyes adjust somewhat.

Addi wandered with her head down, keeping her eyes on roots and rocks, until the smell of a campfire made her look up. The glow of it through the trees in the distance pulled her.

As she walked closer, she could see the fire dancing and hear it crackle. The smoky air was as intoxicating as cologne. The scent was as much a part of Drew as his intense blue eyes.

Faint music started. A sweet melody from an acoustic guitar strummed through the cool, heavy air. Drew, sitting on a bench made from a cut log, had a guitar propped on his lap. His head was low, his hair curling at the ends around an old flannel long-sleeved shirt hiding his tattoos. She edged closer, not wanting to alert him of her presence, but too mesmerized to leave.

His voice entwined with a melody she recognized. It was old, one of those hair bands from the eighties that she remembered he liked as a teen. *Poison.* As he got to the chorus, he looked up at her.

Every rose has its thorn.

Standing across from him while the hot, dancing flames flickered shadows across his face, her heart pounded. His eyes, flashing in the light, blazed blue heat into hers. There was fluttering in every pulse point as she sat, sliding back into a dew-dampened Muskoka chair.

Feelings flooded her, making her want to jump through the flames and run to him. Teenage-crush feelings were strong and as he changed the song to one he'd sung for her way back then, she felt all those early hormone-driven emotions as if they were new. 'I Remember You,' by Skid Row.

And she did. She remembered.

CHAPTER TEN

Drew

Drew plucked the chords of his guitar, singing softly, watching the girl who was once his, the song he sang, once theirs. The melody flowed from the deepest parts of him—he needed to remember, needed her to remember them too.

"Remember yesterday, walking hand in hand..."

He'd sworn he'd never let anyone in his heart again, but Addi had never left and she'd taken up every inch of space inside it. He'd promised himself he'd never hurt another good girl like he'd hurt Addi. But here she was, back in his life, and it had taken every bit of strength inside him to stay away from her earlier.

He'd wanted to hold her, protect her, take her inside him where nothing could hurt her, but more than anything he wanted to bury himself in her... deep inside her soft warmth... and stroke the place within her that would make her call out his name.

God, she was so sweet and beautiful, always, but especially in the firelight among nature. He looked at the strings of the guitar again, breaking their intense stare, and finished the song. There was silence after. Just the sound of snapping firewood, crickets, and tree frogs from the marsh.

He glanced up, wondering if he'd imagined her. But there she was, her hair so dark it was almost black, shimmering in the light. And her eyes, wide, innocent and in awe of him, squeezed his chest. She trusted him. She needed him. But how could he possibly be what she both needed and deserved?

He dropped the guitar. It thrummed hauntingly as it landed. He'd have left, let the lawyer deal with everything, and protected her by being gone, but dammit! Ray had made him promise. And fuck! Ray knew—he knew everything about Drew and his past. He knew about Drew's feelings for Addi. How the fuck could Ray ask that?

How could anyone trust him with a woman like Addi?

Drew lowered his head into his hands, leaning his elbows on his knees. Maybe this was his punishment. Maybe being everything she needed now to get her through Ray's death was karma. He'd survived before. He'd fallen in love with her, but he'd taken care of her then, too. It had killed him to walk away, killed *her*, but he'd have done it all over to protect her, and he'd do it again now—only this time she needed protection from *him as well.*

He'd be there for her. But no way would he allow her to fall for him again. *No fucking way*. He'd have to show her she wanted nothing to do with Drew Fitzer as a lover. *Hell.* He'd have to be an asshole. He was good at that, but with her it wouldn't be easy. God, the way she looked at him tore him up. That trust and vulnerability—those melted dark chocolate eyes.

Drew stood, his long legs holding him steady as he picked up his coat—a plaid jacket he used for working around the camp when it was chilly—and carried it to her. She held his eyes and stood so he could put it on her. They remained silent as he walked her back through the forest. Would they both wonder if this was a dream in the morning? He caught her when she tripped over a stump, and the force swung her around to face him, so he pulled her against his chest. Her breath on his skin was intoxicating.

"It was beautiful." Her words were barely audible so he pretended he hadn't heard them. He turned her back around and started walking again. If he spoke, she'd hear emotion in his voice. If he spoke, she'd turn to face him again. If he spoke, he'd tell her that the song was hers—*theirs—he'd tell her he loved her.*

The crickets still chirped and frogs still sang and it soothed him. It was the music he fell asleep to nightly. He wondered if it would lull her too. How much had she changed? Her hair shined like dark brown silk and her face, although carrying visible stress, was still a golden honey color from her mother's indigenous heritage. Addi's almond-shaped eyes flickered to his.

And still neither spoke.

The moon shimmered in those pensive eyes and he knew part of the shine was emotion she refused to unleash. She needed to cry again, but she'd always been so determined to show the world strength and control—she held onto it like armor. How could he show her there was just as much strength in giving in, shedding tears and sharing her vulnerability?

He opened the cabin door and she put a hand on his chest. He almost moaned at her touch. Light spilled out of the door and her eyes were pleading. "I'm sorry for what I said in the office. I should have known better." Her eyes lowered to the deck. "I feel a connection to you because of Ray, because of this camp, and our past, but we're nothing but strangers." Her cheeks flushed with embarrassment. "I'm a good distraction. And Ray asked. And well, I needed something, too."

"What?" His voice was sharp. "Addianna." Her name both scolded and scalded from his tongue. "Don't." His jaw ticked and he pointed a long finger at her.

"Don't what? Admit the truth?" She looked away, blowing out. "I know this isn't real. I know you're being nice because Uncle Ray asked you to, and because it's easy, but I need some reality to keep me on the ground. And that reality is, outside of this situation, I'm not good enough for you. You're gorgeous and strong and well, I'm just me." She looked down at herself.

"Jesus!" He ran a hand roughly through his hair. "Get your ass in that cabin, little girl." *Her not good enough for him?* The idea was so ass-backwards he snorted, clenching his hands tightly to keep from shaking some sense into her.

Her eyes widened with a start and she stood frozen to the spot. Couldn't she see how he struggled not to rip her clothes off and plant himself deep inside her lush body? He needed to show her, first how she turned him to fucking lava and then why she should stay the hell away from him.

"Baby girl, you'd better move it. When Daddy tells you something, you damn well do it."

She swallowed whatever was on the tip of her tongue and spun, pushing the door open wider. He followed swiftly, making her scramble with a sharp swat to her ass.

When she turned back, mouth agape from his swat, he reached for her, wrapping his hand around the back of her neck, and pushed her with his body against the wall. His eyes went to her mouth. God, he needed to taste her again. Her mouth closed, leaving nothing but a slit between her full lips. He bit the corner of his mouth, trying to hold back but when her tongue darted out to wet those slightly parted lips, he dove for her.

The feel of her lips, so soft and pliable, undid him. The kiss would never be enough. He needed more, but damn, he would take his time with her.

He took her hands from his chest and bound her wrists with one hand, pulling them above her head.

"*Just you* is exactly what I want," he whispered, leaning down to nuzzle the base of her neck with his nose. He breathed in her scent. "You're intoxicating." His mouth closed over her neck and his teeth scraped her collarbone, making her arch toward him before his tongue soothed and she relaxed.

"Those clothes are coming off," he said in a raspy whisper, pulling her off the wall and releasing her hands. "Unbutton your shirt." She blinked at his demand, possibly weighing her options. He took a step toward her and she went for the top button. He took her hands.

"You hesitated." He turned her and put her hands against the wall. "Don't move unless I give you permission." She nodded and he smiled behind her back.

He gave her ass a sharp swat and then slowly slid her hair off the back of her neck to expose her nape. Tracing a lazy figure eight down her neck, he felt her shiver. "That smack was just a taste of what Daddy'll do to you if you hesitate again. Now turn back around, baby girl."

Her lip quivered as she turned but the flush flaming her cheeks told him it was arousal. She was wet and throbbing over his dominance and it had him rock hard. There was no turning back without breaking her and no going forward without being sent to a deeper level of Dante's inferno.

Ah, hell.

He took her wrists in his hands again, this time feeling the thumping of her pulse beneath his thumbs a moment before he let her go and held her with just his eyes. "There are many ways to punish, Addi."

Her breathing changed, coming in smaller pants. His hands cradled her face and he kissed her, hard and unrelenting.

His tongue probed her mouth, to explore and to overtake her before his teeth slid off her bottom lip. "I'm going to make you mine, baby girl, but before I take what's mine, I need to hear it."

She whimpered as he grasped a handful of her thick hair and yanked.

"Are you mine, Addi? Say the words or I stop. *Say them* and I'll make you forget your name."

"I'm…I'm yours—*for now.*" Her lids fluttered and the words all but tumbled from her trembling lips. It was good enough for him. He shoved her back against the wall.

"Damn straight you are." With that he tore her blouse open, buttons plinking onto the wood floor. His hand found her breast and he kneaded a moment before pinching her nipple just enough to make her call out in pain and when she did, he yanked the silky material of her bra down to allow the injured nipple free. He lowered his head and soothed the ache with his hot mouth. He released and looked her in the eye.

"You'll never hesitate to obey my instruction again, baby girl, *never*." He tore the bra completely down her body, leaving it around her middle so he could torment and pleasure both nipples. She squealed and drove her hands into his hair.

"Hands down," he said roughly. "You touch only when I give you permission." He yanked her skirt down, taking her cotton panties with it. She quickly covered her belly and he growled.

"Step out."

She did and he tossed them aside. She was naked except for the bra around her middle. He had to swallow and clench his teeth to keep from throwing her on the bed and taking her before either of them were ready.

He crooked his finger at her, calling her forward and then reached behind her to grab her ass and squeeze. He could tell by the wince around her eyes it was punishing. "Never cover yourself from me, you hear?"

She nodded, closing her eyes in a grimace and slowly moved her hands. His brow cocked. "Baby girl needs training." She bit her lip, nodding and he almost broke free from his jeans. *Fuck*, she was perfect.

"Who am I?" he demanded.

"You're…" He swatted her ass when she hesitated, diving down to devour her nipple again, tormenting it with nibbles and deep suckling. "Gah, D… Daddy!" she called out.

"That's it, baby girl, say it again. Louder. I want the

world to know it."

"Daddy!" she hollered, throwing her head back. "Oh, God, I'm yours, Daddy."

He chuckled darkly as he took her shoulders and walked her backwards, then stopped to boost her up. "Legs around me."

She did as she was told and once again, he pushed her against the wall, diving for her neck and feeling her weaken against him. His hands clenched her ass cheeks, digging into the flesh as he ground his hard, jean-sheathed cock against her mound.

She mewled at the friction and his mouth found hers so he could swallow her cries of pleasure. Dividing his time between her neck and beasts, her breathing labored. When he couldn't stand torturing her any longer, he carried her toward the bed and tossed her on it. Her squeal of shock made him burn hotter.

He took his clothes off, slowly so her eyes followed with a suffering heat.

"You like this, baby girl?"

"Y-yes," she answered, swallowing hard.

"See this?" He looked down at his hard cock. "*This* is what you do to me." He moved closer to the bed. "Does my baby girl wanna feel what she's done to her daddy?"

She pulled her bottom lip through her teeth and he saw insecurity in her face.

"Your body, your curves, drive me wild. I'm so fucking hard for you it hurts. Touch it, babe. Own it like I own the juice dripping down your thighs."

"Don't." Her eyes fluttered closed. "Feet on the ground. I'm no different than any other woman you've been with. Please let me keep my feet on the ground, Drew. I won't survive this otherwise."

His heart pounded in his chest as her eyes opened wide and glossy, staring straight through him. He wished he could clarify, tell her exactly how real things were for him, but he couldn't. He needed her to forget him later—*when it was time to go home.*

"Hey." He fell on the bed beside her and pulled her chin so she faced him. "Whatever you believe, babe, right now this is all you." Her eyes fluttered downward, away from his. "I love your body. I like a curvy woman with something to hold. And babe." He waited until her eyes came back to his. "I'm in charge. *Me.* Your daddy. For as long as we're here together and you want it. Got me?"

She nodded, but her eyes were still glassy. "I can't play like this, Drew. It's too real—too much of what I want for real. Daddies are forever and this," she said, pointing between them. "This isn't forever. It's for right now."

"*Christ.*" He scooted forward on the bed. "You need to learn to let go of the control, little girl. I'm not playing around." He grabbed and yanked her to him, pulling her forward so she fell across his lap.

"Damn, I didn't want to have to spank you again this soon, Addi, not for this, but God, you need it. You're wound too damn tight and you need to learn who's in charge here."

She was naked and there was nothing to protect her heart-shaped rear, so when he swatted her, a pink print marred her right cheek. She yelped and tried to cover the spot he'd branded.

"Hand to the front." She obeyed slowly. He swatted the left cheek and she whimpered. He didn't pause then, but continued until the blush on her backside flourished from the top of her cheeks to the tops of her thighs. She twisted her hips slightly at each swat to avoid his hand landing in the same spot but he adjusted his aim each time. He wasn't spanking her overly hard, it was more to break down her walls, but enough that she felt every burning swat.

"Ow! It hurts! Stop! Please!" she protested on a whimper. He shook his head and smacked her bottom faster, making her bury her face in the bed and squirm more. Her hand came back to her side but she didn't try to block this time. His baby girl needed support so he grabbed her hand and their fingers entwined. She squeezed and didn't fight his hold.

"Who's in charge, Addi?" He swatted slower, waiting for her answer. He instantly felt a change in her. It was as if the tension in her body let go and she relaxed. She needed someone in charge.

"You." The word flew out of her mouth and her bottom went up to meet his hand. He smiled and increased the tempo of his spanking again, her whimpers turning to little moans.

"Yeah, babe, *me*. And I'm going to take care of you, give you what you need, no matter if you realize your needs or not. That's what daddies do. And even if I'm not your daddy forever, that doesn't make our time here any less real. Understand, babe?"

"Yes—*yes, okay*." He continued his rhythm until she added to her answer. "Yes, Daddy."

He pulled her up and tucked her into him. And she let him, this time without hesitation or resistance. Tugging her face in close to his neck, he rubbed the warmth from her bottom, kneading and caressing until she started to make a noise best described as a purr. He chuckled.

"Baby girl, I want to make love to you, but you're not ready." Her purr turned to a disappointed whine. "But Daddy won't leave you frustrated." His hand slipped lower and found the crevice between her cheeks, sliding across her rosebud, knowing it would cause a blip of taboo pleasure, and then went lower still to her wet, hot center.

Her moan made his dick twitch. "Lie on the bed, babe. I'm gonna help you sleep." He moved her onto the bed and she looked up at him, submissive and ready for instruction. "This is exactly what I want to see from my little girl."

He took her knees, spread them wide and slid his hands beneath her warm ass. Lowering himself to his knees, he took a few minutes to nibble and lick her belly, teasing until he decided she could handle no more and found her slit. His tongue traced it with a whisper of a touch and her hips rose.

"Be a good girl, honey. Have patience."

He skimmed her sensitive area several times before sliding his tongue firmer between her folds and bathing her clit. "Mm, babe, you taste so fucking good. I'm going to enjoy this." He sucked and her ass left his hands as she moved rhythmically against his mouth.

"God, your beard. Your tongue. I've never… Oh, oh, oh, *God!*"

He paused. "Never, babe?"

She shook her head and clasped the sheets as he continued with his thumb so he could watch her. "Not this… Just… Sex. Unremarkable sex."

"Aw, baby girl. I'm going to have so much fun with you." He grinned crookedly at her and then took her hands to position them so she held herself open. He dove back between her thighs.

She twitched, squealed, and pushed herself shamelessly against his face but held fast to her pleasure. She didn't seem to want to let go, or perhaps she couldn't. She tensed and stiffened so he flicked faster and suckled harder, running the tip of his tongue along the smooth skin between her lips to flick her nub quickly, and then over again to create a rhythm that caused her breath to huff faster. As he pumped one finger into her tight pussy, a strangled cry passed her lips. He switched his finger for his thumb, stretching her open, circling against her tight wall.

Still she held on. It was part of her need for control, he decided as she was beyond wet and certainly close. Her sweet fluid ran down his hand and into his beard. He found her special spot, stroking and swirling against it with the pad of his thumb until her moisture poured from her down the crack of her ass.

"Babe?" He paused. "You need to relax and enjoy it. You're fighting it." Her eyes were squeezed tight and he stopped.

"Look at me. *Now.*" His voice was firm.

When her eyes opened, she blinked, looking

embarrassed. "I can't. I should have told you. It's not you." She started to rise.

"The hell you can't." He held his moist thumb up before licking it off. She blinked again. "Fucking sweet as honey, babe. You're ready and I'm going to work you as long as it takes because I've been thinking about making you come from the moment I pictured you in that damn bikini."

She bobbed her head but looked unconvinced. He took his hand and wrapped it around the back of her neck, pulling her up and forward to him. "Let me have it, babe."

He went back to her pussy, and began building her up again, working his thumb on her g-spot as his tongue swirled and flicked. He felt her tense again. He kept working his thumb, but used his free hand to push her higher, closer to his mouth. She called out as he squeezed her ass and went over the edge, screaming his name, her thighs twitching against his face.

"Drew, oh, God, *Drew!*"

She pulsed around his tongue and he flicked a few more times to keep her coming.

She tried to shove him back so he flipped her, pulling her up onto her knees, swatting her ass hard three times before easing back and spanking rhythmically to vibrate her sensitive nub. When one orgasm ended, the next began building as he used his mouth from behind. With his nose nestled between her ass cheeks and his tongue flicking relentlessly, he felt his erection straining for release; his own need to come was fierce.

She screamed out in pleasure and he rolled them to their sides to hold her tenderly as she trembled from her second explosive orgasm. After a few silent minutes, her breathing regulated and she turned to her back. She had tears in her eyes and was spread-eagle and limp before him. She was totally uninhibited now, and he loved it.

"I've never," she said on a whimper. She curled into him and her breasts hanging naturally heavy against his chest made him harder still. "I didn't know what the fuss was about." Tears leaked down her face and he swallowed hard at her revelation.

"I'm going to teach you how to let go, little girl." His firm statement was drowned out with the emotion clogging his voice. This woman deserved so much more than she'd gotten in life. She held onto her control so aggressively she couldn't even have the most basic of life's pleasures. How did she release her pent-up stress?

"You need a dominant man to take over, Addi. I know you want more, you want real, but babe, this is *real* as long as you're here."

"Okay." She tipped her head up and smiled shyly. He gave her a half smirk. The trust she'd just handed over blew his mind. How could one person be so beautiful inside and out?

He chuckled. "Okay?"

"Yes, okay." She grinned. "If that's what I've been missing, then yes. I feel so light—so free! I'm yours to teach, Daddy."

"Good girl." He ran a hand sweetly down her hair. "Get comfy, babe. It's bedtime." She opened her mouth and he cocked a brow. "That's an order, Addianna. It's not all about sex, honey. Being my baby girl means I'm in charge of everything. Your health and welfare are important to me." Her mouth closed and he smiled as a flare of heat burned her eyes. Another head bob and she slid that plump bottom lip through her teeth again. "That's my girl."

She rolled over, tucking her fist beneath her chin and pulling her legs up so she was curled in an Addi-sized ball. "An order from my daddy," she said in a small breathy voice. He leaned down and kissed her temple, emotion and tenderness filling him.

What had he done? Could he give her what he'd offered without losing himself? He heard Ray's voice in his mind, asking, and then his own, promising to give her whatever she needed. Did she need this? He nodded silently and rose from the bed.

Addi needed this more than anything. If she kept going with the world on her shoulders, she'd collapse. She was a natural submissive. She needed someone who'd support her, listen, and reassure her of the decisions she made, someone who'd take responsibility *with her* if things didn't go right. She needed both a partner and a leader so she could safely let go and be who she was meant to be.

He looked at her, already breathing deeply in sleep, and shoveled a hand through his hair.

"Even if I'm a broken mess when you leave, I'll give you everything you deserve while you're here." His whisper was raspy with emotion. "You've always been my weakness, but I promise you this… I'll always be your strength."

CHAPTER ELEVEN

Addi

Addi's eyes shot open, her heart aching from a dream about Uncle Ray. She stirred, still entwined in Drew's arms, and he tightened them around her in sleep. She let out a breath, telling herself it was just a dream. Even though she was warm and safe in Drew's arms, she felt restless. She looked at the clock. It was one a.m.

Nothing she could do now, except she *needed* to do something—something for her uncle. The dream had unsettled her and although the vividness was fading, the emotion was still intense. She thought hard about what she could do but there wasn't much that could be done in the middle of the night.

She grabbed her phone on the nightstand and opened her Facebook application. Could she post something? When the group opened, she saw the background banner and smiled. It was a canoe with three boys and Uncle Ray. He was holding up a fish the boy to his right had proudly caught. It hit her then. There *was* something she could do. She could release his rescued fish into the lake!

She breathed in the manly smell of Drew and watched

him sleeping in the moonlight. She should probably wait for him. He did tell her to stay away from her uncle's cabin after all, but that solved none of her restlessness. She moved a little on the bed, testing to see if he'd wake.

He didn't move, but Addi became distracted watching him. She loved the way his dark hair curled around his ears and his beard, dark like his hair, was mussed from more than just sleep.

How was it he could be both scary and comforting—both nurturing and demanding, both angry and loving?

She let her finger trail along one of his angry tattoos—some demon, devouring a colorful bird. His breathing didn't change so she slid out from under his arm.

"I'll be back. I just gotta do this," she whispered.

Taking the small flashlight from her dresser drawer, Addi headed to her uncle's cabin. She was attempting to be as inconspicuous with the beam of light as possible as if she were some burglar, but knowing what would happen if she got caught was reason enough.

She swallowed at the thought. He was her daddy dom for now and he might take a switch to her ass. The idea secretly thrilled her, but also brought a chill of nervousness up her spine. The flashlight beam landed on the cabin, forcing her thoughts back to her mission.

When she tried to open the door it was locked. She twisted it again. Seriously locked. Addi cursed Drew, kicking the green rubber boots on the porch and growling to the star-speckled sky.

How the hell had he known she'd go to her uncle's cabin after he told her not to?

A smile crept up on her face though, because she could pick a lock. Not because she was a badass like him, but because she'd helped Steven out last year by interviewing a hiker who'd gotten trapped in the mountains for several weeks after a storm. The hiker had found a cabin and picked the lock to get shelter. He had shown her how during the interview using a pair of tweezers and a hairpin. She had both tweezers and hairpins in her makeup bag back in the cabin. She crouched to examine the lock a moment before rising and turning straight into a big, strong wall of a man.

"Hi, Daddy."

"Exploring again?" he asked casually, still holding her shoulders to steady her.

"Why'd you lock me out of here?" Her indignant tone was a defense mechanism, but with the grumpy look in Drew's eyes she knew it wasn't working.

"You know why I locked you out, baby girl. It's not safe."

"I wanted a hotdog," she said lamely. His sardonic smile made her heart patter.

"A green fuzzy one?" His right brow rose. "I threw them out, but hey, we could head to the grocery store and check the garbage bins behind it."

She crossed her arms and gave him a grunt. "No, thanks. I'm going back to my cabin."

"Good idea, babe. I wouldn't want you getting into trouble out here." He rubbed his hands together. "How about I grab you another burger from my place? Much tastier than a green, fuzzy hotdog."

"Would you?" Focusing on this new subject felt safer.

"Anything for my baby girl."

"Oh, that sounds delicious!" Her overly chipper tone also didn't seem to fool Drew and he narrowed his eyes.

"You're going to go back to your cabin, aren't you, little one?"

She bobbed her head. "I am."

"I'll meet you there with your burger." His eyes were narrowed, so she smiled sweetly to appease him. She could eat her burger after she released the fish into the lake.

Uncle Ray would want it back in the lake, not festering in some tank. It wasn't much but it was something she could do for him besides pick a bloody coffin and his death wear. Besides, a few minutes in the cabin wouldn't kill her. Drew was just being overprotective.

Drew walked her back to her cabin and listened to her ramble on about her uncle's spider dogs (split at each end so they would curl into spider legs when cooked over the fire). He was a good listener, but damn, knowing she was about to disobey him made her nervous.

After getting the tools she needed and making damn sure Drew wasn't hiding in wait, she went back to Uncle Ray's. She pulled on the rubber boots she'd kicked on the porch earlier and then crouched down and got to work on the lock.

It was easier to pick than she'd thought. Apparently picking locks was like riding a bike. She was thankful for the interviews and research she'd done for Steven and Daniel. She learned a lot: self-defense, first aid in the wild, and eating for survival when you're nowhere near civilization were just a few of the things she'd learned.

Inside, she shone her flashlight beam on the beast in the tank. The fish was still until the beam caught its eye, then it darted forward, hiding behind a pathetic little plastic leaf. Its mouth hung slightly open, showing lots of sharp teeth.

"It's okay, grandpa fish. I'm going to let you free for Uncle Ray."

Addi got closer to the fish before she realized two things: one, it was way bigger than she remembered and two, she hadn't planned her rescue out. How the hell would she get it to the lake? She couldn't carry it with all those teeth ready to bite her fingers off. Besides, it was dark and if he flopped out of her arms, she might never find him before he ran out of oxygen.

She glanced around with her flashlight beam searching for something to carry it in. How long could a fish live without water? The lake was close but what was considered close when you were holding your breath and struggling?

What if she put its head in the bucket and wrapped her arms around the body to keep it from flopping out? She looked at the tiny bucket and then back at the huge fish.

"Why couldn't you just be like a dog and follow the bucket of little fish? Here, fishy-fishy." She huffed and saw a garbage bag on the counter. *Aha!*

Addi filled the bag with water, bucket by bucket, ignoring the small tear that let water and an awful fish smell leak onto her booted feet. Once it was half full she looked back at the tank and grimaced. How was she going to hold the bag and get the fish—and how the hell did you get a fish with sharp teeth out of a tank without getting bit?

She held the bag with one hand and tugged the elastic out of her ponytail, tying the bag closed with it. Once she was sure it was secure, she went to the kitchen area and started opening and closing drawers, mumbling and grousing, until she found what she was looking for.

"Ha! Try and bite through these, sucker!" She put her hands in a big pair of oven mitts and grabbed the bag.

She puffed, out of breath, as she dragged the bag closer to the tank and untied it.

"You think…" She breathed. "You could… jump in?" she asked, holding the bag open and looking pleadingly at the fish. Her voice squeaked as a light clicked on and she let go of the bag. Water rushed all over the floor and her boots while she screeched.

A deep chuckle made her yell, "Who's there?" She covered her eyes, which weren't used to the bright light that was pointed at her face.

"Ah, baby girl, you look quite adorable in rubber boots and oven mitts, but you're in so much trouble."

"Drew?"

"That's right, honey."

"But… How'd you get in here?"

"There's a back door."

"But…"

He flicked on the big light and she saw he was sitting on one of the kitchen chairs she had passed right by in search of the oven mitts. He looked quite comfortable, with an ankle crossed over his knee and a fishing net in his hands.

"Shit!" She pointed at the net. "Why didn't I think of that?"

And at that very moment as if the fates were laughing at her and rooting for Drew, the floor creaked and her foot went straight through the wood, knocking her off balance and onto her butt.

She looked at Drew, who set the net down and crossed his arms. "Appropriate oven mitts, by the way. That fish would have bitten right through them though."

"Oh," she said, looking sheepish. The oven mitts were shaped and decorated like fish. She'd bought them for Uncle Ray last Christmas. "At least the boot protected my foot," she offered, pointing at the hole where her booted foot disappeared.

He only shook his head. She yanked her foot out of the rubber footwear and stuck it in the air, wiggling her toes. "Look, no cuts!"

Drew walked to her, avoiding the puddle and the hole and hefted her up by the armpits, only releasing her long enough to scoop her up properly and carry her out to the porch. He set her down and pointed to the rocking chair. She blinked from him to it and back again.

"Addi," he warned. She stamped the still booted foot and sat.

"What are you going to do?"

"You mean besides spank your naughty ass?"

"Drew!"

"Baby girl, we're going to let this fish go and then I'm bringing you back to your cabin for a bath." He leaned toward her and sniffed, grimacing. "You smell like a pike that rolled in dead fish and fuzzy dumpster hotdogs."

She looked down and sniffed at herself. "Oh, God. I do."

"And once you smell better, you're going right over my knee."

"Really?" She crossed her arms.

He took a step toward her and put his palms on her face, tipping it up so he could look her in the eye. "Was last night a joke? A game?" he asked.

Addi shrugged. He dropped his hands from her face and took her hands instead.

"It wasn't. Not to me. This *is* real and you agreed." When she looked down, he let her hand go to tilt her chin back up. "Have you changed your mind?"

Addi swallowed hard at his words. "No. I want real."

"I'm the boss, babe. I'm taking care of you completely from here on out. You argue, disobey, disrespect, I don't walk away, little one. I correct, teach, and punish however I see fit. Got me?"

"I got you, Drew." She nibbled her lip a moment. "Thank you. I know I'll likely screw up, again and again, but I want this. I want you to take care of me, Daddy." It took a lot for her to say that, but she meant it. She trusted him.

"Good." He leaned down and took her mouth gently again, sucking in the lip she'd nibbled a few seconds earlier. It was a dawdling kiss that created a slow burn deep in her belly and when he released her, she was breathless.

"Come on, babe. Let's get that fish back home."

The net made everything easier, although the fish was heavier than she thought and still fought fiercely so Drew carried it. At the edge of the lake he handed it to her.

"Go ahead. Take it."

"Me?"

"Yeah, babe, but hurry up. This guy can't breathe."

"Okay." She grabbed the net from him. She grunted with the weight and the change made the fish start flopping from side to side again. "Whoa, big guy," she said and waded into the water.

"Careful, it's slippery," Drew warned.

She smiled and put the net in the water but left the top above so the fish couldn't get away yet.

"Should we say something?" She looked at him, unsure if he'd think she was being silly.

"Yeah, babe." He smiled.

"We release you, grandpa fish, in the name of your nemesis, but in the end your friend. This is for Uncle Ray, a fighter for all in need." And she lowered the net completely.

The fish flicked its tail wildly and splashed her with water. She screamed when it turned to her.

"Oh, shit, Drew!" She ran toward shore. "It's gonna get me!" She practically climbed him when he hauled her back to shore, and squealed shrilly.

He laughed, deep and hearty from his belly, and then fell onto the shore. He kissed her neck, sending shivers through her from his scruffy beard.

"Come on, baby girl, let's get you in the tub so I can punish and fuck you good."

• • • • • • •

He ran the bath, throwing another bath bomb in while watching her undress.

"If you didn't smell so bad, babe, I'd be over there helping you." He sat with his hip on the edge of the tub.

"Wimp," she said, wiggling her brows at him.

"A wimp, huh? We'll see who's the wimp when I have you over my thighs, painting that ass red."

"That's not fair. Unless I get to see how you handle a spanking too."

He chuckled, swishing his hand through the pink water. "Me, Daddy, you, baby girl."

"Smart like biker," she mocked.

"Hmm and what shall I spank that naughty *and* saucy ass with?" He looked skyward. "Hand? Belt?" She followed his eyes to the sink. "Ah, how about the hairbrush over there."

"Drew!" Her voice spiked higher.

"That's Daddy, babe."

"Fine! *Daddy!*" she pouted, but didn't feel any fear whatsoever, not with her clit swollen and her core burning hot and slick for him. Down to only her underwear and bra, she looked at her feet, using her long hair like a veil. She felt shy. How could he possibly find her attractive?

"Come 'ere," he said holding out his hand for her. She

went to him.

"Look at me."

She obeyed, staring into his blue eyes, admiring the dark blue ring.

"Every inch of you is beautiful, got me?"

She nodded and he stood. "Arms up."

She lifted them and he took off her bra and then bent, lowering her panties.

"That's my girl." He took her hand. "Step in."

When she sank into the water, it felt amazing, but it was nothing compared to how she felt when he washed her. By the time she stepped out of the tub, she felt as languid as a puppy after a long run. He dried her and nodded toward the brush.

"Grab that, honey."

She swallowed hard. "Yes, Daddy."

He took her hand when she complied and led her to the bed, still crumpled from them sleeping in it. He sat and nodded to the floor. "Kneel down and I'll brush your hair." He ran the brush through her locks and the gentle tugging on her scalp made her feel languid.

"Up you get now, babe," he said and patted his thigh. "Let's get you over my knee."

She set herself over, closing her eyes as her breasts fell heavily.

"You okay, honey?"

She nodded and he tapped her thigh with the brush hard enough to make her squeak.

"Yes, Daddy."

"Better. You were a naughty girl tonight, weren't you?"

"I guess."

He swatted her thigh harder and she lurched forward on his lap, feeling her balance waver. His big hand pulled her hip closer to his abdomen, securing her.

"Yes, I was naughty!"

"How, baby girl?"

"I broke into my uncle's cabin."

"A cabin that I forbid you to go into, yes?"

"Yes, sir."

"Because it isn't safe, yeah?"

"Yes, Daddy."

"And you gave me your trust to take care of you, right? To care for you, protect you, and punish you if I see fit?"

"Yes, sir."

"Then, are you ready? This won't be a sexy spanking, babe. It's gonna hurt."

She nodded and peeked at his hand rising over her bottom in the mirror of her dressing table across from them.

"Wait!"

He stopped, noticing her in the mirror, and looked her in the eye. "Give me your hand, baby girl." She reached back to give it to him. "Daddy's got you." He smiled at her and let his arm fall. The spank was crisp, loud and shockingly solid, the sting so much more biting than his hand, especially on her still damp skin.

"Ouch!" she hissed.

"Uh huh. I'm pretty sure you'll remember to obey me after this." He smirked at her through the mirror and despite the burn on her butt, she smiled back. God, he was a hot biker daddy. "Now let's get this spanking going, young lady. You need to squirm on my lap before you wiggle under me."

Before she could come completely undone by his words, the brush was searing her backside again—this time without pause. He obviously believed in swift correction, because it wasn't like his other spankings, the more sensual ones. She called out, squeezed his hand, kicked, and burst into tears as the burn and sting overwhelmed her.

"The floor is rotten. You could have been hurt. What if the floor caved in just a few more feet to the left and the fish tank fell on top of you?"

When he stopped, she continued weeping.

"That hurt!" she said in a wet sob.

"It was supposed to. I meant business when I said don't step foot in there."

"I never thought of that." She sucked in a shaky breath and let it out on a long whimper. "I just wanted to do something for Uncle Ray since all I seem to be doing is getting tangled up with you."

He helped her up onto his lap, tucked her hair behind her ear, and kissed her temple. She leaned against his shoulder, grabbed the brush from his hand, and threw it across the room.

"I hate that thing!"

Drew chuckled, but patted the part of her bottom he still had access to.

"Go get it, babe. We don't throw fits of temper after we've been spanked, do we?"

Her brows crunched and her frown deepened to a pout. "But I hate that thing."

"Do you need more? Another spanking to get that naughtiness out?"

"No," she said, crossing her arms.

"Go get it."

She huffed loudly as he helped her up. A swat landed against her ass, making her clutch her cheeks with both hands.

"Ow!"

"Brush now, babe."

She narrowed her eyes but stepped quickly away so he couldn't reach her. Grabbing the brush, she gave it a dirty look.

"Bring it here."

"You're not going to use on me again, are you?"

"Babe. Bring. It. Here."

She shuffled her feet, but handed him the brush. She stood at the ready to jump back if she needed to though. He set the brush down and she relaxed, but then he grabbed her and yanked her back over his lap, giving her three sharp spanks with his hand. She gasped and smacked her hand on the floor.

"Babe, I'm okay with you bratting, that's part of being a

baby girl, but you need to be okay with the consequences, too." He rubbed and squeezed her cheeks and she mewled. "Now let's see how you really felt about this hairbrush." He chuckled and his hand slid from her cheeks, down her slit, and settled at her opening.

"Seems awfully slippery down here for the hate you were showing that brush, honey."

She felt her face flush. "That's for you, Daddy, not that damn brush." She growled and he smacked her thigh, making her whimper. "No more, please!"

"More, please?" The offending hand went back to her slick center and began exploring, sliding through her lips, circling her nub, and then rubbing her moisture up her crack and over her bottom hole, before sliding back to her pussy opening and gliding his long sturdy finger into it.

"More of this, yes?"

"Mmm, yes, please."

He chuckled again, and the deep raspy timbre made a shiver run down her spine. He pumped his finger into her and she arched her back as he grabbed her hair, entwining it in his fist.

"Tell me what you want, babe." He leaned down and licked the shell of her ear, breathing hot moist breath into it. Suddenly she wanted to conquer her fears with this man. She felt stronger with him, ready to challenge herself and her fears.

"I want… God, Drew, I want to fuck on your bike." Her words surprised her, but they weren't a lie. She did want to fuck on his bike. There was something freeing about it, as if the scared little girl she became after her mother's accident wasn't the real her, but a coat of armor she wore to protect herself.

He pulled her up and turned her head with her hair. His eyes were clouded with arousal.

"Take me for a ride and then let me ride you, Biker Daddy."

His hiss of breath made her hotter, slicker, and she felt

in control of his desire for the first time. She felt like a beautiful goddess.

"Let's go." He peeled off his t-shirt and put it on her. "Panties only." His brow shot up to challenge her, but she only bit the corner of her lip.

It was dark and still; even the night sounds had quieted. She wore her wedge sandals, his t-shirt, and white cotton panties, and as she flew through the forest led by him in just a pair of jeans and his sturdy black boots, she felt as if she were a giggling aroused wood nymph that had tempted the manliest of catches.

He led her to the Norton, but she shook her head and pointed at the Harley. "That one." She licked her lips. "The one you were riding when I first saw you pull up behind me."

His smile came fast and wide and his eyes sparked with both mischief and arousal.

After he put her helmet on, buckled it, and warned her where to keep her legs so she didn't get burned, he got on the bike and held it steady for her. Her middle throbbed as she slid forward on the leather seat and pressed herself against him. The warmth of his skin set her on fire. She clasped her arms around his hard middle and kissed his back.

"Hang onto me tight, babe."

She planned to.

CHAPTER TWELVE

Addi

The wind rushed through her hair and against her bare skin. It felt amazing. She was free. Freer than she'd ever been. And pressed against a man she trusted, she was completely safe.

They rode for half an hour before he pulled off the gravel road to a lookout spot and cut the engine. The rocky escarpment was dark except for the stars lighting the sky.

Drew held the bike while she got off, then flipped the kickstand. As soon as he was off the bike and they had taken their helmets off, his hands found her face and drove into her hair. His kiss was hot and demanding. He released her hair with one hand and grabbed her ass to boost her up. She didn't wait to be told to put her legs around him.

"That's… my… good… girl," he huffed, between kissing and biting her lip. One arm banded under her bottom so the other could unbuckle, unzip, and shuck his jeans down.

He'd gone commando. His hot thick cock poked her bottom until he set her down on his bike seat. Pulling the shirt up and off her arms, he sucked her nipples, while tearing her panties until they were just bands of cotton in his hands.

The cool air on her nipples and the risqué way she was exposed to the world made her pussy pulse harder.

He climbed on and pulled her to him, grabbing her hair to hold her head so he could access her neck. He bit first, then ran the flat of his tongue along it and sucked, making her belly quiver.

"Lean back, babe. I got you," he said with a deeper than usual rasp to his voice. She leaned back on her hands, holding the seat, and he grabbed her ass to pull her closer as he bent to take a tightly beaded nipple into his mouth.

"Ah, that's… ooh…" He stopped to wet his finger and thumb with his tongue so he could roll her other nipple between them. He went back to his suckling and she called out when he sucked so deep she felt the tug right to her clit.

She released the seat and shoved her hands through his hair, tugging, and he bit down hard enough to make her cry out into the darkness.

"Hands on the seat, babe. Daddy's in charge out here, too." He took her mouth when she opened it to complain, first sucking away her words and then making her forget what they were.

Drew slid off the back of the bike and yanked her ass closer to the edge of the seat. His mouth nibbled down her rounded tummy, but because she was holding her breath in anticipation of his tongue heading for her pussy, she didn't give it a second thought.

When his mouth came down over her shaved mound and his tongue slid inside her slit, she threw her head back. He wasn't teasing her this time. This time, he sucked, nibbled, and flicked her up the crest of the hill, and in minutes she howled his name with an explosive orgasm. And when she sat forward on his bike, she slid on the wet leather beneath her. She'd soaked it.

Her breathing was labored and she felt almost dizzy with the waves of pleasure that pulsed on.

"Come 'ere, babe." He climbed back on, grabbed her ass, and lifted her until she was impaling herself slowly on his cock. "God, you're fucking tight and wet. Baby, you're so fucking hot. Come on, fuck me on this Harley." He helped her move her hips up and down, his shaft thrusting deeper and deeper.

"I wanted to…" she panted. "I wanted to suck you, but gah… you feel so good inside me." She sped up slightly and saw pleasure blossom on his features. He started rhythmically swatting her ass every time she rose. One cheek and then the other was lit with his fiery spanks. Her cries went from pained to pleasure whimpers as he slammed his cock up harder when she came down. His cock reached what seemed an impossible depth.

He groaned and fisted her hair with his free hand and continued to spank her ass.

"Baby, fuck me hard. Show me what a badass you are."

Her pussy clenched and dripped at his words. She was not some scared woman, she was his badass baby girl. And only he could control her—no one else and only because *she* gave him that power.

She leaned down as the tension increased in her abdomen. Her mouth clasped over his shoulder, over the tattoo of a horned creature, and as she bit down into his fleshy muscle the most amazing coiling spring in her belly released and ripped through her. She screamed into his shoulder. His moan of release followed.

•••••••

"Did I hurt you?" She looked up from her spot between his legs in the cool grass. His beard tickled her face.

"No, babe, but if Daddy's little girl bites again she's going over my knee." He kissed her forehead and she snuggled deeper into his arms.

She'd run a finger over the teeth indents on his shoulder after they came down from their orgasms and smiled. She had marked him as hers, just as he'd marked her. She felt sad a moment, knowing both markings would fade just like them.

"It's getting late," she said, looking at the sky.

"More like early," he countered. The sky was lightening as they sat in the dewy grass beneath a tree.

"Thank you," she said again, looking up at him.

"For what, babe?"

"For everything." Her eyes welled and she knew her emotions were running high because of everything they'd done that night. He'd given her another explosive orgasm—another first of its kind for her, and so much more. With his dominance, she felt her confidence growing. It didn't make sense but she knew it to be true. Not in a million years would she have ever thought she'd ride on the back of a motorcycle.

"You've been here for me every second… whether it's to comfort, protect, or correct. I was resisting because I felt guilty for enjoying you while I'm here to grieve. I'm at Tonalonka for my uncle and instead I'm falling for you. It seems so wrong, you know?" She felt him freeze against her. Was he holding his breath?

She swallowed and kept talking, hoping to clarify. "I mean not like falling for in like a long-term way…" She chewed the inside of her cheek. "I just think, knowing my uncle, he'd want me to be supported and cared for during this time. I think he'd be happy I'm not sitting somewhere bawling over the loss, right?"

"Yeah. Right." He started to shift beneath her. "Come on. I'd better get you back."

"Drew?"

He looked at her, his expression hidden.

"I… I… didn't mean to…"

"Don't worry about it, Addi. We're all good."

Her heart sank. He didn't call her babe, or baby girl.

When he got her back, he tucked her in and left her, claiming he had something important he needed to do. She nodded, feeling like her insides were filled with acid.

God, how could she be so stupid and say she was falling for him? So what if they had a past. So what if they were connected because of their grief for Uncle Ray. It would mean nothing once she went home and back to her reality. She would mean nothing—forgotten.

She didn't bother trying to sleep, but stayed in the bed for a while simply staring at the light changing outside her window.

Her mind tortured her with thoughts of why she wasn't good enough for him—of why she was just a temporary distraction. Of why her father spent all his time hidden in his office and why her mother was always off doing wild things. The only correlation with every relationship was her.

Feeling as if the walls were closing in on her, she got out of the bed. Drew seemed to really like her, to want the same things as she did, so why did he go from hot to cold so easily? Why did he seem so angry at times? She took a breath and held it, grabbing her hairbrush and taming her 'just fucked' hair before releasing the air in her lungs.

It was easy to just say she wasn't good enough or she was just a distraction. Easy, but maybe a bit narcissistic. Not everything was about her. And her gut told her something else was up. Things between them weren't as black and white as they seemed.

She glanced at her uncle's letter. She still couldn't do it. What she wanted to do was go to the cliffs. See the place where everything began with Drew. Maybe there was more to their breakup than she remembered.

Already in Drew's shirt, she pulled on a pair of loose cotton sleep shorts and some shower flip-flops she'd found in her gym bag. Even if nothing came from her going to the cliffs, the walk would do her good.

She couldn't even remember where the damn cliffs were but walked along the lake knowing it would eventually bring her there. The bugs were biting in the early dawn as she walked along the marsh. They buzzed in her ears and left welts where they bit her, but she ignored them and as the sun rose higher, it amped up the heat and they disappeared. Cicadas buzzed and she panted as the sun beating down on her made the steady incline seem steeper.

It would be a scorcher that afternoon. The kind of day that was good for swimming and lazing by the lake and not much else. Maybe she'd take her notebook and sit by the lake and write Uncle Ray's eulogy. Forget all the drama of Drew and her twisted feelings.

Before the cliff came into view, she saw the house. It was sprawling and gorgeous, probably close to five thousand square feet along the edge of the forest where pine needle and damp earth beds turned to rock, greenery, and moss. The house was made of logs, but with the windows, huge and tinted so she couldn't see in, and the glass wraparound veranda, it looked modern. Was this the house Brent had spoken of? Was this where Uncle Ray had painted?

As she got closer, she saw the door swing open in the slight breeze that had picked up as she neared the cliff. Addi looked around. A flash of blonde caught her eye and the short-shorts on the blonde told her exactly who it was.

Layla.

She wanted to follow, but looked back at the door. Which was more important? She moved faster to follow Layla. She could go back and see the house after. The way the door flapped and Layla ran told her following was more important. She was up to no good. Unless, was Drew in the house? She looked back and shook her head.

As she got closer to Layla, she slowed, knowing the noise could alert her. Layla had slowed, herself, pulling out her phone. She pressed some buttons and stuck the cell to her ear.

"Rebecca? You aren't going to believe what I found. Call me as soon as you get this. You're going to shit. Trust me." She took the phone from her ear and pressed a few more buttons before putting it back against her head. "I'm sending you some pictures."

Addi paused, looked back at the cliff house and then at Layla. What had she found? Making a split-second decision, Addi turned back. What was in the house?

The lock hadn't been broken. A key was in the mechanism as the screen door creaked open and closed. Had Layla been trying to steal her uncle's paintings? Was Drew trying to hide them from her here? Was he trying to distract her with his dominant biker daddy routine so he could sell them before she found out about them?

She held her breath, turned the key, and pushed open the inner door. The room that opened before her was vast, with cathedral ceilings and skylights to allow more natural light to pour in. Paintings were hung on walls, sat on easels half complete, and set against crates, closed and packed labeled for shipping. Drop cloths splattered with color and brushes in glass jars cluttered the room and the intense smell of oil paint and turpentine accosted her nostrils.

He *was* trying to hide this from her. She walked deeper into the room, spinning around to look at all the amazing art pieces. Emotions battered against her and she held strong against them. Her uncle was amazing. The paintings were overwhelmingly beautiful.

Scenes of the camp, cliff, lake, and marsh were all around her. There was even a self-portrait of her uncle watching the sunrise at the lake. He was holding a steaming thermos cup and a fishing rod, and it was so realistic, it took her breath away. The way his shoulders stooped slightly with age and his favorite plaid shirt was wrinkled and faded, and even the way his smile was slightly tilted, made it so real, it was as if he were alive standing before her.

As she passed through the room into a kitchen, she felt her strength waning. The beauty through the wall-sized windows overlooking the cliff was astounding but she barely noticed. Her eyes were stuck on the paintings hung perfectly on the walls.

Her. They were all of her. Tears welled as she went closer. She was sixteen, chubby, and innocent, her hair hanging in dark braids, but the truth of the painting lay in the stubborn pride painted brilliantly in her eyes and the tilt of her chin. It was like going back in time and looking in the mirror. She was on the cliff, her mouth a willful curve and her eyes flashing determination. The boys were all there too, but none held the focus or detail of her in the painting.

Her uncle hadn't been there. He hadn't seen what had happened. As far as she knew he didn't even know it happened at all. How could he have painted this?

The portrait beside that one was of her as well, her face down in concentration as she read. The shade of a willow tree shadowed her face. This time there was no obstinate look on her face, just one of peace and wonder.

She looked around again—every portrait was of some moment that summer. Except for the one sitting on the easel closest to the bay window. It was her as an adult.

Addi's mouth fell open. *Her* in the big floppy hat and flowered skirt. The first day she'd met Drew in Last Resort. Her hand flattened against her mouth.

Uncle Ray was not the artist. Drew is.

It clicked suddenly that *he* smelled of turpentine and paint and what she thought was grease on his fingers could very well have been remnants of his latest work. Why hadn't she realized this before? He'd drawn her many times at camp and they'd discussed his dream of being an artist. *Shit!*

Addi closed her eyes, letting a memory from camp play out in her mind like a movie.

"Sit still, squirmy!" Drew said, with his one eye peeking over his sketchpad. "Keep moving and I'll give you something to squirm about." She tipped her head back and laughed. He was always threatening her. The pad flopped into the dirt suddenly and he lunged at her, tackling her to the ground gently. His big strong fingers clasped her two wrists above her head and his free hand found her ribs. She squealed as he tickled her.

"Stop... no... please!" Giggles burst from her and echoed through the clearing as she wiggled relentlessly for freedom.

When he stopped, she was out of breath. His eyes found hers and her stomach fluttered. Those blue eyes were so filled with adoring, she felt it right to her soul. The dark blue ring she loved so much seemed to pulse and he leaned down and kissed her nose.

"You, gorgeous, don't cooperate at all!"

"Lemme see!"

Drew turned the pad her way.

"It's amazing. You'll do it, you know. You'll be a famous artist."

She smiled, opening her eyes. He'd succeeded in getting his dream. Addi wandered the house, finding paintings everywhere, more of her and camp that summer, and even some more of her uncle. Those she stared at for a long time, feeling both grief and joy at the sight of them.

Drew really captured him well. He had a way of painting beyond a simple expression. He told a story with each face. You felt as if you knew the subject. You knew what they were thinking, what they believed, and what they felt. It was quite amazing really and she didn't doubt why his paintings sold for hundreds of thousands of dollars. He was brilliantly talented.

Why though? Why did he hide his talent? Her brow furrowed. And where was all the money? He lived in a trailer, and it wasn't a new one either. And why were so many paintings of her?

She got to a room with a closed door and twisted the handle. It didn't turn, but the door opened a crack anyway. The jamb was broken. The room was full of paintings too, but without light she couldn't see them in detail. They weren't like the others though—that much she could tell. They were dark and gave her chills.

"Christ, Addi, did you break into my trailer and steal my keys?" Drew's accusing voice startled her and she spun to see his deep frown and sleep-tousled hair. Her heart pounded in her throat. He still had faint bed lines on his cheek.

"You startled me."

"That tends to happen when you're caught being naughty, baby girl."

"Are you mad that I'm here?" she questioned when he looked around, sighed. He walked past her and shut the door to the room. Scrubbing his hands over his face, he gathered a breath.

"Only that you broke into my trailer and invaded my privacy." His brow quirked up. "But I think Daddy knows how to deal with naughty little B&E bandits." His mouth hitched at the corner and her heart fluttered as he reached for the buckle of his belt.

She stared, her heart doubling its pace as the belt buckle jingled. Her core clenched and heat spread from her middle outward, weakening her as it went. She even considered keeping quiet to see where things went. The thought of that leather against her ass titillated her.

"I couldn't have stolen the keys, Drew. I found this place while I was out walking. Brent mentioned a cliff house but I wasn't sure what was out here." His hand paused in unbuckling and she swallowed. "The door had the key in it and I saw someone running away. But if you wanna keep sliding that belt through your loops I just might confess to something I didn't do." Though her tone and expression were flirty, his was not.

"Someone?" His hand fell from the belt and he strode toward her swiftly, his eyes wide and worried. He grabbed her upper arms firmly and looked her up and down. His jingling buckle no longer thrilled her with concern plastered on his face. "Babe, are you hurt?"

"It was Layla, and she didn't see me. I followed her for a bit before I came back here though." His brows rose in question and he scratched at his beard. She could see he was deep in thought. "She called someone named Rebecca, eager to tell her what she'd found. Do you think it was the reporter?"

He looked away and swore.

"I have questions too," she said softly. "About what I

found." She gestured to the paintings of her. "And about things between us."

"And I'll answer them all, Addi, but first I gotta get rid of these paintings."

She didn't understand any of it. Why would he hide his talent and why would Uncle Ray take credit? "Why? Why can't anyone know you're the artist?"

"Babe, I need you to trust me. Can you do that?"

"Yes."

He gathered a breath and looked around again. "This problem isn't going anywhere." Rubbing the back of his neck, he bit his lip. "The damage is done. She probably took pictures." He reached for Addi, pulling her close enough to hear his heartbeat pound steadily in her ear.

"She did. She sent them to Rebecca."

"Dammit. I should have just given her some fluff, but Ray was private and as you now know, we had shit to hide."

"But why?"

"Babe, I warned you I'm not a good guy."

"I don't believe that for a second, Drew."

He kissed the top of her head and she traced one of the pained figure tattoos on his bicep. "I know you don't, baby girl, and that's the biggest problem of all."

"Uncle Ray didn't either." She pulled back and glared at him—steady, sure, and determined. "He wouldn't have asked you to take care of me if he didn't trust you. And he wouldn't trust you if you weren't good." She ran her palms from his arms to take his hands.

His head hung a moment and even with his hair falling in his face, she saw both pain and hope twisting his features.

"I promise I'll tell you everything, Addi. You deserve the truth. I just need to digest and settle some shit first. Can you give me time for that?"

"Of course."

He pulled her against his warm chest and she wished they could stay like that for at least a few more days. She knew things were about to get complicated and with Uncle

Ray's funeral tomorrow, she didn't think either of them deserved complicated.

"I'm going to town to get some new locks, and ask a friend to watch over the place while we're gone tomorrow. How about you relax and I'll bring back some pizza for lunch." His mouth quirked to the side as he pulled her back from his embrace to look at her face. "That's an order, baby girl."

"That sounds unbelievably good, especially that it's an order."

He leaned down to her ear and whispered, "You know we still have the old projector and white screen in the mess hall. We can pull the blinds down and put on one of the old movies like Ray did during rainy days at camp. Throw some gym mats, sleeping bags, and pillows down. I just put a brand-new air conditioner in last year." His brows wiggled and his raspy voice took on a sexy lilt. "We can cuddle up and watch *Homeward Bound* or *Free Willy*."

"You are so turning me on right now," she said sarcastically, knowing the only options for movies would be the kid-friendly kind. "But you had me at air conditioner." She laughed and he joined in with his deep chuckle. He kissed her head and then tipped her chin so he could do the same to her lips.

"Do you want to stay here or go back to your cabin?"

"Well, it feels a little weird staring at myself and all my adolescent angst in these paintings, so yeah, I think I'll go back."

"I like them." He looked around at the paintings. "They remind me you were always a determined little brat."

"It was all the time I spent with bossy, overbearing boys."

"That so?" He swatted her ass. "Well, now you have a bossy, overbearing Daddy." He took her hand and they walked in silence back to the main camp.

Concern was hidden in his expression and her own churned in her gut, but for now they'd let sleeping beasts lie.

CHAPTER THIRTEEN

Addi

Fell County and the town of Fell near Tonalonka Camp weren't big, but when the residents all gathered in the small funeral home, they certainly filled it.

Addi couldn't believe how many people came to what she'd thought would be a small service of close friends and family. She'd figured it'd be done in an hour. That's what she'd wanted. The true tribute would come from the memorial weekend she'd planned for October. Where all the people Ray had shaped would come to tell stories and enjoy the camp once more.

With all the mourners chatting and milling about, she felt overwhelmed. Who were they all?

"Babe?"

Startled, she blinked at Drew. "Who are all these people?"

"He was loved, Addi. He was always there when someone needed a hand. Hell, more mamas came to discuss their wayward boys than men called him for fishing—and he was called to fish a lot. He had a way with kids and adults alike. This community adored him."

Tears pooled in her eyes. "My God. I just didn't realize." He took her hand and gave it a squeeze. "I feel like I've talked to a million people today."

"Oh, here you are!" A woman with short dark hair wearing a floral-patterned dress came rushing to her as soon as she was in sight. "Finally I get to meet Ray's little girl. He was always talking about you, honey." She grabbed Addi's hands, pulling the one from Drew's. "I'm Nora. I run the diner in town. Your uncle ordered eggs up, ham, and home fries with a side of steak every Sunday at the diner. He was a small man but he could pack it away." Her laugh was infectious and Addi found herself smiling at the woman.

She went on to tell Addi all about her three boys and how they were always up to no good until they started going to Ray's camp. "He changed my hooligans into proper young men."

"That sounds like him." She looked around. "I didn't expect this kind of turnout." She nervously wondered about the sandwich and light lunch offerings she'd had the funeral home order in. "I don't think I ordered enough food." She sounded spacey even to her own ears, but if Nora cared, she didn't show it.

"Hon, my place was doing the catering. Don't you worry. I'd been asking around and knew there would be more people here. I adjusted the order myself on the house. You'll be fine. You just go around and meet everyone and hear stories about your uncle. They'll go a long way in the days to come."

"Thank you, Nora." Her nose tingled with emotion, but she was quickly swept away under Nora's arm and met more people, heard many stories, and was hugged so much she felt as if she'd collapse if one more person dragged her off.

The service had been beautiful and several of Ray's fishing buddies got up to speak, but she was sort of numb to it all until Drew stood.

"I met Ray when I was a teenager. I'd been sent to work at the camp after getting out of juvie. His good fishing buddy Judge Darren Mackie had asked him if he'd take me on as a favor." He pointed to a tall thin man sitting in the first row behind the pew reserved for family—well, for her. He turned and waved a big hand at the congregation behind him and then nodded at Addi and smoothed his gray goatee.

"I was ready and willing to learn, earn my keep, and prove to the world I wasn't worthless, but I didn't expect to be treated very well. I was wrong." He glanced around.

"Ray treated me like a son and never once doubted me or my potential—even when I hurt him. And I did hurt him. I had my reasons, and he understood them, but he didn't have to take me back with open arms and he did, without hesitation." Addi sniffed and Judge Mackie passed a tissue forward.

"I don't know what he saw in me, but there was never a doubt that he loved me. He changed a lot of lives." He smiled as he looked at Addi. "He even changed the life of the giant pike he finally proved lived in the lake. We campers and leaders tried not to believe it, but we still swam like hell when no one was looking just in case." There were chuckles from the crowd. "A few weeks before he died, he rescued that pike and nursed it back to health. His niece and I released it a few days ago and I'm sure Ray was smiling down on us and probably yelling at us to do it his way." More laughter filled the room and Drew continued weaving a picture of Ray that made everyone smile and wipe tears from their eyes.

It was evident to everyone that Drew loved Uncle Ray, and when he continued to speak of Ray's love for his only niece her cheeks were wet with tears. By the time he finished, she was sobbing along with everyone else. Even he had red glassy eyes.

As the man from the funeral home rose to end the service, Drew whisked Addi to the private family room off to the side where they could still see and hear but also have some privacy. The only thing she saw as he pulled her away, besides the sniffling teary crowd, was the redhead sitting at the back.

"You okay, babe?" he asked, after sitting Addi down and crouching in front of her. She nodded, wiping her eyes and he scrutinized her in that weird way as if reading her mind for what she wasn't vocalizing.

"That was beautiful, Drew. I'm so glad you had each other all these years."

"You and me both, honey. I don't know where either of us would have been." He stood, shoveling a hand through his hair. "Well, no, I'm pretty sure I know where'd I be."

There was a gentle knock on the door and they both looked to see Carter.

"What the hell do you want?" Drew growled in a low, but threatening way.

"I'm just checking on Addi. I stopped by the camp yesterday but no one was around. She looked pretty shaken up just now, so I thought I'd see if she needed anything."

"It's okay, Drew," Addi said and he looked at her in disbelief. She took his hand, squeezing it like he had hers moments earlier. "I'm good."

His mouth hitched slightly on the side and he nodded before shooting Carter a threatening look. "I'll get us some coffee."

"Thanks." When he was gone, Carter spoke.

"Those speeches were hard to hear, sweetheart." He sat next to her on the sofa. His genuine smile made her wonder how much people could change over the years.

"Thanks for checking on me, but I'm fine."

"Let me take you home after?"

"I came with Fitz."

"On his bike?" He stood, slamming his fists on his hips. "God, Addi. You have no idea who that guy is. He's dangerous."

"I know he was in some kind of trouble as a teenager but has he done anything recently for you to believe that?" She crossed her arms and watched Carter press his lip and look away. "Can people change, Carter?"

He turned back to look at her. He smiled at her but it didn't reach his eyes and felt more like it was mocking her than anything else.

"I believe some people can. I know I have." He relaxed his arms and shook his head. "Stay safe, Addi."

"I will."

He walked out, leaving her with a rolling stomach and a headache brewing.

"Did he upset you? What did he say?" Drew handed her a coffee and sat down.

"I'm fine, but I'm ready for this to be over." She looked at the coffee in her hands, resting it in her lap. "I want you to tell me everything." She looked at him and grinned. "And then I want you to make me forget my name."

•••••••

As Addi went through the motions of socializing with her uncle's friends, she saw Daniel and Steven walk in.

"I'm so sorry we're late." Daniel's eyes shot to Steven. "Someone forgot to grab the plane tickets and we missed our flight."

"I see you eye-pointing at me, Daniel," Steven groaned and leaned in to grab Addi up in a big hug. "How are you? How was the service? God, I am so sorry!"

"She's shitty, Steven, shitty. Can't you see? And we weren't here for her." Daniel hugged her then, too.

"I'm so glad you guys made it." She took their hands and dragged them toward the food. "You must be starving!"

They pulled her back and a look passed between them. "You're kidding, right? Look at you! Have you eaten at all since you've been here? You look like you've lost ten pounds!"

"I've been trying to feed her." Drew's deep voice sent tingles down her spine as he sidled up next to her. Another look passed between her two best friends. Addi wanted to roll her eyes and laugh at the same time.

"Guys, this is Fitz. He's the caretaker at the camp, and was my uncle's closest friend." Drew stuck out his big hand, which swallowed Daniel's but only dwarfed Steven's slightly. His arm quickly settled around her waist and he winked as she looked at him sharply.

They had never discussed their relationship and when she had even brushed up against the idea of having feelings for him he practically ran away screaming. Was this his jealous boyfriend act again? Why was it he felt the need to metaphorically pee on her leg every time people were around?

"These two are more likely to be eyeing you than me and besides they're married, Fitz. No need to get all caveman."

"Oh, I think the caveman suits him, Addi. Don't discourage. Do. Not. Discourage." Steven fanned himself.

"Steven," Daniel warned. "Your filter is broken again."

"You gonna eat?" Drew said, pointing to the food table. "I highly recommend the…" Addi tuned them out as they headed for the food, choosing to find an empty table instead of being further mortified by Drew's possessiveness.

The noise of the chattering crowd, the heat of too many bodies all pressed into the room, and the dull ache behind her eyes had her feeling nauseated and lightheaded.

She wanted to get home so badly. *Home?* Her cabin, and the camp with Drew really did feel like home. Unlike the house she still shared with her father.

Looking around, she wondered if anyone would notice if she slipped away. They were occupied. She turned, eyeing the door, her brow cocked as she wondered what Drew would do later when he found her.

"Hi, Addi." She spun, startled by the small voice. Brent stood smiling at her. "My mom said I could come." He pointed. "She's over there with Trevor." His mother, wearing an inappropriately short dress, was standing at the coffee station next to the bartender from Last Resort. He looked annoyed, but so did she.

Addi crouched down and wrapped her arms around

Brent. "I'm so glad you came." She saw some frosting on his nose and she wiped it off, showing him. "I see you found Nora's strawberry cupcakes."

He bobbed his head. "They're even better than the bakery's, Addi."

"They are pretty darn delicious." She saw Nora watching them with a smile and waved. "I bet Nora would give us the recipe and when you come by to paint with Fitz, we can make them."

The boy's head dropped and he kicked the tip of his dress shoes against the floor. "My mom says I'm not allowed to talk to Fitz anymore."

"Brent!" His name was called sharply and both Addi's and Brent's heads snapped toward Layla.

"Let's go!" Layla spat and grabbed his hand roughly.

Brent looked at Addi as he was dragged away, his eyes owlish and sad. She mouthed she was sorry and he just turned away.

"And what was that all about?" Steven asked, joining her with a plateful of goodies.

"I don't know."

"Well, if you ask me, good riddance. That woman has been upsetting everyone."

Addi looked around and saw the mourners were no longer milling about chatting with each other. They were gathered in small pockets, staring at Drew, whispering.

Had Layla told everyone Drew was the artist?

"I'll be right back," she said, leaving the table.

As she headed for Drew, still standing with Daniel, several people stopped her, asking her if she knew.

Knew what? What the hell was going on?

The word murderer was spoken in a hushed whisper behind her, making her spin. Nora and a few others were standing in a group, pale-faced.

"Oh, honey, I'm sorry." Nora reached for her, but Addi just turned to look at Drew.

His eyes locked on hers, concern immediately crossing

his features and then his brows furrowed and he looked around. Daniel stood frozen with a tea sandwich poised in front of his open mouth. Steven, who'd followed her, put a hand on Addi's shoulder.

Addi heard her blood rushing through her veins.

Drew, looking determined, started toward her in big strides, cutting through groups of people as if they were fall leaves in the park. His pace was shrinking the space between them, but not fast enough. Her heart, beating a hummingbird's pace, called to him. He would explain. Her uncle knew Drew, trusted and loved him and Drew had promised to tell her everything. He warned her it was big.

She started for him, first in a walk and then in a run, but before they reached each other, Trevor stepped between them.

He was a wall of bald, goateed, rock-hard muscle, which under normal circumstances would have her breaking out in a nervous sweat, but she was Drew's. She wasn't afraid of Trevor.

"Get out of the way," she said before Drew could speak.

"Hey, little lady, I think we should have a talk before you go anywhere."

"No, we shouldn't." She sidestepped the big man as he tried to take hold of her wrist and she grabbed Drew's palm. "The only person I need to talk to is Fitz."

"Do you have a phone at least?"

"She's got one," Drew answered tightly. The big bald man nodded solemnly and stepped back.

Drew's jaw was tense, but he didn't say anything else, just followed Addi out into the Saturday afternoon sunshine. She was shocked over her own reaction, but his even more so. He was letting her take the lead—like he knew she was capable and not just pretending for once.

She paused as they got to his bike, released his hand, and texted Daniel to meet them at the camp. Drew handed her his spare helmet and got on the bike to hold it for her. She took a moment to kiss him full on the lips, while cameras flashed and recorded them. She took off her cardigan, wrapped it around her waist, hiked up her dress, and climbed on the bike.

"Shit! Put your helmet on now," Drew said, shooting a dark look past her at the cameras.

"Is it true you're the real artist, Mr. Fitzer? Or is it still Mr. Trigger?" Rebecca Snow shouted and Addi wrapped her arms around Drew's waist.

"No comment."

Rebecca pelted them with questions as Drew backed the bike out of its parking spot. His gut was tense beneath her arms and she wished she had the power to calm him like he calmed her.

"Is it because you murdered Officer Doug MacAfee when you were a member of the Skull Grinders Motorcycle Club?"

Addi swallowed hard. *Murdered an officer? Skull Grinders?*

"Is it because no one would buy art from a murderer?"

Addi pulled away from Drew's sturdy body to spin and spear Rebecca with a cold look. She didn't know if Rebecca's accusations were true or not, but she knew Drew and he was no cold-blooded killer.

"Baby girl, tuck into me now!" His voice held panic she had never heard from him before, but she ignored his demand.

"Maybe it's because fame-hungry vultures like you twist everything around and make a story out of nothing, ruining good people's lives!"

"Are you implying the death of an officer of the law is nothing?"

"Goddamn it, Addi, don't say another word." He'd spoken through clenched teeth so she tightened her arms around him again and clenched her mouth shut. He started the motor and they rode off, leaving the reporter and her crew to run after them.

The ride wasn't long enough, Addi decided as she climbed off. She enjoyed the escape of it, like when he dominated her. She wasn't in control, and when he leaned to go around a corner, she had no choice but to lean with him—as if she was both a part of the bike and him. The first time she rode with him she fought it, but once she gave into it, she truly began to appreciate its power and that made her feel powerful, too.

She thought the camp was fenced completely, but there was a small hidden gate in the corner of the property that she hadn't known existed. She assumed very few knew about it since it was a rough single rutted path that led them through the thick forest to the edge where the cliff house stood overlooking the lake.

He had taken the path slowly and told her to tuck in tight so she wouldn't be whipped by branches. She hadn't needed to be told twice, especially when her bare arms got scratched.

She enjoyed the sight of the rocky outcroppings and water when they broke through the thick forest, but once they turned toward the main camp her nerves had kicked up. It seemed easy to ignore the issues they were facing with the warmth of their bodies pressed together and the rumble of the bike so loud she couldn't think, but that was about to end. She needed to know what was going on, but what if she couldn't handle it?

When they were off the bike, she held her breath, watching his expression as he pulled off his helmet. She hadn't known him long even including their summer together, but his handsome face had become so much to her. He was a hardened man to most, but with her, there were cracks. She released her breath noting the concern, anger, and worry on his face, but when he scrubbed a hand over it, it was gone.

After years of people-watching, attempting to understand them, she knew this man was afraid. Not the kind of fear she carried daily for all things risky, but fear of losing someone. *Her.*

She reached for him and he looked away, chewing the

inside of his cheek.

"Babe, I think you need to read your uncle's letter before I say anything. I don't know how much Layla told everyone at the funeral, but I've got a pretty good guess and it's going to require some damage control. I'll tell you everything after, but it's true. I am partially responsible for that cop's death." He looked down at the helmet he held in both of his hands now. "I know I don't deserve you, no matter how much I've loved you all my life, but I want you to know if I could trade my life for that cop's I would." He looked her in the eye. "He should never have died."

"You what?" She couldn't believe what she'd just heard. He stepped forward, dropped the helmet with a thud into the dusty dirt and gravel and placed both hands on her face.

"Baby girl? Are you paying attention to me now?" His tone was stern. The one that gave her nervous tingles everywhere and throbbing in all her sexy places. The fear all gone from his features, he was the man she'd come to depend on—the man who took control.

"Yes," she whispered in a breathy voice. Her stomach flipped and her heart kicked up its pace. All her worries and troubles paused. He calmed her, quieted her mind.

"I'm partially at fault for that cop dying. And I've loved you since we were nothing but screwed-up teens. Even when I broke your heart, it was for your own good, not because I didn't love you. I've never stopped loving you—not once. There's been no one in my heart but you all these years. You got me, babe?" His brow quirked up.

She swallowed audibly. "I got you, Daddy."

His hands left her face and traveled down her arms until he held her hands. "And you said you trusted me, yeah?"

She nodded without hesitation. "I do, but I have so many questions. I can't comprehend you being responsible for someone's death, especially when you're responsible for saving my life." She looked away. "In more ways than one." Fearing everything like she'd been doing her whole life was no way to live. When her eyes found him again, so sexy in his suit and tie, his face was patient and his smile gentle.

"Was it an accident?" she asked in a whisper.

"My part of it was, yes."

"How?"

"He was shot in the chest."

"And you pulled the trigger… by accident?"

He gathered a slow breath and released it before stepping forward to cup her cheek. "No, baby girl. My father did."

She bit her trembling lip and let go of the breath she'd been holding, relief flooding her. His thumb stroked her face.

"Did you order him to be killed?"

His brow furrowed. "No, I was twelve, Addi." More relief came.

"So…"

He stopped her by taking her chin between a thumb and forefinger. "Go read Uncle Ray's letter…" He paused to look her from head to toe, a hungry glare replacing his stern one. He untied her cardigan and let it fall atop the helmet. "Before Daddy rips off that dress, spanks your ass for disobedience, and fucks you right here in front of the main office of the camp."

The right side of her mouth hiked up and she gnawed the corner of her bottom lip. "What if I need that right now?" She did. She needed to feel consumed by him. Reassured by his firm physical touch. Owned by the strong dominant man *that cared. For her.*

"Babe, I need you to know everything before we make love again." He looked toward the gravel road that led to the entrance of the camp. "Besides, your friends should be here soon."

"You never said *make love*, Drew. You said *fuck*. I want to be *fucked* right here in the middle of the camp."

His eyes shot back to hers and widened a moment before they hardened and pinned hers, making her stomach flip-flop.

"Baby girl, you're trying Daddy's patience again." He took another step forward, but she was the one that closed the gap completely when she launched herself at him.

He caught her despite the surprise on his face. She wrapped her legs around his waist, her dress hiking high, and before he could get a word out, she kissed him.

The kiss was urgent and wanton, and she fisted his hair as she plundered *his* mouth for once. She was in control. His hands held her ass, squeezing and kneading as he held her up and she thought she had him, but then he lowered her until her feet touched the ground and held her back at arms' length.

"I need you to know everything, Addi." His eyes pleaded with her. "Including what happened that day when we were sixteen and the Skull Grinders came for me."

Her heart kicked up a notch. She didn't want to think about that now. Not with so much going on, not on the day of her uncle's funeral—not when she was starting to think that maybe there could be more than just *right now* between them. Not when she needed him and he needed her.

"No. Please not now. Not today. Please."

He pressed his lips and his brows teepeed in… empathy? Regret? What? How could she read him when back then she thought she knew him better than she knew herself.

When he continued, her heart clenched. He was going to force this.

"If they knew how I felt about you, Ray, and this camp…" She glanced at him, hearing the vulnerability in his voice. He looked down and scrubbed his hand over the back of his neck. A look of pure anguish marred his features when he dropped his hand and looked back at her.

"They would have used both of you to punish me. I pushed you away to protect you. I never wanted to but I had to keep you safe—both of you. And you had to believe it." He shook his head, anger cinching his brows together. "My dad always goes after the ones you love to hurt you."

She nodded, but the weight of hurt and confusion was

heavy in her gut. It made logical sense but there was so much more she didn't understand. Why couldn't he have told her once he was back with Uncle Ray? Did he think by then it was long out of her mind? Did he think his rejection hadn't affected her and every relationship she'd had after?

She took another step back. "You're right. I should read the letter."

She turned and jogged, needing distance. Even though it wasn't far, she was out of breath when she reached her cabin, mostly because of the panic attack building.

Inside, she shut and locked the door. The whole day had been too damn much and she couldn't think straight with all the thoughts rushing around in her head like a room full of rubber balls bouncing off the walls.

She watched him leave on the bike through her window before she kicked off her high heels and sat on the bed, tucking her right foot underneath her. She grabbed her uncle's letter and spent a few minutes just running her fingers along the edge of the envelope.

Finally tearing it open, she read…

My dearest Addianna,

You are my little girl. Never forget that. I may have moved on to another place, but I'm still with you. It doesn't matter that you are my brother's daughter. He didn't have the capacity to love you the way you deserved, your mother didn't either. She was always chasing her next adventure. I'm not sure how two selfish people ended up with such a giving child. You have more capacity to love and forgive than anyone I know.

I'm sorry they couldn't be the parents you needed and I'm sorry I wasn't closer. Just know I love you and am proud of you for everything you've accomplished despite the crappy upbringing you've had.

You need someone strong enough to put you first for once, and I think you probably know by now who that is. At least you will if my plan has worked out.

Drew is a good man, Addi. No matter what he's done in the past (and I know it all). Hopefully he'll explain all of that to you one day, and you'll see things the way I do, but until he does, I just want you to trust me that he's the best kind of man and he'll love you like you deserve, if you let him. If you look at his, yes, his, *paintings of you, you'll see it in every brushstroke.*

You'll likely have to convince him he deserves your love too. And he does, Addi. He deserves you, just as you deserve him. He needs nurturing too, honey, and if anyone can convince him of that, it's you.

As for the will, just know I gave you each partial ownership of the camp. Not only because I was playing cupid, but because you're both my children. Maybe not by blood, but in my heart, which is the only place it matters to me. I want you both to be happy and I believe being together is the best possible way for that to happen, but I can't force you two together any more than I have by using this camp. The rest is up to you.

The other reason is because I'm hoping you two can bring Tonalonka back to life. That was always my dream. You know your aunt, God rest her soul, was my everything and it killed me when she died with my unborn son. I made this camp for them. I want it to live on through you and Drew in its basic original purpose—helping kids—but if you can't do that I have offered it up to a company that can. The lawyer will explain everything.

Anyway, sweetheart, just remember I love you and I want you to be happy.

Uncle Ray xo

Any doubts she had about Drew fell away with the tears that ran down her cheeks and she couldn't wait to be in his arms again.

CHAPTER FOURTEEN

Drew

He didn't chase her when she ran. She needed to process, needed to read her uncle's letter and he'd let her.

Drew went the back way by the cliffs, the same way they came into the camp, to avoid the media and rode out of town to the spot where he and Addi had made love on his Harley. He sat under the same tree, this time in an expensive suit, and pulled his sketchbook out. She needed time and he'd give it to her even though they had little. The Skull Grinders would know where he was soon. As soon as Rebecca's story broke, they'd come for him. He'd need to lure them away from Addi and the camp. And then he'd convince them that he'd paid the price for leaving by taking full responsibility for the murders they'd committed, keeping them out of jail. And that he'd never be the kind of person that could run a one-percenter club.

Drew shook off the thoughts of his father, Mauler, and Dingo, and started sketching Addi's face, the way *he* saw her, powerfully sexy and strong. Not the woman she saw herself as. He knew she saw herself as weak and only playing the part of competent.

She was beautiful and pure of heart, but what would this truth do to her? Would she hate him, or worse, would she compromise herself to be with him? Would she convince herself that it was worth the risk to be with him?

His portrait complete, he looked at the sun hanging low in the sky. It was time to head back. The time he'd spent working had settled his mind. He was ready to face his past and the consequences of his time with Addi.

•••••••

There were still a few cameramen and reporters hanging out by the front entrance, but only the diligent. Most had given up for the day. They perked up when his bike rumbled past, some rushing for their cars, but he'd already tucked into the entrance by the cliff house and killed the engine before they drove by.

He left the bike, needing the walk, and made the half-hour trek to his studio. His heart pounded when he saw Addi on the cliff. First, because she'd taken a dive from that cliff years ago and second, because with her hair whipping around in the wind and her dress fitting flush against her curves, she looked stunning and haunting—it spoke to his artistic side, just as the danger called to his protective side. His hands itched to paint her, but also to turn her across his knee for standing too close to the edge.

Paper fluttered in her hands, which she struggled to fold neatly, before turning back to the house. At the sight of him, her mouth widened enthusiastically.

Her smile was contagious and putting a firm look on his face was harder than he thought. He headed for her, but once again, she ran to him, jumping into his arms carelessly, before he got to her. He spun her around, overjoyed she didn't hate him, even though that would have been easier.

"I love you, Mr. Biker." Her mouth crashed into his, mashing their teeth together ungracefully and he laughed into her mouth.

"I love you too, now tell me why you're out here in the wind, dangerously close to the edge of that cliff, young lady? And how come you're not back at your cabin?"

"I needed you to know something. I figured you'd come back this way."

"Okay." His eyes narrowed and he set her back on her feet.

"No matter what your past holds, no matter how guilty you feel, I love you and I'll always love you. You don't even have to tell me what's going on, because I trust you." Her eyes tilted in a flirtatious way. "And if by chance you want to spank and fuck me, my friends are busy unpacking in the cabin next to mine."

His chest fluttered and his gut sank simultaneously. Now that he had her, he couldn't bear to lose her. He couldn't help but picture a life with her, but she deserved better than him. Way better. Some normal guy not running from his past, someone with a nice family that could become hers too.

"Come on," he said and grabbed her hand. "I've got something to show you."

"I hope it's your…"

He covered her mouth and his brow shot up. "Baby girl," he warned in his deep timbre. She gave him a toothy grin when his hand left her mouth to find and swat her plump, sexy ass.

He led her inside to the bedroom with the locked door and took his keys from his pocket. Unlocking it, he pushed the door open and flipped the lights on. The windows in the room had blackout blinds and the paintings on the walls were hung not as art should be, but lined up in a sequence of sorts. Each with its own dramatic lighting to show the shadows of evil that encompassed him when he saw them.

He watched her as she went to the first. The only other thing in the room was a desk with newspaper article clippings piled on top and notes about the Grinders, their whereabouts and activities.

"Is this you?" Addi asked, looking over her shoulder at him. He nodded. The painting was of him on his dad's bike, sketching in the lamplight of the dingy alley the night Officer MacAfee had been killed. Every detail was in that painting, from the trash on the ground to the look of pure evil on his father's face, everything was perfectly captured.

"How old were you again?"

"Twelve."

She looked closer, pointing at the man with the tattoo of the devil on his neck. "He was here."

Drew nodded. "The acting vice president of the Skull Grinders, Mauler."

"Acting?"

He looked down a moment. "Acting because I was the true vice president. As soon as I was old enough, Mauler was going back to his position of sergeant at arms." Drew figured that might be another reason why he hadn't been found. Some of the Grinders wouldn't want him back.

She nodded and moved on to the next painting. This one focused on a man rounding the corner, a bag of Chinese food in his hand. Drew painted the scenes as if they were a graphic novel but in realism. His face in the scene was in shock, his mouth open in a shout.

"What were they doing to this guy?" Addi pointed at the man that Mauler held as his father, fist extended, was about to hit him.

"Teaching him a lesson, I suppose." Drew stepped further into the room to point out his father to Addi. "This is my father, the president of the Skull Grinders. This is Dingo, acting sergeant at arms here." Drew pointed to the victim. "I don't know what this guy did, but he crossed my father so they were going to make an example out of him." Drew shoved a shaking hand through his hair.

"My job was to keep six."

"Keep six?" Her bows scrunched and he fisted his hands to keep from pushing her hair back from her face. He wouldn't touch her now. Not until she knew everything.

"Lookout, babe. I was the lookout."

"But you were just a kid." She frowned, and managed to look both angry and sad. "You should have been at home, doing schoolwork or playing basketball or street hockey."

"I was the future president of the Grinders, babe. I had my place. It was what was expected of me."

"You didn't want to be a biker?"

"Not the kind the Grinders are." He drew in a breath. "These clubs can be really great places for guys like me to feel like part of a brotherhood where everyone has each other's back. The Grinders were into bad shit though. I've never been interested in hurting anyone."

She narrowed her eyes, scrutinizing the painting of Drew's dad and then moved on. The next scene was of the shot, a flare of orange at the front of the gun, and the guy lying lifeless in the filthy street. Addi covered her mouth and squeaked as she saw the boy in the alley. His pants were wet and his eyes wide in horror.

"A child, a baby?" she stammered.

"The off-duty cop's son. He witnessed his father's murder." Drew swallowed hard at the memory, his chest constricting as if an anaconda had him.

The next painting showed his father shooting the other man, Drew holding his hands over the cop's wound, blood seeping through his fingers and a shadowy form hovering over Drew. The form was hooded and dark, a sickle in its hand. He'd painted more details, like a sketch pad on the ground beneath the bike's tire and the bag of Chinese food tipped to its side, but it was the reaper she stared at. It was what drew his eyes too. It was his interpretation of what had happened as the man died beneath his hands. He'd become the reaper. That would've been his patched name.

The paintings were his living nightmare on display before the woman he loved and it chilled him when he watched her face examining them.

Addi moved to stand before the final painting. It was of Drew shoving the boy behind the dumpster.

She stood for a long time staring before going back to look at the others again. And finally when he didn't think he could stand another second in the room confronted by his demons, with the walls closing in on him, she turned to him. Tears streamed down her cheeks.

"Oh, Drew. I thought I had it bad. But you… you had it so much worse."

"I know I was too young to walk away from my father and the Grinders. I know those deaths weren't my fault. For years I blamed myself but Ray helped me see things differently. The thing is, I still witnessed two men lose their lives and a kid lose his father. I was still the one that called out. And I still took the place of those killers in jail. I've been making fucked-up decisions my whole life, babe. This shit has shaped me." He pulled off his suit jacket and rolled up his sleeves, holding out his arms for her to see.

"Look at me. I'm a man who will never escape my demons. You deserve better."

"You know what I see when I look at you?" she asked and he swallowed hard. "I see a hero. A man who has always put others before himself. Me and my uncle included."

"You really believe that?" His brow furrowed tightly.

"Don't you?"

He shrugged and sat in the desk chair staring. Addi climbed onto his lap. "I give all the proceeds from my art to a couple of charities I founded."

"You do? Is that for them or because you feel like you don't deserve it?"

He gave her a sad smile. "You know me so well already, baby girl." He brushed her dark hair back from her face. "Both. I want to help them, but I don't deserve good things either. I helped put that kid through university, and countless others but it'll never make up for what I did." He looked at her pointedly. "I don't deserve you." She leaned against him, her head cradled in the hollow of his neck and shoulder.

"When I was twelve my mom was in an accident. She

was in a coma." His hand went to her head and he began stroking her. He knew some of this story from Ray. He didn't stop her though. She needed to tell it in her own words.

"I had to decide whether to keep her on life support or take her off." He felt Addi tense against him, so he left her hair to knead her shoulder. "My dad left the decision up to me. I chose to stop all life-saving measures because I knew it's what she would have wanted, and what my dad and the doctors wanted, but I hated them all for it. Her for needing the adventure and screwing me out of a mother, my dad for not wanting the burden of a family but especially a bedridden wife, and the doctors for taking away my hope. I hated my mother as she struggled to take her last breath."

"Of course you did, baby girl. You were sixteen. You should never have had to make that decision."

"*I* wasn't enough for her. She always had to have the next adventure. *I* wasn't enough to get my father to leave his office."

He felt her hot moist breath against his neck. Her hurt was crushing him. He wrapped his arms around her, holding her tight.

"Addi, you're the fucking strongest woman I know." He leaned his forehead against hers, keeping his eyes pinned to hers. "You've had to deal with so much and you're still not only upright and functioning but an amazing person. Your parents were self-involved narcissists." He released her face to wipe her tears away.

"I'm so sorry you had to go through that. Neither of us deserved what we were dealt in life." He kissed her mouth gently. "I love you, baby girl." He would do whatever it took to keep her safe from his father and the Grinders.

"Drew?"

"Yeah, babe?"

"Make love to me. *Please.*" Her eyes were glossy from emotion and he could see she was still haunted by her confession. He needed to take her mind elsewhere, bring her to a place she couldn't think of her fucked-up childhood—a place she couldn't think at all. One where they could both forget what they were up against.

"I thought you'd never ask." His mouth quirked up to the side and she pressed her lips to his mouth. It started as a peck, but morphed, slowly, into a hot mating of tongues.

"I want to paint you," he said, his voice husky with desire and breathy across her face. Her eyes fluttered open, widened and darted to his. Lifting her, he carried her, legs around him, her ass resting on his arms, out of the room. He watched her throat work as she swallowed.

"You've painted me hundreds of times." She pointed to the various paintings of herself around the kitchen.

"That's not what I meant, baby girl." His crooked half smile had her biting her lip. She was nervous and he loved it. Her mind was already focused on what he would do to her, not on her mother, her father, or even her uncle.

He took her to the big bright room with all his painting supplies and let her down, loosening his tie and tearing his shirt open. He palmed her cheek and as he leaned down to her mouth, his fingers weaved through her hair and he gripped her head steady. His mouth took hers, thoroughly and completely, until her knees went slack and she had to wrap her arm around his neck. Her right hand stroked his bare chest. His free arm swung around her waist and he held her as her knees gave away fully.

When he set her back on her feet and pulled away, she looked dazed. He smiled fully then. He loved kissing this woman senseless.

Shedding his clothes, all but the tie, he stood naked before her. His cock, fully erect, glistening at the swollen tip where his pre-cum beaded for her. By the longing on her face, he could tell she wanted to touch him. And he wanted that, too. God, did he ever, but he wanted something else more.

"Stay."

Her head bobbed eagerly and he grabbed a drop cloth

and spread it out on a backless settee in the corner. Shoving away crates, easels, and anything else he could trip on, he pulled the couch to the middle of the room.

The lighting was perfect in the room with the cloudless sky. It would bathe her skin in a glow.

"You have a great ass, Drew." His eyes shot to her and her face bloomed pink.

"Is that so, babe?" He smirked.

"Your penis is pretty magnificent, too."

Tipping his head back, he laughed. She was too damn cute when she was nervous and the way she chewed the corner of her lip was making him ache with want. "It's a cock, sugar—and if you keep nibbling your lip like that you're going to make both my cock and I forget we're gentlemen."

Pulling his tie over his head, he nodded to the settee. "Sit." Once she'd obeyed, he wrapped the tie around her head to cover her eyes and kissed her nose. "I fucking adore you."

"You're painting me with a tie around my eyes? Is this going to be the cover for another one of *those* novels?"

He just chuckled and started unbuttoning her dress.

She reached for his hand. "No!" Her face paled and all the playfulness gave way to her nerves. Her teeth sank deeply into her bottom lip.

"No?"

"I don't want you to paint me naked. I…" Her voice cracked and he tilted her face up with his finger. She looked instantly calmer.

"Babe, do you still trust me?"

"Yes." Her lip trembled when she released it, so he kissed it still. "But I…" Her mumbled words against his lips made his mouth quirk. God, she was adorable.

"You're beautiful—every single part of you, inside and out—and you're mine to do as I please with."

"I don't want my body, in all its inglorious detail, immortalized forever on canvas, Drew."

"If you put yourself down again, babe, you know what's going to happen, don't you?"

She lowered her head and licked her lip. "I do."

"What's that, baby girl?"

"You'll spank me?"

"Mhmm. Daddy will spank your naughty ass crimson." He used a dry paintbrush to swirl around her nose and across her lips lightly. She shivered and he blew out to keep from losing control. Her reactions were so damn sexy.

"Okay. I'm sorry."

"Good girl. Now I want you naked and lying down." Her brow furrowed and she bit her lip again. He cleared his throat.

"You aren't painting on canvas, are you?"

"Nope. *You're* my medium today." He ran his thumb over the apple of her cheek, which was pink and warm to the touch. "I do have another one of you started. You can't see it until it's done, though."

"Okay."

He took the sides of her dress and pulled it off. Unhooking her bra, he let it slide off her arms while eyeing her thong panties. They could stay, he decided, tracing the little triangle covering her bare mound with his paintbrush. He liked it naked and smooth.

"You were going to wear this at the charming little old lady B&B?"

"No, they're my motivational panties. I've never worn them. I just keep them packed to push me to remember to eat properly and jog while I'm away. I only wore them today because my only funeral-appropriate dress was a clingy material and I didn't want panty lines."

"Do you know how amazing you look in them?"

"Don't tease me, Drew." Her mouth was a flat line and it made his jaw tense.

"Get up," he said firmly. She swallowed audibly and he grabbed her arm to pull her up before she could disobey. Bending, he tossed her over his shoulder. She squealed.

"Drew!"

"It's Daddy," he grumbled.

"Fine! *Daddy!*"

"The sarcasm doesn't impress me, babe." His palm cracked against her naked flesh again. It sounded sharp and her gasp said it felt that way too. "Be a good girl now."

He flicked on the light switch as he walked into the large bathroom down the hall from the kitchen. Lowering her to her feet, he spun her to face the full-length mirror and yanked off the blindfold.

"Look at yourself."

She crossed her arms and looked skyward, stubbornly.

"God, with that attitude, babe, you're asking for a spanking so badly right now. Is that what you want?"

"No." It was sullen and she sighed forcefully.

"I had other plans, but I'll always give my baby girl what she needs."

He propped his leg on the edge of the soaker tub and grabbed her, pulling her over his knee. Her legs flailed without purchase, but her hands grasped his leg. His hand whaled on her naked bottom, making crisp spanks and squeals echo throughout the bathroom. Her struggling was no real deterrent. He was strong enough to keep her steady over his knee and continue reddening her ass.

"Are you ready to behave and lose the attitude?"

"Yes, Daddy. Jesus, *yes!*" Her legs scissored and he leaned forward, opening the drawer beside the sink.

"Language when you're being spanked, babe, language." He swatted her bottom with his wooden-backed hairbrush and she hollered. He got in half a dozen whacks when she started shouting.

"Oh, God! Sorry! Sorry! Yes, I'm ready!"

"That's better," he said, dropping the brush to rub the sting away. "I'm going to put you down now."

She sniffed and nodded. When he set her on her feet in front of the mirror she rubbed her bottom and pouted, looking through her lashes at him. He wanted to comfort her right there, but he needed her to see what he saw.

"Look at yourself." He pointed at the mirror.

Her eyes swung slowly to her reflection and he moved to stand behind her. He towered over her and he was wide enough to block her from view if he stood in front of her. He couldn't see why she thought she was fat. Her distorted body image was way off base.

He watched as she sniffled and her eyes perused her body. When they stopped on her breasts he reached around and cupped them. "Beautiful. Round and full. They feel fantastic in my hands." Her nipples budded beneath his palms and his cock twitched. He pushed it against her ass so she could feel it.

When her eyes went lower to her belly, she shut them and whimpered, "Please don't make me do this."

"Open them, baby. You're gorgeous. This belly is cute, and supposed to be a little rounded." His hands smoothed down her front before making a heart shape with them. He waited for her to look. When she had, he grabbed her hips, making fingerlike dimples in her flesh. "These are nice to hold, and squeeze," he added through clenched teeth, as he once again ground his even harder cock into her ass.

She pushed her bottom back and hissed. He chuckled and his hands smoothed back up. His left hand grabbed her tit and tweaked the nipple, but his right palm slid to her mound, beneath the little patch of silk and his fingers pressed down between the crevice of her pretty shaved pussy.

"Watch your face," he demanded and slid further between her folds to get his finger good and wet with her juices. He stroked her nub, and her bottom lip quivered. He stroked again, a little harder and her knees wobbled. Pulling her lip through her teeth, she moaned.

"Mm, babe, does that feel good?"

"Yes," she answered breathily.

"Hands on your head," he demanded, while rolling her nipple between his thumb and finger. She obeyed and he stroked her clit again, faster this time. "Spread those legs."

She opened for him and he smiled over her shoulder at her in the mirror. Her head tipped back and her eyes closed as she leaned against him. His fingers stopped playing and he pulled his hand away. Her eyes burst open just as his palm swatted her mound and his fingers slapped against her clit. It wasn't too hard but enough to make her lurch.

"Watch."

"Yes, sir."

He grunted approvingly and his fingers started their gentle explorations again. Her cheeks were glowing and pink as she got closer to climax. She began rocking against his hand, her breathing steady puffs.

"Take Daddy's gift of pleasure. It's yours. Pleasure is good, your body was designed for it. Take it like you own it, because right now, in this moment, you do. That won't always be the case, babe."

As he worked her, they both watched. He loved her expressions, the way her eyes lit and her face flushed. And damn it, that wobbling lip would be the death of him if he didn't capture it between his own teeth soon.

She started to make a mixture of moaning and heavier panting sounds and he kept up his pace, then suddenly wanting more than anything for her to come on his tongue, he dropped, turned her around, and brought his mouth to her. She had been so close to going over, it only took moments of his suckling and flicks before she came in a shudder against his mouth. He immediately looked up to watch her face as the spasms took her away from this world.

"Baby girl, that was magnificent. I've never seen someone look so beautiful mid-orgasm in my life." His heart pounded as he continued watching her from his knees. He could easily see himself in this position proposing to her and it scared the hell out of him. But she was *his* in his heart and now that he'd come clean, and she'd confessed her own secrets, he felt that more than ever.

"Alright, babe, let's get you back on that settee." He

stood and ran his hands up her still warm ass. "I want to paint that gorgeous, hot pink ass someday." He gave it a pat and Addi smiled shyly.

He helped her to lie on the cloth-covered settee, admiring her body and then fiddled through a box of paints until he found the ones he wanted.

"Put your arms above your head." He adjusted her arms so they were crossed at the wrists hanging over the side of the settee. He pulled her hair back from her face and let it lie over the side as well. One leg was bent and leaning and the other, hanging off the couch. She was open to him just enough. The swollen pink flesh between her thighs still glistened from her orgasm.

"Are you comfortable?"

"Being naked or lying here?"

"Addianna," he warned. She licked her lips at his stern tone. "Do you need another spanking with that brush?"

"I'm comfortable." She giggled. "It hurt, by the way, but it was damn hot, Daddy."

He shook his head, but couldn't hide his smirk. "Close your eyes and no peeking. I have no clue where the tie went." He picked up a tube of paint. Read the label to make sure it was what he wanted, opened the cap, and squirted some on his palette. They were the nontoxic, water-based paints he used with Brent.

Using his biggest brush, he scooped up some paint—a shiny black, but it didn't seem quite right so he added some cobalt blue, making it a vivacious blue-black. "That's better," he murmured and began at her throat.

He ran the brush along her jawline and down, stroking across her jugular and circling in the hollow of her shoulder. He kissed her other side, starting in the same spot on her jaw. His tongue continued the pattern, causing her breathing to spike. Using a smaller brush, he painted the shell of her ear on her right side. And again, he used his tongue on the left.

He ran his palm from her throat to her breast before

using the brush to swirl around her nipple. The stroke had her arching her back and moaning. Addi's nipple engorged and tightened to a stiff peak, encouraging his cock to swell. He licked his lips, and unable to resist, took her other nipple into his mouth for a quick taste. It wasn't enough so he thoroughly laved it before gently blowing it dry. Both nipples were alert for him now. His paintbrush continued, swirling the paint around her sensitive nubs and around her breasts. He used another brush and painted from the sides of her breasts across her ribs to her navel. She squirmed and he ogled.

"That's it, baby girl, feel each brushstroke. So fucking beautiful."

"Oh, Drew, it feels so good."

"Mm, does it, babe?"

He completed her stomach, spending some time suckling the hollows of her hips before painting them too. He coated her front with the paint all the while teasing her into arousal. When the front was complete he got her to stand and painted the back of her too. Last, he worked on her face, starting with the eyes. He used a vibrant green on her lids. He swallowed hard when she was complete. It was just like the sketch he did earlier, but now realized on the perfect medium—*her*.

"Eyes stay closed, babe." He led her back to the bathroom mirror and once again stood behind her. "Okay, open them."

She gasped, mouth wide. She had been transformed into a sleek, powerful and incredibly sexy human panther. The blue-black shimmered and every stroke of his brush had created a realistic fur look all over her. He'd shaded her using his pallet of grays, whites, and blues to make her every sinewy muscle stand out. She looked so formidable and sexy he wanted to take her right there.

"I look…"

"Gorgeous, strong, and sexy. This is how I see you, baby girl. This is the woman I can't get out of my mind. This is who you are. Who the world sees. And honey, when you give me control, you become my kitten. There's nothing more erotic than turning a feral wildcat into a kitten."

She turned slightly, looking at herself and for once, seeming to appreciate what she saw.

"Drew, it's incredible. You make me look and feel *incredible*." She eyed him, and this time he saw a feline temptress glaring. "Will you take some photos? So you can paint me like this on canvas? I never want to forget how I feel right now."

"I will and then…"

"And then?" Her hips swayed as she went to him, running a black painted paw complete with retracted claws down his chest.

"I'm going to mess you up. First, right here on the floor and then in the shower." His eyes blazed as he raked them over her body. "I'm going to undo you, kitten."

She dropped to her knees. "Fuck it. You can paint me like this again." She took his cock into her mouth. He swore, but she only looked up coyly at him and took him in to the hilt, sucking hard and swallowing his tip before sliding off and back on, once again to swallow his tip.

He moaned, feeling his control waver, letting her go on for just a few more strokes… He fisted her hair, pulling her off his cock. "On your hands and knees, babe. You seemed to have forgotten who's in charge." When she obeyed, he pulled open one of the vanity drawers to grab a condom. He swatted her ass as she wiggled her feline painted bottom at him and went to his knees behind her. Taking her hips, he admired the print he left in the paint on her skin. "Stick that ass out, kitten. I wanna see that slick pussy as I slide into it."

He pushed her front down so her chest was close to the floor and her ass high. It looked so plump and ripe he bit her cheek just enough to make her gasp. His fingers found her ripe inside too, so he took a moment to play, making her mewl.

"Mm, you're hot and wet for me, kitten." He unwrapped the condom and slid it on. She turned to watch over her shoulder so he gave her a firm look and twirled his finger so she'd turn back around. Before she was fully around, his cock slammed into her, making her arch and call out.

"Ohhh! God, yes!"

He pounded into her for a few minutes before pulling out and rolling her over. He kissed her long and deep while sliding his cock into her. His thrusts were slower this time as he enjoyed the pleasure that blossomed on her face. She arched her spine and called out in pleasure. The sound echoed in the small room. He got to his knees, sitting back on his legs and pulling her ass up his thighs so he could slide in and out of her and still access her button.

She called out again, louder and freer as his thumb stroked her clit like a string on his guitar. Her fists clenched and her head turned. She was caught right at the cusp.

"Come, kitten. Come for me."

Her face flushed and her forehead wrinkled as she closed her eyes, clamping her teeth over her lip. A moan of pleasure burst from her and she grasped his forearms, squeezing as her release came. And just as she pulsed around his cock, his own orgasm ripped through him.

As they panted, spent, he looked around the room. "Baby girl, we've made a helluva mess in here."

"I may not know how to clean up this one, but I just thought of how we can clean up the other mess."

She had no idea. With the Skull Grinders coming, it was more disaster than mess and for now he'd keep it that way. She didn't need anything else on her plate.

CHAPTER FIFTEEN

Drew

The bar was packed and Drew wanted to turn around and leave but he had to face Trevor, and he needed to talk to the Grinders when they showed up and this was where they'd come first. Steven and Daniel were with Addi, and the media were still camped out and chomping at the bit for answers, so he knew she was safe. Daniel was a bit on the small side, but Steven was built and both seemed protective of Addi, so he had no concerns about leaving her for a short time.

His true worry was the Grinders anyway and the media would stop them for now. As long as Addi stayed put, she would be fine. The back way was well hidden and unless someone walked the perimeter, which was a quarter of a kilometer from the road and in the thick of the forest, they'd never find the back entrance.

Television crews from all the major stations were standing vigil at the entrance of the camp, in the parking lot of Last Resort, and even at Nora's Diner. At least they were getting some extra business from it. Seeing a few bikers at the bar wouldn't alert anyone, unless they wore the Skull

Grinders patch and not even Dingo was dumb enough to do that.

A wave to Trevor got him a nod and he knew the second his friend had a minute, Drew would get his usual. He wouldn't snub Drew over gossip. Trevor didn't believe unsubstantiated rumors.

Drew looked around. The bar was filled with strangers in leather and some regular sorts—most likely reporters. They nursed their beers and glanced awkwardly around. One of the bikers, someone he'd never seen before, was blatantly staring at him. Drew assessed the big blond man and he looked away to pick up his drink. Curiosity perhaps, Drew decided. Maybe he was a cameraman. He looked hardened and ready for anything though, so if he was a camera man he'd seen some bad shit.

Of course, Layla was having fun wiggling her fringe-skirted ass around enticing the leather-clad men and this time she had a friend with her. Trevor looked annoyed as he glanced at Layla and Drew couldn't blame him. First, Layla was trying to encourage two of his drinking customers to go home with her and her friend and second, he was pretty sure Trevor'd had enough of her crap.

Trevor grunted, threw a napkin down, and set a drink roughly in front of Drew on a beer coaster.

"Sorry about earlier, but Addi's a real lady and I needed to know she'd be okay."

"I know. Thanks for looking out for her."

"You do what they're saying?" Trevor questioned, eyeing Layla. Drew spun his glass, watching the dark liquid slosh around the glass.

"It's complicated. According to the law I did it because I confessed and my prints were the only ones at the scene." Trevor's eyes widened slightly and Drew shrugged. "Truth though?"

Trevor nodded.

"I was just the lookout and I was a kid." Drew shoved the glass back. "How about something that won't burn a hole in my gut?"

"It's about time, my friend." Trevor smiled widely. It looked odd on him. The man wasn't a smiler. He turned and grabbed some top-shelf whiskey and poured Drew another glass, dumping the other one down the sink with a sneer. When he looked up, his good mood suddenly soured. Drew turned to see Layla sitting in some guy's lap.

"Woman trouble?"

He swore and fisted his goatee before grabbing the bottle off the counter and pouring himself a liberal shot. He threw it back and gave an appreciative sound. "That woman is gonna put a hole in *my* gut."

"She needs to be straightened out, Trevor, and I'm not sure there's a man alive with the patience." Drew took a swig from his glass. Trevor crossed his arms and continued to watch, pouring himself another shot and added more to Drew's glass.

"It's been on again, off again for seven years, Fitz, and still that woman gets under my skin."

"You know I didn't know that when I…" He stopped talking when Trevor gave one sharp nod, still staring at the blonde and her friend.

"I know."

There was some ruckus in the bar to their left and Trevor went to deal with it. Drew swallowed the rest of his drink with a grunt, ignoring the stool that was pulled out beside him. One casual glance to his right had his chest tightening though.

The biker Layla had been flirting with had a devil tatt on his neck. *Mauler—patched that for his love of lying on top of his victims and covering their noses and mouths with his hand until he felt them go limp. Sometimes just until they passed out, but more often until they were dead.*

The news had only broken around noon and Mauler was already in town. Drew rose silently, while the beefy biker had his back to Drew. Pulling his sketch pencil out of his jacket pocket, he grabbed a napkin.

"Hey, babe, what're you drinking again?" Layla looked up at Mauler, but as soon as she saw Drew her smile faltered.

"Hello, Fitzie. See all the new friends I'm making since you kicked me out of your bed." Her eyes darted quickly to Trevor and Drew shook his head. All along she'd been using him to passive-aggressively torment her ex. Mauler glanced over his shoulder dismissively and was turning his attention back on Layla when he took a double take.

"Reaper?"

Drew was already at the door. The only thing left in his spot was his empty glass, a twenty dollar bill, and the napkin with his cell number on it.

"Hey, hold up," Mauler called just as Drew reached for the door. "Dingo, I think that's him, the fucking prodigal son! Layla, that your man?"

"Pfft, no, but he's still in love with me. Reaper?"

"It's a nickname, sugar tits. He's an old friend."

Drew's jaw clenched but he didn't dare turn back. His goal was simple. Lead them out of town, away from the camp, and set up a meeting with his father.

Even though Drew had taken the fall for the murders, his father hadn't forgiven him for leaving the Grinders or refusing his role as vice president. He'd left. Without a word, Drew had disappeared. John Trigger's words rang out in his head…

"There's only one way out of the Grinders, kid, and that's in a body bag."

Drew wasn't going to hide anymore. He was done being a prisoner.

Drew sat on the hard wooden chair, a plainclothes youth officer beside him, but he didn't feel safe. His father sat on his other side looking odd, clean shaven and wearing an expensive suit. He looked nothing like the man Drew knew, but he hadn't changed in the important ways.

His eyes were still those of a cold-blooded killer, and his body was tense and ready for a fight in the place full of authority. His father's beard had been long, clasped in a braided leather cord with steel beads hanging, only the day before, but now only a rashy pointed chin was exposed. Drew supposed he should feel good his father had shaved and dressed nicely for his sentencing. Then again, he knew it was more to ensure Drew didn't change his story and tell someone it was his father that had pulled the trigger.

Drew looked at his father's chin again, thinking of the beads that once hung there. Each one symbolized a murder he'd committed. His father always said each bead was a man who had crossed him. Now Drew had witnessed the truth. His father had added two more beads after that night in the alley. Although, when someone had truly crossed him, his father never went after them personally—he went after their wives, girlfriends, sons, and daughters. Hell, even mothers or grandmothers sometimes.

"Go after the ones they love, son. That's what really hurts."

When the youth officer rose to speak to another guard, Drew's father turned to look at him. His mouth, normally hidden behind his facial hair, was thin and pressed into a cruel curve. His father wasn't pleased with him. And suddenly, Drew was happy he had no family besides the Skull Grinders—no friends either—no one for his father to take from him. And Drew had better keep it that way for the rest of his life.

"Boy, I'll find every person you even think about caring for and julienne them like fucking carrots if you fuck this up!" Spittle sat on his father's chin and Drew blinked, clenching his jaw to show no fear. But the fear was so strong he felt dizzy.

That fear was gone and nothing was more important to him than a life with Addi. He'd protect what was his… even if it meant taking down the club brick by fleshy brick.

Drew headed out of town. He stopped at a joint a couple of hours away from the camp and had a coffee while he waited. It was only a matter of time.

He took the last guzzle of his coffee and pulled out his cell as it buzzed in his pocket. His jaw tightened.

"Yeah?" Drew cracked the tension from his neck.

"Reaper, it's been a long time."

"Not long enough, Trigger."

"C'mon now, son. Is that any way to talk to your father?"

"Father or president? You were always more one than the other."

"Right down to business then." Trigger growled an order at someone. "Here's the thing, kid." There was a long pause. "Mauler's got your girl. He's bringing her home to me. I'm thinking about passing her around to the boys when she gets here. The club whores could use a day off."

Drew's insides went cold. His whole body froze and the hushing in his ears made it hard for him to hear the rest of his father's words, but he breathed through it.

"I've got her kid, too. He yours? Doesn't matter." Trigger chuckled. Her kid? Drew's head dropped. Fucking Layla. Her games had gotten her and Brent into real trouble this time. He rubbed a hand across his forehead. *Fuck!*

At least Addi was safe.

"Here's your choice. You can save one of them. You get to watch the other die. That's your punishment." His father's laugh was wheezy but still cruel and more familiar than Drew cared to admit. It had been in his nightmares since he'd been born.

"Once it's done, you stay here at the clubhouse and work your way back into our good fucking graces. You'll be fully patched and back with the Skulls soon enough and if not, the other dies, too. I got a new guy and he'll escort the woman or the kid back to town and stay until I know you're committed to us again."

Drew swore and smashed his fist off the outdoor picnic table he sat on. It throbbed but nothing like the pain he felt inside. His shitty life was like herpes, always coming back and ready to infect everyone he loved.

"Who the hell's this new guy?" Drew asked to keep his father on the line longer.

"Someone loyal, unlike you, who fucking ditched your family."

"You use the word family loosely, Father. And I went to jail for *your* family."

His father laughed humorlessly. "You went to jail because you just had to be a fucking hero." The phone went silent and Drew squeezed it in his fist so tightly he thought it might break into pieces.

He tossed his coffee cup into the garbage and got on his bike. No matter how much he didn't want to be like the Grinders, he was heading there. Violence was the only thing his father understood.

First he needed to hide Addi somewhere just in case they figured out they'd fucked up and taken the wrong woman. But before he could tuck away his phone and ride back to her, it rang again.

"What?"

"Fitzie? You gotta help us." It was Layla. There was a thump over the line and a whimper. "Save Brent! And tell Trevor he's the father."

"Enough, bitch." Another scuffle and a slap. "Reaper, I gotta say your snub hurt."

"Mauler."

"We'll be at the clubhouse in a few hours. You've got till noon tomorrow." There was a scuffle and a scream in the background. "I really hope you choose the kid, though. This bitch is pissing me off."

The phone went silent and Drew's mouth dried. There wasn't time. Looking up the number for Fell County Police, he shook his head. Carter may not be his favorite person, but he would protect Addi.

CHAPTER SIXTEEN

Addi

Drew had dropped her off at the main camp to hang out with Steven and Daniel before he came to town to talk to Trevor and she was glad. She had her own plan and with him so mercurial around people, especially people like Rebecca Snow, it was better she start her plan on her own.

The best way to deal with Drew's problem was by utilizing Rebecca and her urge for fame and fortune. They'd offer her an exclusive interview with the real painter Andrew Trigger, and explain about his past and why he'd kept it a secret, if *and only if* she agreed to follow Addi's questioning guidelines. Drew would finally tell the world the truth, while promoting his charities. The world would finally see what a good man he was.

"Your turn, Ads," Steven said, leaning back in his chair with his arms crossed. "TALKS onto Daniel's CAMP for the triple word score."

She glanced up from her notes to see he'd clobbered both her and Daniel with his turn, but she still could have kissed him. His words gave her an idea.

She tossed an A in front of the M in CAMP and stood

up from the table in the mess hall where they'd been hanging out playing Scrabble. She suddenly knew how they could fulfill Uncle Ray's wishes for the camp!

"Where are you going?" Daniel crossed his arms, shot a look at Steven, and stepped in front of Addi. "We were under the impression that Drew wanted you here, where you'd be safe and out of trouble."

"With us!" Steven added.

"Guys, I'm perfectly capable of handling myself. I've actually been doing it for years." She grabbed her purse. "I'm going to talk to someone I think can help."

"Who is this woman?" Steven asked Daniel.

"I don't know, but our Addi would stay safe in this situation." Daniel shrugged.

"Oh, for heaven's sake, I'm just going to the front gate to talk to Rebecca Snow. Not fight the whole town for Drew's honor."

"Rebecca Snow? I know that name." Steven scratched his chin, his eyes narrowed in concentrations. "She's a tabloid reporter, isn't she?"

"She won't be for long." Addi smiled. "Not if she agrees to my plan."

"I still don't think you should go." Daniel crossed his arms.

"Me either. Besides, we're here to hang out. You need to show us around, talk about that hottie, and maybe go skinny dipping in that sparkling lake I saw."

"And we will. Just as soon as I finish my chat with Miss Snow."

Steven looked at Daniel with a frown. "She just agreed to skinny dip… she's definitely not Addi."

"God, you two!" Addi growled. "I'll be back in ten minutes. Stop analyzing my every move."

"You've changed since you've been here, Ads. Spill. We want to know what this hot biker has done to you."

Addi smiled. "I'll tell you all about it as soon as I get back. Promise."

"That's fine, just as long as you know we're calling Drew." Steven held up her cell phone in a wave. Daniel smirked, looking at his husband with both love and admiration.

"God, Daniel, you can use the time I'm gone to rip his clothes off." She looked pointedly at her other best friend. "And you can call him all you want. It'll be worth the spanking he'll give me."

Their jaws dropped. "Spanking?"

"Oh, don't look so scandalized." She rolled her eyes. "I friggin' love that he daddy doms me."

Daniel tipped his head back and laughed before turning to look at Steven with a serious look. "Maybe if I spank you when you screw up our deadlines and lose articles, you'll become more organized." Daniel winked at Addi.

"Only if you want me to lose stuff on purpose. I am thoroughly turned on right now, but don't you dare expect me to call you Daddy." He looked at Addi. "No offense but gag." He shoved a finger down his throat.

Addi giggled and snatched her phone from Steven on her way out the door. "Spank him good, Daniel, he needs it."

•••••••

"Let me go, Carter." He had her handcuffed to a hotel bed since the evening before. She had at least spoken to Rebecca and worked out a deal before he showed up, handcuffed her, and threw her in the back of his cruiser.

"Oh, you're awake. We talked about this last night and my answer's still nope. You wouldn't have had to be handcuffed if you hadn't tried to take off."

Addi struggled against the cuff attached to her wrist and his bed.

"Drew asked me to take care of you and as much as I hate that dick, we have a common goal. Keeping you safe."

"Carter Lerner, Drew's the one in trouble, not me!"

"Yeah, I imagine he is, but I don't give a fuck about him." He jabbed a finger at her. "You on the other hand…"

"Why the hell should you care about me?"

"Because instead of telling you I had a crush on you when we were sixteen I made up that stupid bet and you damn well got hurt. Can't a guy make up for the shitty things he did in his past?"

"By handcuffing me to the bed in a shitty motel?" Her voice rose in pitch.

"Don't make it sound so lecherous. It's for your own safety. I can't have you taking off and getting involved in whatever mess Drew's in. Okay? I want us to be friends, Addi."

"Yes, me too, but handcuffing me is not the friendliest gesture, so how about letting your *friend* out of these shackles, Carter?"

"Not a chance, honey."

She sighed and slammed her palm off the bed. Carter shot her a warning look.

"Why would anyone want to bother with me," Addi said with a sigh.

"It's not as simple as you think, Addi." Carter's face looked pained. "The Skull Grinders, his old biker club, have taken Layla and Brent. They're hell bent on payback for him leaving."

"What?" She broke out in an instant sweat and her heart pounded against her ribs. "Why Layla?"

"Because Layla was mouthing off that she was his ex and that he was still in love with her." He ran a hand through his hair and groaned as he sat on the end of the bed. "They've given Drew a choice. Brent or Layla and the other one dies." He looked gravely at her. "He has till noon today."

"No!" She yanked hard on the cuff, growling. Carter stood, facing her in the bed. He opened his mouth to speak but before a word escaped his lips, the door burst open, splinters flying, and a big blond man wrapped his massive arms around Carter's neck.

It took ten seconds for him to slump to the floor. Addi screamed and the hulking man leaned over her, placing his hand over her mouth.

"Addianna?" He blinked as if waiting for a response so she nodded. "Don't scream. I'm not going to hurt you." She nodded again. As soon as he released her mouth, she gasped and scooted back as close as she could to the headboard.

"Did you kill him?"

The blond blinked again and looked at Carter. "Him? No, just choked him out. Cut off the blood supply to his brain. He'll be fine, disoriented when he wakes up but fine." He reached down and came back up with the handcuff key. A big metal thing that looked nothing like a regular key. "You're coming with me."

"And you are?" she asked as he unlocked the cuff around her wrist.

"Hacker is my patched name with the Skull Grinders." He helped her from the bed by her arm and pulled her toward the doorway. "But my real name is Sean MacAfee."

Addi's eyes widened. Sean's focus turned to Addi, his eyes softening slightly before he continued guiding her out of the motel.

"I know you're his real girlfriend, Addianna."

Addi threw herself to the ground. She'd taken Brazilian Jiu Jitsu and knew her strength was on the ground, but Sean caught her, twisting her arms behind her back. "Relax, honey. You won't get hurt if you cooperate."

When she struggled, he nudged behind her knee and her leg buckled, adding more pressure to her arms.

"Drew didn't kill your dad and he saved you!"

"I know," Sean said. "I'm going to let you go, but you need to listen to me. We don't have much time." He released her and put his hands in his pockets as a show of faith.

Addi got herself into a position with her legs shoulder width apart, her knees bent, and her arms up. She didn't fist her hands, but kept them open and ready to hit him with the heel of her hand, preferably in the nose or cheekbone where his eyes would water and she'd gain a few seconds' advantage.

"Andrew saved my life and now I'm going to save his and get justice for my dad." He gathered a breath. "They're luring him into a trap. They plan on killing both hostages and Andrew, and then going after Trigger."

Addi's trembling hand went to her mouth, adrenaline still pumping through her.

"I was more than happy to wait and let Mauler and Dingo kill Trigger and take over the Grinders before I handed the evidence I collected while in the club to the RCMP, but when I found out their plan for the woman, her kid, and Andrew, I knew I had to stop them. I work for a private security firm and I've gotten all the information to them. They're with the authorities now presenting them with evidence, but there's no time."

"How do we stop them? I'll do anything."

"Walk and talk, Addi." They headed to the car Sean had in the parking lot while he continued speaking. "So Andrew took off from the clubhouse one night, a week after they picked him up from the camp when he was sixteen. They couldn't find him, but they've never stopped looking. Most of the club members are pissed at the old man's obsession, but Trigger wants his son to run the club with him and take over eventually. They want the old man out and they'll kill Andrew to make sure he won't come claim his place."

"He won't be easy to take down."

"I know that, too. But I'm afraid after they've killed the woman and her kid, he won't fight them. Especially if he thinks they don't know about you and his death will end everything and keep you safe." He took his hands out of his pockets and pointed the fob at the car to unlock it.

Addi's nose tingled with unshed emotion and she nodded, knowing it was true. He would give his life if it meant ending it all and saving her. Sean opened the passenger side door and waited for Addi to get in.

"If I show up with you and tell them I found the real girlfriend, it'll confuse them long enough for me to take them down and you to get Layla and her son out safely. Hopefully before Trigger arrives. The boss trusts me, but they don't. If I hand you over, it'll hopefully prove I'm one of them. They'll never expect me to turn on them then." His eyes were a deep brown and with his blond hair he reminded her of a teddy bear.

"I won't let anything happen to you, Addi. I promise." He took out a roll of duct tape. "But you're going to have to pretend I will."

CHAPTER SEVENTEEN

Drew

Drew's bike rumbled purposely loud as he drove into the parking lot of the Grinders' clubhouse. It was an old house on a shitty street where the neighbors never complained and the yards were all overgrown. The place was even smaller and a helluva lot more run down than he remembered. The whole neighborhood looked like shit.

Drew watched for Trevor through the unfenced yard. He'd sent him down the alley that ran between the back of the houses. Trevor had walked his bike through to avoid alerting anyone but also to have his bike close in case they had to move quickly. Drew gathered a breath.

Parking his bike, he got off and plucked his helmet from his head. He watched for movement in the house through the filthy windows as he walked up the stairs onto the veranda with the peeling gray paint. Beer cans lined the windowsills like other houses might have flower boxes. He kicked a milk crate out of the way and frowned at the cigarette butts littering the ground. He shook his head. The way the place was falling apart it was only a matter of time before the whole damn thing burnt to the ground from one carelessly flicked butt.

He banged his fist on the door and walked in, his boots clomping loudly to alert his former brothers. The front hall had been opened up to join the front bedroom by removing a wall and creating a sitting room. There were a few chairs and high tables as well as a bar fully stocked with liquor. A big screen television took up one wall. More empty cans were scattered about the room, along with overfilled ashtrays and empty liquor bottles. Rhonda, the house mouse hadn't cleaned up from the night before apparently. He wondered if she was even still around. She'd been young back then but maybe she'd moved on.

Drew stepped further into the clubhouse, hearing some pool balls clacking in the dining room where the pool table was housed.

"Reaper?" More pool balls cracking off each other. "We're in here." Mauler, cue in hand, reefer in his mouth, poked his head around the jamb. Drew followed when Mauler turned back into the room.

The dining room was open into the kitchen and Drew saw Brent at the table, tied around the waist to a chair. He grit his teeth, but remained outwardly calm. Dingo was across from him, leaning his chair back on two legs, chewing on a toothpick. The remnants of a meal sat on a plate in front of him. A full plate in front of Brent indicated he'd chosen not to eat.

"You okay, buddy?"

"Yeah," Brent answered, shooting a Dingo a dirty look. "They've roughed up my mom though."

"Shit, kid. You ain't seen nothin'."

"And he better not." Drew stood taller and cracked his neck. Dingo gave him a half smile.

"I gotta say, Reaper, you've really grown into that name. You look scary as shit."

Drew only grunted and walked to Mauler. "Where's Trigger?"

He nodded toward the stairs. "In his office."

Drew glanced into the back room that also served as a sitting room to see Layla was tied to a chair with her mouth taped. Some guy sat on the sofa beside her using a cell, probably to play games. It was only eleven, so they were passing the time. Drew was glad the guy was looking at his phone and the others at him rather than out the back, because Drew caught a glimpse of Trevor sidling up to the house.

When he'd told Trever that Brent was his son and he and his mother had been taken, Drew couldn't keep him away. Trevor wanted his kid and his woman and he was willing to fight to the death if it came to that. Drew understood. He'd have been the same way if it were Addi and their child.

The thought gave him pause. He could easily see Addi heavy with child, glowing with life and sassing him. It made his heart beat faster. He wanted that. He was desperate for it. But his gut told him things weren't going to go well with the Grinders and he might not walk away from this. They wouldn't stop looking for him and they'd kill Brent and Layla the minute he wasn't around to protect them. That meant he had to end things, one way or another.

His skills hadn't been honed in a long time. He learned to fight young in the club, and then in juvie and he'd continued to keep in shape, but besides helping Trevor with the occasional bar brawl that ended too swiftly, he hadn't used his fighting skills.

How would he handle himself with Mauler and Dingo? They used their skills regularly. Drew scratched his chin. Mauler and Dingo were bullies, dealing with scared men who had crossed Trigger. None of them put up much resistance. They hadn't the skill or brains for that. Drew wouldn't back down and he certainly wouldn't cower to them.

"Jesus Christ. We're a little busy to be entertaining, Hacker," Mauler said, slamming his cue down. Drew's head spun. His jaw was tense and his eyes narrowed, but his heart was cracking off his ribs like a deer surrounded by wolves.

A big blond man had Addi's arm clasped in his grip. Her hands and mouth were duct taped. He didn't look like a Grinder except for the leather vest with the patch. It was the same guy who had been watching him in the Last Resort.

Addi struggled and yelped through the tape when he yanked her roughly. Drew saw red but kept his feet planted. He had to be smart, not impulsive.

"This is Reaper's real girlfriend." The blond's voice was deep and condescending.

"How do you know?" Dingo said, jumping up and letting his chair slam back onto all four legs.

"Because I took the time to ask people rather than listen to the drunk and bitter rantings of the town lush. Besides, have you watched the news at all? These two are all over it." He shook Addi and pointed between her and Drew. "She was on the back of his bike."

The sliding doors to the back were open, letting in a cool breeze and their words flow out. Trevor could hear everything the blond man said, but Drew didn't have to worry about Trevor rushing in to avenge his girl's honor though. First, Trevor knew it was the truth, and second, he knew enough to stay put until the opportunity was right. Not too many people knew it, but Trevor had done a tour in Afghanistan back before he came to Fell County to take over his brother's half of the bar after he'd been killed by a drunk.

"It makes sense, this one's prettier and look at those curves." Mauler left his spot by the pool table and wandered to Addi, ripping the duct tape from her mouth. Drew's insides burned with fury and his fists clenched at his sides as Mauler ran his hands over Addi's breasts and down her sides to her hips. He wanted to crush the guy's skull, but before he could take a step, Addi leaned back on the blond and kicked Mauler in the gut with both legs, sending him stumbling back.

"Fuckin' bitch," he spat, and backhanded her.

Addi spit blood on the floor. "Keep your filthy hands

off me."

"Should we let this one go?" Dingo asked, eyeing the kid. "I ain't keen on killing a kid."

"I'm not leaving my mother." Brent crossed his arms and narrowed his eyes at the bikers. "Drew'll kill you all and I'll leave with my mom and Addi."

Mauler and Dingo both laughed and Brent's hands fisted. "Sure, kid." Mauler took Addi from the big blond, pulled another kitchen chair out and sat it next to Layla, shoving Addi in it roughly.

"No one's going anywhere, moron. The kid'll just run to the cops."

"Fine, I gotta piss. Can you two handle this?" Dingo was clearly annoyed by Mauler's insult and that's when Drew saw his opportunity. He knew Trevor would handle Dingo as he went out the back door. He probably needed air as much as he needed to piss and the lawn was as good as the bathroom to him. The guy was constantly whipping it out in public to piss when Drew was a kid.

Mauler leaned his face so close to Addi's she could probably smell his putrid breath and then grabbed her breast while his eyes flickered to Drew's. Out of the corner of his eye, Drew saw Addi slip both hands out of the duct tape, and lift both knees while Mauler was distracted. She flew forward as his head turned back to her and she clapped both palms over his ears. Drew winced, knowing that was not only painful but it was disorienting as hell. Addi fisted his hair and yanked him to her, head-butting his nose. And while Mauler was stumbling, holding his nose and attempting to clear the tears from his eyes, Addi's legs sprang out into his gut, sending him flying back again.

Mauler wasn't a small man and the fucker was laid out.

"That's for touching me again," she spat.

Drew turned his attention to the big blond, who hadn't done anything to protect his brother from Addi's attack, and frowned in confusion. He was already untying Layla.

What the hell is going on?

Drew grabbed Addi as she lunged for Mauler, who was back on his feet again. "Untie Brent and get them out of here."

She nodded, but before she obeyed, she spun and kicked Mauler in the balls with the top of her foot. Thankfully she kicked him hard enough to make him drop to his knees and not just piss him off. Drew grabbed Mauler by the scruff of his shirt and grinned at Addi as she headed for Brent. "That's my baby girl."

"Drew, he's a good guy." She nudged her chin toward the big blond who had already untied Brent. His eyes narrowed at the blood on her forehead. She had hurt herself head-butting Mauler. Dammit.

"His name is Sean and he's on our side."

Drew nodded. "Head out back, Trevor's out there."

She took off with Brent and Layla and he slammed his fist into Mauler's jaw, hearing a satisfying crunch.

"That's for having such a hard fucking head and hurting my baby girl."

Trevor was dragging Dingo into the clubhouse, blood spurting from his nose, when shit went bad.

There was a flash of silver and Trevor went down with a blow to the head. Three Skull Grinders stepped over him to walk in the clubhouse.

"You know what we do to traitors and runaways?" the biggest one said as another three guys walked in holding Layla, Brent, and Addi.

Shit.

With the six guys and one gun pointed at him and Sean, and the other pointed at Addi, he knew they were pretty much screwed. Especially when John Trigger walked down the stairs.

"Well, look who's finally graced us with his presence." He looked much older than Drew remembered. He was thinner, slightly bent in the shoulders, and his skin was scarred around the cheeks. Drugs, he assumed.

"Trigger," Drew acknowledged, buying time as his mind

worked through scenarios for getting out of the mess they were in.

"Boys, if you wouldn't mind getting rid of the witnesses, I'd like to have a word with my son and his girlfriend." His hard dark eyes, slitted in anger, turned to Sean. "Give Hacker a good send-off. Anyone who betrays the Grinders needs to be made an example of." His mouth, a little crooked, turned up cruelly. "Video it. We'll watch it at the next prospect meeting."

Drew's muscles tensed as he readied himself. He planned on rushing his father as soon as the others left. Mauler was useless, still clutching his gut and gagging and Addi could handle him if she needed to. Dingo, still holding his nose, was eyeing Trigger, probably awaiting instructions.

"Let Addi go." Drew stepped toward his father, but stopped when he pulled his gun, a black Glock, out and pointed it at Addi.

"Mauler and Dingo were going to betray you," Addi said in a rush, her voice high and panicked, making Drew feel as if he'd been kicked in the gut.

"Shut the fuck up, cunt!" Mauler choked out and started to rise. The others paused in their attempt to subdue Sean so they could hear what came next.

"They were going to kill you and Drew and take over the Skull Grinders MC themselves."

"I can prove it," Sean added. The three guys jumped on Sean as he attempted to pull something from his pocket.

"Stop!" Trigger yelled. He turned back to Addi. "Don't lie to me or I'll put a bullet in every joint, grab some popcorn, and watch you writhe in agony on the floor."

"Enough." Drew's voice was still his usual deep and raspy but was so cold he didn't even recognize it. "This has gone on long enough. I took the fall for the murders. I spent my youth in jail and then became a goddamned recluse. All because I didn't want to be in your damn motorcycle club. We can both walk out now and end this. We'll start fresh. We'll lead this club together. No one will dare try to overtake the two of us. I'll come home, Dad." Drew took a sure step toward his father. "Let the girl go. She means nothing to me. She was a distraction, a hot piece of tail, that's all."

Trigger shoved his gun in his pants and clapped his hands. A smile, wide and genuine, brightened his pocked face. He focused his gaze on Addi.

"You're the girl from that camp, aren't you?" He took a few steps further down the staircase until he was on the main floor and looked at Drew. "I knew as soon as Mauler said you were back in that shitty little town that you must have been hiding at that camp." He went to Addi and took her chin with his thumb and forefinger, turning her head to examine her face. "You're the girl, aren't you? The one my son was in love with when he was sixteen." He chuckled. "Don't look so shocked, Andrew. A father knows."

"You hurt her, you'll have to kill me or have a guard with you every minute, 'cause I'll fucking beat you to death when you're sleeping."

Trigger's brow rose. "I haven't made any decisions yet, Reaper." His eyes swung toward Sean. "I wanna hear your proof." Trigger cocked his head to the side and gestured for the guys to back off. As soon as they did, Sean elbowed the closest one in the face and smiled when his jaw made a crunching noise.

"You deserved that one, Cowboy." The guy with the cowboy boots swore through his hands.

"He fucking broke my goddamn jaw!"

Sean pulled out his phone, pressed a few buttons and held it up. Mauler's voice came from the little speaker, but before anyone heard anything damning, two things happened. First, there was the loud rumble of at least twenty bikes coming down the road and second, Dingo shot Sean's hand. He was probably aiming for the phone but he missed.

Sean hollered, did some fancy-ass moves and had Dingo on the ground. The gun skittered across the floor and both Drew and Addi lunged for it, but Mauler was closer and diving for it too.

By then the noise from the bikes had stopped and Mauler's voice was explaining how he and Dingo could take down Trigger and Drew.

"Addi!" Drew yelled, shoving Addi down and diving on top of her as Mauler grabbed the gun and swung it toward them. Two shots rang out and Drew felt his ears explode in pain, but he didn't care, Addi was out of the way of the gunfire. Then there was silence. He rose and looked down at himself, checking for wounds and then noticed blood on the floor. He checked Addi quickly.

Mauler was clutching his gut, looking pale with an expression of disbelief. At least twenty guys walked through the door then, but none of them wore the Skull Grinders patch.

They were all from the Iron Code. They'd come to help their brother, Gunner.

The Iron Code MC took care of the remaining Skulls and Drew pulled Addi into his arms to calm her trembling and reassure himself she was safe. She pointed after a few minutes and Drew looked up to see where Mauler's bullet had gone.

His father was on the floor, eyes wide and lifeless.

Drew pulled Addi's face into his chest and rocked her. He watched the organized chaos around him as the Iron Code held the living members of the Grinders in the front room, fixed Sean's hand wound and tended to Trevor and Layla, who were both pretty battered. Brent was physically unharmed but was clinging to Layla's legs looking stunned and pale.

Drew rose and helped Addi up from the floor. "Babe, let's go check on Brent and Layla."

She nodded and stayed close under his arm. When the sirens started, Drew felt Addi relax further into him.

"Drew?" Sean called to him before they'd made it to Layla and Brent.

"You undercover RCMP?" Drew asked, sizing him up.

"No, and actually, we've met before."

Drew was puzzled and now quite pissed that this guy put his woman in danger when he wasn't the authorities.

"We have?" He scratched his beard, keeping his calm. "You one of the Iron Code?"

"No, I work for a private security firm, hired by the MacAfee family."

Drew swallowed hard, still comforting Addi, his free hand stroking her hair. "Babe?" He looked down at Addi. "This is where I pay my penance. Just remember how strong you are. How beautiful and how proud I am of the way you took these assholes down. I love you." His hands dropped and Addi reached for him but he stepped out of her way. Drew looked back at Sean and straightened his shoulders.

"You'll let her go, yeah? We'll deal with this alone?"

"Sean, tell him. Please," Addi begged, emotion strangling her vocal cords.

Drew frowned. His baby girl was in shock and talking nonsense. He wondered how long it would take her to get over all of this without him. She would, he had no doubt of her strength and resilience, but it would take time and she would grieve the loss of him.

"We haven't been properly introduced, Andrew Trigger. I'm Sean MacAfee and you saved my life." He reached out to shake Drew's hand, but Drew was too dumbfounded to move.

"Sean MacAfee?" Drew asked, and Sean nodded.

"You shoved me behind the dumpster and saved my life. I regret it took years of therapy for me to talk again. Otherwise, I may have been able to give testimony to prove your innocence." He reached out further to take Drew's hand, shaking it firmly. "Thank you for saving me."

Emotion welled inside Drew and it was mirrored on Sean's face. He shook his head and pulled Sean into a bear of a hug.

"You have no idea how good it is to hear you've forgiven me." Drew released Sean and rubbed the back of his neck with his hand, a little embarrassed.

"Forgiven you?" Sean's question was paired with a furrowed brow. "How could you possibly blame yourself for any of it?" He gathered a breath and Drew glanced at Addi.

"My uncle pulled some strings, cashed in favors, and used his influence to make sure you were locked up and I regret I wasn't able to stop any of it. You were only a little older than my sister and being held responsible for a murder you didn't commit. Any other twelve-year-old in the same situation would have been protected, given therapy and care, but you were condemned because of my uncle and my weakness." Sean's hands shook as he placed them on Drew's shoulders.

"I need *you* to forgive *me*."

"You were just a kid."

"And you weren't?"

•••••••

It was later, after Sean left to debrief his firm and the RCMP was satisfied enough with all the statements to let everyone leave, that Drew took Addi on the back of his bike down to the river where he used to draw as a kid.

"Are you okay, babe?"

"I'm fine. I'm okay." She nodded excessively as if she were convincing herself as much as him. The last thing she sounded like was a person that was okay.

"Honey, Daddy's here."

Her eyes filled with tears and she threw herself into Drew's arms. "You almost had me convinced, Daddy." And her tears spilled hotly against his chest.

"Convinced of what, baby girl?" He tilted her chin up and wiped the tears from her face.

"That you were going back…" she sobbed and took a shuddering breath. "And that I meant nothing to you."

"Aw, I love you, sweetheart. And I will spend the rest of

our lives convincing you that you're the most important person in the world to me." He shushed her when she buried her face in his chest again.

Addi's cell buzzed in her pocket. Drew was going to take it, but Addi was too quick in answering.

"Yes, Dad?" she sniffled.

Drew waited as she listened on the line. Addi rolled her eyes at whatever he was saying on the phone.

"Dad, you're a grown man, I'm not your wife, your assistant, or your goddamn slave. Grow a pair and take care of yourself for once. I'm done!" She pressed end and tossed the phone into the river.

She looked at Drew and smiled. He beamed back at her.

"Have I told you lately how fucking amazing you are?"

She laughed. "Yeah, but now I finally believe it."

CHAPTER EIGHTEEN

Drew

The interview with Rebecca Snow went so well it was picked up by international news stations and broadcast all over the world. Rebecca sat down with both Drew and Sean and followed Addi's questions to the letter.

The world finally knew the truth about what happened and who the real artist of the famous Ray Moore paintings was. There was a flurry in the art world to buy copies of anything with the wrong signature and art dealers were begging for anything new from Drew, including the paintings in the background during his interview. The paintings of the events that shaped both Sean's and Drew's life.

But the true success had nothing to do with the truth being out there or Drew's art becoming even more sought after; the actual achievement was the camp. Tonalonka had become a place where kids could get over their trauma from violence by learning to express themselves through art.

They offered classes in painting, writing, and even martial arts and self-defense to empower their bodies and minds, as well as all the usual camp bonding activities. They had therapists and child trauma specialists to help with curriculum and counseling and had a plan to get some therapy animals.

People were calling from all over North America to get their kids a spot at the camp when it officially opened. Drew had even decided to start winterizing the cabins so they could run it all year long.

"So do you think Uncle Ray is proud?" Addi asked, looking at the sun rising over the flat lake. They had postponed his memorial by eight months to correspond with the grand opening of the new camp.

"Proud? I'm just a dumb biker so I gotta ask. Isn't there a stronger synonym, Miss Moore?"

Addi shot him a dirty look. "It's baby girl, Daddy. Don't make me start calling you Mr. Biker again." She turned, jabbing a thumb at her back where she wore her property patch. It read, 'Property of Daddy,' the bottom rocker read 'Lone Wolf,' and in the middle was the insignia of a wolf and the small MC patch. The front of her leather cut had her own MC name, Baby Girl. She had designed and had it made but she'd be packing it away soon. Drew had finally agreed to become an Iron Code prospect and she knew he would be getting his Iron Code top rocker soon, but she'd still be wearing his property patch. Whether he was a Lone Wolf or in the Iron Code, Addi would always be his Old Lady.

"You've been spanked for that already. I don't advise doing it again."

"Pfft, you wouldn't dare today." Her eyes narrowed at his crooked grin.

"Oh, really?" He reached around her waist and pulled her tightly against him before releasing her to smack her bottom sharply.

"Not today! It's Uncle Ray's memorial and if there was ever a time where he was watching us closely from above, it's today." Her voice rose in pitch at the end as his grin turned more wicked.

"I think your uncle would enjoy seeing your naughty ass get blistered. He told me himself you needed spankings."

Drew's brow flicked upward as hers slammed down.

"He did not!"

Drew stayed silent and turned his attention to the sunrise.

"He didn't, Drew, right? He wouldn't." She huffed and crossed her arms. "Drew!" She stamped her foot and Drew looked down at her ankle-high boots.

"I'm so glad you're wearing appropriate footwear now, but babe, Daddy doesn't like when you stamp and throw a tantrum." He patted her on the head.

"Don't change the subject!"

"Don't be bossy," he warned. "And no, he didn't say it in so many words." His smile widened. "But he implied it, and who am I to deny a dying man his wish." He grabbed her arm and turned her to face him. He was full of mischief and Addi frowned deeper.

"You wouldn't."

"I would." Drew nodded. "And as you pointed out, you're my property."

"But we've got guests arriving soon." Her eyes were wide now and he loved the trepidation in them. He looked at his watch.

"The memorial doesn't start until noon, babe. It's not even seven yet." He gave her a firm look. "Don't move." Bending his knees, he lowered to undo the button and zipper of her jean shorts.

She grabbed his wrists. "Daddy!" Her voice spiked in alarm.

"Move them." His voice was deep and demanding and her reaction was the sweet blush he loved. And when she clamped her lip and put her hands on her head, his cock fought for release.

Dropping her shorts, he grabbed the string of her sexy thong panties. He lowered them slowly while eyeing her trembling knees. She wasn't frightened, not really. It was all part of their dynamic, but he knew the anticipation of his crisp spankings always caused her frisson. Her clit would be throbbing and her pussy slick with need, but her ass would also tingle knowing the sting his hand would bring.

He'd provide her sexual release after, but for now his baby girl needed to be reminded who was in charge and that meant a red, hot, sore ass before he made her come with the force of a storm.

"Step out." She obeyed and he looked up at her with her shorts and panties in his hands. "Shirt too." It was a warm October morning where the worst she'd have from being naked outdoors was hard nipples and a cool breeze blowing across her soaked pussy.

"Daddy!"

His brow flicked up and her intake of breath was sharp and audible.

"Yes, sir." She licked her lips and removed her shirt, handing it to him. He rewarded her with a smile and then looked at her luscious body like a man looked at a lake during a heatwave. God, she was gorgeous, especially now that she'd lost her insecurity and body shame.

"To the log, babe." Since they watched the sunrise every day as a tribute to Ray, he'd put a huge fallen log on the beach for them to sit on. He'd used it to spank her before and he would again, of course only during the times when the camp was closed. One week each month the camp shut down so Addi and he could have a break and some privacy.

She loved outdoor spankings, at least after the fact, and sex—hot, roll-in-the-dirt, randy sex. It got her engine revving knowing they could be caught by anyone who stopped by.

And Steven and Daniel had a habit of dropping in unannounced. They'd moved to Fell County so they could help with writing classes and ran their business from their cottage not too far down the road.

"Lean your hands on the log, little girl."

She gave him a pouty frown but bent to put her hands on the log. Her round ass was high and her tits hung heavy like ripe fruit that he longed to taste. He meandered around her, touching her back, shoulders, and thighs, but keeping her ass quivering in anticipation.

"Should I pick a switch this time?"

"No, please!" Her words rushed out and her ass jiggled.

"My belt then?"

"No, Daddy, just your hand. Please."

"Mm, yeah?" He placed his hand solidly on her sacrum and leaned down to look at her face. "Do you deserve a hand spanking?"

Her head bobbed and her ponytail swung, making him smile.

"Okay, baby, we'll put you over my knee for some warming up but then you're going to get into this position again, you hear?"

She nodded and he twisted her ponytail around his hand. "What are you going to do then?" she asked, not quite hiding the tremor of expectancy in her voice.

"You'll have to wait and see, babe."

He sat and used her ponytail to guide her across his lap. His cock poked into her. She said nothing about it but wiggled, causing an almost painful but delicious friction.

"Young lady, what are you doing?"

She turned her head and looked at him innocently. "Getting comfortable, Daddy."

He grunted and swatted hard, hard enough to make her lurch forward and swing her feet up to her bottom.

"Nuh-uh, baby girl. Feet down or I'll send you for the brush."

She whined but lowered her booted toes back to the pebbled sand. His hand landed lighter this time and then he built up the intensity. Her whimpers were mixed with moans of arousal and he had the urge to stop and drive his cock into her hot mouth.

"Please, no more," she begged as if her spanking were more than just uncomfortable. Her ploy was revealed when she slid between his open knees and unzipped his pants. He wasn't the only one thinking of her mouth on his cock.

He closed his eyes and let her take him in her mouth, even enjoying it, for a few minutes before he scolded her for getting out of position.

"I was going to fuck you with your ass up and hands on the log, but since you can't obey the rules, I think a few strokes with my belt will remind you." Her lips slid off his cock with a pop and his eyes rolled back as he barely held it together.

"Aww, but I was having fun," she whined.

"How many times did you slide me into your mouth, babe?"

She looked down at his cock, still wet from her swollen mouth. "Maybe ten?"

"Is that a guess?"

She bobbed her head.

"You sure you wanna go with that number?" Again, she nodded. He stood and unbuckled his belt. "Up into position, babe. Ten strokes with my belt."

She gasped when the belt slid through the loops of his jeans, but the quiver of her lip was purely arousal.

She put her hands on the log and stuck her ass in the air. It was blushed a nice pink already. He ran his hands over the warm flesh, soothing it before sliding between her cheeks, past her pucker and right to her hot center where he stroked until she spread her legs, eager for more.

"You are so fucking wet, babe. It's almost a shame I have to belt your ass before I drive my cock into that needy little cunt."

"A daddy never breaks the rules, so hurry and whip my ass then."

"You're right, but what kind of a badass biker would I be if I didn't break the rules now and then?"

She giggled and he wanted to snuggle her in his arms like a daddy dom should.

"You're a badass lone wolf who takes what he wants, aren't you?"

"Damn right I am," he growled, and before she even

expected it, he'd dropped his jeans and rammed his pulsing cock straight into her tight, fiery cunt.

She called out, howled loud like an animal without concern for being heard. It was just how he liked her, free and unashamed of her body or her impulses.

"Oh. Fuck. Yeah."

•••••••

Addi

Tonalonka was packed with former campers and even Sean came to show his support even though he had never met Uncle Ray.

Sean had had so much evidence compiled on the Skull Grinders they'd never see freedom and the few lower ranking members who hadn't done enough to get locked away weren't loyal enough to stick around, especially after Sean, Drew, and the president of the Iron Code had had a talk with them. Drew was finally free of his past.

Addi was free of her father as well. Dear old Dad managed to snag himself a new woman to do his bidding and she seemed happy to take care of him.

Former campers shared stories about her uncle that made her laugh, cry, and gape in shock and everyone had a wonderful time. Trevor brought Brent, but Layla had stayed home. Brent came regularly to paint with Drew and work on journaling with Addi. Since the trauma of being taken by Mauler and Dingo, he'd been having nightmares and slept with his mom or dad nightly.

Poor Layla had been pretty shook up from the whole ordeal and hadn't been around town or the bar much since it had happened, but Addi saw her regularly for self-defense classes with a wonderful instructor Addi had hired for the camp.

Everyone was gathered around the fire chatting but when Drew stood, a hush fell over the crowd. There was a canvas draped in a cloth that he put a light on once dusk fell. She wondered what it was, but Drew had forbidden her to peek.

"I want to thank everyone for coming to remember Ray Moore. He was so much to all of us and we'll never forget him. He gave me a place to stay, a purpose, and his trust even when I didn't think I deserved it." Drew looked to where Addi sat in a Muskoka chair. She was warmed by the fire and the love for her uncle that surrounded her. Drew's eyes flickered in the firelight and he winked at her. Her heart fluttered and she couldn't wait for them to be alone.

"He gave me one other thing." Drew reached into his pocket and held up something tiny in his hands. "His wife's engagement ring and his blessing to marry his precious niece." He bent onto one knee. "Addianna Louise Moore, or as I like to call you, baby girl, you're already my Old Lady, but will you also be my wife?"

Before she could answer, he yanked the sheet off the canvas and beneath was a painting of her on his bike, looking fierce, confident, and mesmerizing in leather. Her eyes were tilted sexily and her lips red and crooked in a smirk. He had once again painted her in a way that showed how he saw her and she loved it. She was that strong, fierce woman, not the easily frightened woman she'd always thought of herself as.

Addi stood, her knees shaking and tears blurring her eyes.

"I'll be anything you want me to be, but more than anything I want to be Mrs. Biker."

"Is that a yes?"

"You bet your badass biker butt it is."

He chuckled and caught her as she flew into his arms. He leaned down and put his lips next to her ear. "No, baby girl, I believe you bet *your* butt."

THE END

STORMY NIGHT PUBLICATIONS WOULD LIKE TO THANK YOU FOR YOUR INTEREST IN OUR BOOKS.

If you liked this book (or even if you didn't), we would really appreciate you leaving a review on the site where you purchased it. Reviews provide useful feedback for us and for our authors, and this feedback (both positive comments and constructive criticism) allows us to work even harder to make sure we provide the content our customers want to read.

If you would like to check out more books from Stormy Night Publications, if you want to learn more about our company, or if you would like to join our mailing list, please visit our website at:

www.stormynightpublications.com

Made in the USA
Coppell, TX
13 May 2021

55565980R10127